KILLER
CONTENT

KILLER CONTENT

A Brooklyn Murder Mystery

Olivia Blacke

BERKLEY PRIME CRIME
NEW YORK

BERKLEY PRIME CRIME
Published by Berkley
An imprint of Penguin Random House LLC
penguinrandomhouse.com

Library of Congress Cataloging-in-Publication Data

Names: Blacke, Olivia, author.
Title: Killer content / Olivia Blacke.
Description: First edition. | New York: Berkley Prime Crime, 2021. |
Series: Brooklyn murder mysteries; 1
Identifiers: LCCN 2020022171 (print) | LCCN 2020022172 (ebook) |
ISBN 9780593197882 (paperback) | ISBN 9780593197899 (ebook)
Subjects: LCSH: Murder—Investigation—Fiction. |
Brooklyn (New York, N.Y.)—Fiction. | GSAFD: Mystery fiction.
Classification: LCC PS3602.L325293 K55 2021 (print) |
LCC PS3602.L325293 (ebook) | DDC 813/.6—dc23
LC record available at https://lccn.loc.gov/2020022171
LC ebook record available at https://lccn.loc.gov/2020022172

First Edition: February 2021

Printed in the United States of America
1   3   5   7   9   10   8   6   4   2

Cover design and illustration by Rose Blake
Book design by Alison Cnockaert

Don't forget to tip your server.

1

Odessa Dean @OdessaWaiting · June 24
I did a thing, y'all. Williamsburg, here I come! #adventure #NYC
#Williamsburg #blessed
Brooklyn, NY

I ALMOST DIED ON my way to work today.

Dodging between two enormous food trucks, each racing for the single open spot along Brooklyn's Metropolitan Avenue, I didn't notice an oncoming biker weaving around a jagged pothole roughly the size of my head—until he slammed into me, knocking me backward. As I stumbled into the path of the oncoming behemoths—focused intently on each other instead of the out-of-control, petite brunette in a neon green polo shirt, homemade floral skirt, and well-worn cowboy boots—my life flashed before my eyes.

And I have to admit it was as boring as a fence post.

I spent the first twenty-three years of my life in tiny Piney Island, Louisiana, just outside of Shreveport. Calling my hometown a one-horse town would vastly exaggerate the number of horses. There were no pine trees in Piney Island, nor was it an island—it was a chunk of dry land surrounded by more dry land, or at least as dry as it gets in the swampy bayou state I call home. According to the sign demarking Piney Island city limits, there were 2,014 residents, which, as far as I could tell, was at least a hundred thousand less than the population of my new neighborhood.

Ever since I could remember, I dreamed of seeing the world, but that was never in the cards. Not for me. That is, until my aunt, Melanie, asked me to pet-sit her cat for three months. Taking a much-needed break from the obligations of my marshy hometown, I packed a bag and boarded the next Greyhound bus to Williamsburg.

Williamsburg, Brooklyn, New York City, New York. It's quite a mouthful. It's also extraordinary. And fascinating. And terrifying, especially when I was inches away from becoming a grill ornament for the Lucky Stan's Stuffed Croissants truck, the trendy neighborhood's latest craze.

I bounced off the food truck's bumper, tripped into the same pothole that had started this whole mess, and landed face-first onto the hot sidewalk. As I tried to catch my breath, I couldn't help but notice that the passing pedestrians steered clear of me in a wide arc instead of offering a helping hand. I guess it could have been worse. They could have trampled me.

"No, no, I'm just ducky. Don't worry about me," I said, panting loudly as I got to my feet, dusting off my skirt. With its wide elastic waistband, long length, and flowy cut, it was one of my favorite skirt patterns—one I'd made in a variety of colors. "Thanks for the offer, though." The passersby continued to ignore me. Luckily, I wasn't too much worse for the wear. There was a mysterious new stain on my messenger bag that I absolutely did *not* want to know the origin of, but I was in one piece. More or less.

"Hey!" I glanced over my shoulder at the speaker. The Lucky Stan's Stuffed Croissants truck driver, the one who had bullied his way into the coveted spot, was hanging halfway out the window shouting at me.

I'd never seen food trucks in real life before leaving Louisiana, but they were a staple here in Brooklyn. In my hometown, I'd had the choice between eating free lunch at the Crawdad Shack on my break or running across the street to the Dairy Queen. Piney Island wasn't big enough to warrant a Sonic, much less a McDonald's. Now, I had seemingly unlimited choices from a dozen new mobile restaurants a day as enterprising young chefs converted trucks into rolling kitchens serving anything from savory vegan cupcakes to authentic street tacos.

"Watch where you're goin'!" the driver shouted.

Head down, I scurried away. I'd only been in New York a few weeks. That was long enough to figure out how to navigate the complicated maze of subway lines (with help from the MTA app on my phone), but not quite long enough to break a lifelong habit of Southern manners. If it had been, I might have shouted something nasty in return, even knowing my Gammie would somehow find out and march all the way up here to wash my mouth out with soap.

Williamsburg was starting to have a bad influence on me.

Prior to the nineties, Williamsburg was a run-down, industrial neighborhood of Brooklyn overlooking the polluted East River, which separated the outer boroughs from Manhattan. Then gentrification came and the abandoned warehouses and poorly lit streets were transformed into one of the hippest—and most expensive—neighborhoods in New York City. Decaying factories were replaced by chic parks. Bodegas—tiny corner grocery stores that carried everything from box wine to off-brand laundry detergent—now had to compete with Whole Foods. As rent skyrocketed, street art and expansive murals covered decades of graffiti.

I entered Untapped Books & Café, the hybrid independent-bookstore-slash-cramped-luncheonette where I worked, and the first thing I heard was, "Odessa! You're late!" The front door hadn't even closed behind me before the manager started yelling. Yep. It was going to be one of those days.

"Sorry, boss," I replied, with an apologetic smile.

Todd Morris, the general manager and de facto boss, was a short man with thinning hair streaked with gray that he thought no one noticed. He wore rimless glasses and had a hairy mole above his eyebrow that made it hard to have a serious conversation with him without staring at it. He was nearabout the same age as my dad, but liked to believe he was still young and cool. He listened to bands like Nine Inch Nails and Pearl Jam and the other oldies. In other words, typical Gen X-er.

"What on earth did you do to your shirt?" he asked in a salty voice. "Those aren't cheap, you know."

I looked down at the large rip running from the bottom seam to my armpit, exposing the side of my plain white bra. Yikes. "Nearly got into an accident on my way here," I explained, clutching the shirt closed. "Don't worry, I've got a sewing kit in my bag." I pretty much always had an emergency sewing kit. I'd drag my sewing machine with me everywhere I went if I could.

"No time for that. Grab a new one from the back and get to work."

"Yes, sir," I replied. He scowled at me. Todd figured I was being sarcastic when I called him "sir," but I was raised in a household where manners were drummed into me from an early age.

"And while you're at it, grab a case of Hopping Rad. We're running low."

"How can that be?" I glanced up at the clock. "We just opened." Todd gave me a look that I interpreted as meaning he'd forgotten to stock one of our most popular beers in the cooler this morning, but he didn't want to admit it.

Back home in Louisiana, Bud was king. Then again, that could be because most of the time, it was the only beer option. Here in Brooklyn, craft beer—microbrewed, flavorful, independently brewed and locally created beers like Pour Williamsburg Pale Ale—reigned supreme. Boasting fresh, often local ingredients created in small batches, each was named something fun and punny. The first time I tried one, I thought it would be my last, but the taste grew on me. Except for the sour beers. I thought I didn't have the palate to appreciate them, but then I sampled a sour I genuinely liked and I had to reconsider my tastes again.

I detoured toward the Employees Only door behind the cash register of the bookstore. Untapped Books & Café had been one of the first stores that opened in the new-and-improved Williamsburg back in the mid-nineties, so in terms of the rest of the revitalized neighborhood, it was practically prehistoric. The thin carpet was atrocious, a stained gaudy pattern that would have been right at home at one of the more run-down casinos in Atlantic City. The owner called the flooring unique, but I think he was just too cheap to replace it. The rest of the bookstore was at least tasteful if a little peculiar, from mismatched floor-to-ceiling bookshelves jam-packed with all of the books no one had ever heard of before to huge windows that drew in customers looking for a cozy hideout for a few hours. If someone wanted a unique book, especially something fringy and edgy, either we had it or we could get it.

A dozen café tables were squeezed in behind the rows of shelves. They were almost always full, with additional seating in the courtyard out back. A counter ran along the wall separating the tiny kitchen from the eclectically decorated dining area. From pink flamingo party lights strung up along orange carnation wall-paper to the shiny contact paper that wrapped the steam pipes, no matter how hard I looked, there was no coherent theme to be found. The stools lining the counter should have been registered with the U.N. as torture devices, but that didn't keep people from lingering for hours nursing lukewarm beers with their friends as they argued over the symbolism in *Moby Dick* or traded esoteric quotes from *Anna Karenina*.

Between the food truck invasion and the ever-revolving pop-up eateries, it was a miracle that Untapped remained popular. We had air-conditioning (such as it was), a primo location, and were clean, so we had that going for us. Our book selection was niche, which led to a wide range of choices but hardly paid the bills. Customers really came back for the beer, sandwiches, and salads at the café.

But mostly the beer.

Along with whatever craft beer selection was in stock, we fea-tured a revolving menu, which was a trendy way of saying that we served whatever the cook felt like making that day. We offered savory sandwiches stuffed with plenty of local produce served on warm artisan bread, with a side of house pickles and tasty chips made right here in Brooklyn. Because there was no telling which creations would be available on any given day, a ton of repeat clientele kept us busy from ten in the morning to eleven at night.

There were two boxes of uniform shirts in the storeroom. I bypassed the box that held the tiny ladies' polos with their sleek lines, cap sleeves, and jaunty collars. On my first day, Todd had taken one glance at me and declared, "We don't have any girls' shirts in your size, but maybe one of the men's will fit."

Unfortunately, he was right.

As much as I would have preferred the contrasting piping and shorter hem of one of the ladies' shirts, Todd only ordered female polos in small and extra small, neither of which would fit my curvaceous body. I dug out one of the plainer, larger shirts from the men's pile. Between the inconsistent sizing and lack of pockets, women's clothing was impractical at best, but I hated how men's clothes hung on me like sackcloth. Whenever possible, I made my own clothes or tailored off-the-rack outfits to be more flattering on my body shape. Not that the neon green polos that all Untapped Books & Café employees—even Todd—wore were flattering on anyone. I tugged on the shirt before snagging a case of Hopping Rad and hurrying toward the café tables.

On the way, I carefully stepped over Huckleberry, the approximately two-hundred-year-old shop dog that loosely resembled a golden retriever. If I squinted. He had the shaggy yellow fur and huge friendly eyes of a retriever, but that was where the resemblance ended. He had a short, thin tail; long, floppy basset hound ears; and fat rolls around his ankles and neck.

Huckleberry wandered into the bookstore one day and never left. Most nights he slept here, if he didn't follow one of the employees home. His job was to greet the customers, give Untapped Books & Café a homey, cozy feeling, and scare off potential burglars. As far as I could tell, he napped in the aisles all day, waking only long enough to beg for scraps from the kitchen. "Heya, Huckleberry," I said, shifting the case of beer so I could squat down to give him a quick scratch on the top of his head. He opened one eye partway and thumped his skinny tail once on the ground in greeting. "How ya doing today, buddy?"

"Odessa, thank goodness you're here!" I looked up and saw my friend Izzy Wilson, who worked the cash register at the front counter. Her super short hair was sunset orange this week. With a four-energy-drink-a-day habit and the metabolism of a squirrel, Izzy was a constant ray of sunshine.

She was also the first person I'd met in New York who'd given me the time of day, even going so far as to show me the ropes. If it weren't for Izzy, I'd probably still be roaming around lost and homesick. "Todd was threatening to make me put on an apron and cover the café for you if you were any later." She rolled her eyes at the ceiling. "Troll."

Izzy was a vegan, along with a surprisingly large number of our customers. And while there was always at least one vegan option on the menu every day, plenty of carnivores frequented the café, too. Izzy got the willies even looking at meat, and had threatened to quit the last time she had to ferry meat-based meals to the tables. Although, to be fair, the special that day was bacon-wrapped ham fritters, and they kept trying to roll off the plates.

"So sorry I'm late. You wouldn't believe the morning I've had."

Izzy nodded sympathetically before gesturing toward the dining area. "And you can tell me all about it on our break."

I scanned the café. Each tabletop featured a different bold pattern sealed under an easily cleanable plastic shell. My favorite was faded fabric printed with cartoon spaceships in an epic outer-space battle. The most popular was a paper map of the old subway lines.

Despite having opened only fifteen minutes earlier, half of the twelve tables were already occupied, along with two of the spots at the counter. No one looked particularly happy. Bethany, the only other server on the early shift today, was taking orders at the far end of the narrow room. Wishing I hadn't stopped to pet Huckleberry, I slid the case of beer into the bottom of the glass-fronted cooler and dashed back to the ladies' room to wash my hands, grabbed my apron off the line of hooks in the hall and tied it around my waist, and got down to work. Starting at the closest table, I made a sweep, taking orders, serving drinks, and delivering food that was sitting in the window getting cold.

"Thank goodness," Parker Reed, the day-shift cook, said, as I balanced six plates along my arm. Parker worked in the tiny kitchen, which meant instead of the ugly green polos, he got to wear a long-sleeve shirt. Right now, the sleeves were pushed up to reveal arms covered in cuts and burns. His shaggy blond mop was stuffed into a hairnet and, as usual, a cheery smile was plastered on his face. He didn't look like my idea of a chef, but he was one of the culinary geniuses that kept customers coming back for more. "I was about to deliver those to the tables myself."

"It's gonna be one of those days," I agreed.

"I hope not. If we have a lull, I need to go check on my bees."

Parker kept 3D-printed beehives up on the roof where he managed a small colony of bees that helped pollinate some of the local community gardens, as well as providing the freshest honey I'd ever tasted in my life. He even sold some to a local brewery for their Bee's Knees Lager, which we stocked in the café. If that wasn't the perfect analogy of the Williamsburg ecosystem, I didn't know what was.

"Hey, I whipped up a new hummus recipe you just have to try." He picked up a salty kale chip and got a big scoop out of the bowl. Since I had my hands full, I leaned forward into the window and he popped it into my mouth. "Whatya think?"

One of the things I loved about Williamsburg was that I got to try new things all the time. Tasting novel twists on dishes from all around the world was my new favorite thing. As I chewed, Parker stared at me with intense puppy-dog eyes that were just begging for approval. "It's great."

"Yeah?" he asked.

"Not *quite* as delicious as your raspberry Nutella crepes, but I love it," I assured him.

Parker glanced over at the pile of tickets I'd clipped to the counter before grabbing the waiting dishes and shook his head. "Hot plate's on the fritz. Again. No avocado toast today. Push the sweet pepper sandwich instead. Tell 'em it comes with a side of my special roasted garlic white bean hummus."

"Will do."

I dropped off the plates before returning to the table to tell them we were out of avocado toast. Before coming to Williamsburg to cat- and apartment-sit for my favorite aunt while she explored Europe for three months, I thought that all New Yorkers were as rude as the food truck driver I'd run into—no pun intended—on my way to work. I soon learned that wasn't the case. First and foremost, there was no such thing as a "typical" New Yorker, any more than there was *any* typical person. But with a few notable exceptions, like my boss Todd, the people I'd met so far were nice. Friendly. Helpful.

Take Parker for example. If I had shown up even five minutes late to my shift at the Crawdad Shack back home, the cook would have threatened to boil me alive in his enormous crawdad pot. If I'd told a customer that their order wasn't available that day, they would have given me a steely-eyed glare and said something particularly Southern that sounded pleasant but was secretly nasty, like "Bless your little heart." Here, all I got was a shrug and two orders for the sweet pepper sandwich that Parker had suggested.

Then again, up until a few weeks ago, I hadn't even *heard* of avocado toast. I hadn't known that avocado was good for anything other than mashing into guacamole, but to my surprise, avocado toast was not only delicious, it was also more complex than the name suggested. There were dozens of ways to prepare it, but here at Untapped, it was two slices of locally produced multigrain bread, lightly toasted, topped with creamy avocado chunks, a slice of heirloom tomato, a squirt of lime, a sprig of cilantro grown in the next-door rooftop garden, and feta cheese crumbles, with a perfectly poached egg on the side. It took me several minutes to work up the nerve to try it the first time, but it's quite tasty.

"Hey, Bethany." I caught the other server's attention. She was several inches taller than me, with blonde hair tied back in a green ribbon that matched our polo shirts. She wore heavy makeup and despite washing her hands dozens of times a day, her nails were always perfect. Bethany had a turquoise owl tattoo on her wrist and wore a fake medical bracelet big enough to set off a metal detector. "Parker says no avocado toast today."

"Again?" she asked.

"Hot plate's on the fritz," I explained.

"Sounds familiar. Sometimes I think the only thing that ever works around here is us. Speaking of which, you mind covering me for a few minutes? Half an hour at most."

2

I GLANCED UP AT the clock on the wall. It was a little past ten thirty. "What do you mean cover for you?" I asked Bethany. "You can't just leave me here alone."

"I know, and I feel absolutely horrible, but it's an emergency. Life or death. If Todd asks, tell him I'm in the bathroom or something. Don't worry, I'll be back before the lunch rush."

I frowned at her. I wasn't terribly keen on having to handle the café all by myself, and I didn't like lying. "Why can't you wait until after your shift?"

"Because reasons." I gave her an exasperated look, so she elaborated. "I have some business to take care of at Domino. I'll be back in a flash." She took off her apron and draped it over my shoulder. "Thanks. I'll make it up to you. Promise." Without giving me another chance to object, she slipped through the Employees Only entrance that led to the back door.

"Hey, miss?" a voice called out over the low-level hum of conversations and nineties grunge rock piped in over crackly speakers. I plastered my best customer-service smile on my face and approached the table where the customer was waving at me. Behind me, I heard Parker ring the old-fashioned call bell on the pick-up window. One of our orders was up.

I grinned at him and asked, "Mike, right?" I made a point of trying to learn the names of all of our regulars. He nodded, looking pleased that I remembered. "What can I get for you?"

"Got any of that Hopping Rad?"

"Not cold," I told him, fighting the urge to ask if ten thirty a.m. on a Monday was the best time to order a beer, but my job was to serve the patrons, not judge them.

I'd made a point of memorizing everything I could about our ever-revolving selection of craft beer, but few of our patrons ever asked for details. Either they were certified brew-philes already or they couldn't tell the difference between Pabst Blue Ribbon—aka PBR—and lemonade. "But I think I saw a few bottles of Many Hippy Hoppy Returns in the back of the case. They're not brewing any more of that until next spring, so get it while it lasts."

"Is it made from local hops?"

"Grown in a co-op upstate," I assured him. For being one of the most densely populated places in the United States, New Yorkers were obsessed with eating locally grown produce, whether that was a rooftop garden in the Bronx or one of the big factory farms up near the Canadian border.

He nodded. "That'll do."

I detoured into the kitchen to stuff Bethany's apron into the cabinet the employees used to store bags and purses before taking care of his order. I waited on both my and Bethany's tables as the café continued to fill with the usual noisy lunch crowd. At night, when we're swamped, there's usually someone dedicated to pouring brews and beans, with two servers inside and one outside in the courtyard. But since I was alone, everything fell to me.

Despite what some people might think, waitressing is taxing work. I had to be friendly, but not too friendly. I kept the tables turning over without rushing anyone. I was on my feet all day, shuffling food and plates back and forth between the kitchen and tables. I was always covered in mysterious bruises, cuts, or burns. And at the end of the day, I made just a fraction of minimum wage, plus tips. If I was lucky.

Days like this, when we're shorthanded, I worked twice as hard to keep up, but most of the customers got frustrated by the mediocre service and left little to no tips.

My aunt, Melanie, covered the rent and utilities, paid automatically out of her account. She'd all but begged me to take a few hundred a month to thank me for babysitting her longhaired cat named Rufus and taking care of her apartment—a cavernous space in a converted warehouse that hosted both her living space and her art studio. But being a well-mannered Southern woman and dutiful niece, I'd refused to take any money. I'd saved up a few dollars working at the Crawdad Shack back home, so I had a little run-around money. How expensive could New York be?

Turned out the answer was *very*.

Very, *very* expensive. Twenty-five-dollar-sandwiches expensive.

It didn't take long for my meager savings to run out, and as much as I would have liked to spend every day exploring Williamsburg or listening to true crime podcasts in Domino Park, I needed a job. Untapped Books & Café was hiring. I had experience waiting tables. Now, here I was, the new girl in an ill-fitting men's neon green polo working all of the café tables by myself until Bethany returned.

"Odessa!" Todd barked my name, and I swear I shriveled a little inside. When I'd been hired, my job title was waitress. My job description was a little more varied than that. And by a little, I mean a lot.

So far, I'd covered the cash register several times, taken Huckleberry on more walks than I could count, and helped unload the delivery trucks almost every day. "Let me drop off these drinks and I'll be right with you," I told him, in case he didn't notice the heavy tray I was expertly balancing on one hand. Drinks delivered, I rejoined him at the double-wide doorway that separated the bookstore from the café.

Todd stood at the top of the three steps leading down into the café area. I was an incredibly average and extremely respectable five-foot-five, and on level ground, I would have been nose to nose with the manager. I couldn't be certain that Todd was self-conscious of his height, but I did notice he took every chance he could to pass down his orders from the highest position he could manage to find.

"Where's Bethany gone off to?" he asked.

"Ladies' room, I think." That wasn't the truth, but it wasn't exactly a lie, either.

"Well, somebody needs to update the Twitter."

I resisted the urge to correct him. I get it. I'd grown up in the "digital generation" and could type before I could write in cursive, which I'd never fully mastered if truth be told. Todd wasn't that much older than me, but he grew up in an age of dot matrix printers and rotary phones mounted to the kitchen wall. It could have been worse. My parents still looked at computers with suspicion and since I'd come to Brooklyn, they'd called me twice asking how to open "the Google." True story.

Bethany was in charge of Untapped Books & Café's social media accounts. Being from a small town, my daily interactions had been limited to customers at the Crawdad Shack, my parents, and anyone I bumped into at the grocery store. Twitter, Instagram, and Facebook were my only connection to the outside world. I didn't post every single day, and I don't think I'd ever gotten more than a dozen or so likes on a post before (and when I did, I felt like a superstar!). But still, social media was in my generation's DNA.

Bethany, however, was a YouTube guru.

Bethany was a bona fide influencer, with scores of loyal fans. Last I checked, her YouTube channel had almost a hundred thousand subscribers who tuned in every week to watch her make naturally scented soaps and lotions. She had six-figure followers on all of her social media pages, and made almost as much selling her soaps on Etsy as she pulled in with tips. It made perfect sense that she also put her talents to use promoting Untapped Books & Café by posting a few updates a week. Highlight a new book release here. Feature one of Parker's culinary creations there. Advertise upcoming events, like Poetry in the Park, or when we landed an author for a signing. Pose Huckleberry the shop dog strategically around the store for cute pictures.

"I'll post something real quick. Can I see your phone?"

He handed me his phone and I opened the Twitter app. After verifying that he was logged in as the store and not a personal account, I posted a quick update advertising Parker's new hummus.

As soon as I hit submit, the screen refreshed and a tweet with an embedded video titled "Flash Mob Proposal Gone Horribly Wrong!" caught my eye. It had only been uploaded a few minutes ago, and it already had tens of thousands of views.

I didn't know why I enjoyed surprise proposal videos as much as I did. It's not like I was itching to get married. I've never even had a serious boyfriend. Sure, I dated, but back home the single men had dwindled down to a nineteen-year-old with a third-hand Camaro; a few thirty- or fortysomething recent divorcés; and eighty-five-year-old Walter, who had buried four wives already and came into the Crawdad Shack at least once a week asking when I was gonna break down and agree to become wife number five.

There were plenty of single men my age in Williamsburg, but I didn't plan on being here long enough to start anything. I'd met several guys that might be fun to hang out with, but none I'd consider dating, much less marrying. I guess maybe that was part of the appeal of proposal videos. I could fantasize about getting engaged without any of the messy relationship drama that went along with it.

"Have you seen this yet?" Todd asked when he noticed my gaze lingering on the video. "You should totally watch it. It's insane."

"You really shouldn't throw words like 'insane' around," I told him, but I doubted he would take it to heart. Todd didn't seem to notice—or care—when he used offensive language.

I clicked the full-screen button. The video opened, and after the obligatory YouTube advertisement played, I recognized the familiar backdrop of Domino Park. The remains of the old Domino Sugar Refinery and four of its thirty-six-foot-tall syrup-collection tanks were some of the few remnants of Williamsburg-that-was, back when it was the center of industry instead of the vibrant residential neighborhood it is today. Now, the factory's skeleton served as the backdrop of the lovely six-acre Domino Park, filled with lush lawns and multiple activities. A fifteen-foot-tall elevated metal walkway ran five blocks along the length of the park, providing spectacular views of Manhattan and the Williamsburg Bridge. I loved to lean against that rail and watch the sun set over the New York skyscrapers.

The video playing on Todd's screen was perfectly framed. The park had been designed to reduce hiding spots for would-be muggers and other creeps, which left stealth cameramen with nowhere to conceal themselves. From the low angle and the steadiness of the camera, despite being zoomed to its limits, I assumed that the camera was propped up on a tiny tripod, probably concealed in the bushes that separated the sidewalk running along the river from the manicured lawns.

A blanket was spread out on the grass. A couple in their twenties sat on the blanket sharing brunch. He was cross-legged, and despite the rising temperature, wore a knit hat. She had her legs stretched out in front of her, crossed demurely at the ankles. She wore a crop top with high-waisted shorts—the official Williamsburg summer uniform. Her sandals rested on the blanket beside her and the wind whipped her hair into a frenzy around her head until she gave up and twisted it up in a knot at the back of her neck.

The picture-perfect couple sipped their coffee and chatted. The camera was too far away to pick up their conversation over the sound of the river slapping against its rocky banks, but then the first strains of Beyoncé's "Crazy in Love" started. A woman jogging by in the background stopped abruptly and began to dance. She was joined by two more people, and then four more, all dancing in sync.

The couple, now surrounded by elaborate choreography, abandoned their coffee to watch the spectacle as more dancers appeared. "I thought flash mobs were dead?" I asked.

"Shush. Just keep watching," Todd told me. "It's about to get good."

At the crescendo of the performance, the boyfriend reached into his pocket and withdrew a small ring box. The woman stared at the box, glanced back at the dancers, at her boyfriend, and back to the box. Her mouth moved but whatever she said was drowned out by the music. He shifted so he was down on one knee and held out the box. She made a high-pitched sound that cut through the rest of the noise. As she reached for the ring box, something fell from the sky behind her.

One of the dancers screamed, the choreography abandoned and the proposal forgotten. There was another terrified scream, joined by shouts for someone to call 9-1-1 and more voices raised in alarm over the last notes of the song. A shadow fell over the camera as someone leapt over the bushes onto the lawn, toppling the camera to one side. I could hear his voice loudly. "Is she okay?" I had to strain to hear as other voices answered, "I don't think she's breathing!"

I had to tilt the phone to keep watching, now that the camera listed hard to the right. A crowd, originally drawn in by the flash mob, gathered in a huddle. From the camera's point of view, I could only see their backs. Then someone moved and I caught a glimpse of green surrounded by onlookers.

Neon green.

Bright neon green, the exact same shade of bright neon green as the Untapped Books & Café uniform shirts.

It was just a split second. If I'd blinked, I would have missed it. But that was plenty long enough for me.

I was a seamstress. I loved making unique creations with a variety of fabrics and patterns. I loved experimenting with colors, textures, and lines. I noticed cloth, and clothes. And I recognized that shirt as sure as I was breathing. I glanced down at my own neon green polo shirt and a chill ran down my spine.

What was it that Bethany said right before she left? She was gonna meet someone at Domino. Unless she'd gotten a sudden hankering for pizza, she had to have meant Domino Park, which was only a few blocks away.

It couldn't possibly be a coincidence that Bethany ran off to Domino Park, and then a few minutes later, someone uploaded a video featuring a person wearing an Untapped Books & Café shirt falling off the park's elevated walkway. I untied my apron and handed it, along with his phone, to Todd.

"What's all this?"

"I need to check on Bethany. I'll be right back."

"Wait a sec, you can't up and leave. Who'll take care of the tables?"

I didn't have time to argue. "I'm sure you can handle it," I told him. Then, as an afterthought, added, "Table Three is ready for their check, Table Six needs refills, and we're almost out of ice."

"Which one's Table Three?" Todd yelled after me.

Ignoring him, I hurried toward the back exit. It was early, but the dumpsters in the alley were full of trash bags and beer bottles—even the recycle bin was overflowing—and the sun was high. The smell hit me like an almost physical force, but I pinched my nose and ignored it as I jogged toward Kent Avenue and Domino Park.

Perched on the banks of the East River, Domino Park was a lush, landscaped getaway from the bustle of New York City. Featuring interactive fountains, a fenced-in dog run, a kids' playground built out of some of the remnants of the old refinery, and a sand volleyball court, it was one of my favorite places to spend a quiet afternoon with a riveting podcast.

Today, all I noticed was a large crowd forming near the north end of the park, on the stretch of lawn I recognized from the proposal video. An ambulance was parked on the grass, lights flashing but siren silent. I pushed my way through the lookie-loos.

A body-shaped lump lay on the ground under a blanket.

My breath caught in my throat. I'd hoped to find Bethany embarrassed or maybe injured, but the person under that blanket wasn't moving and the paramedics didn't seem to be in any real hurry. I closed my eyes and reminded myself that it could be someone else. Out of Williamsburg's hundred and fifty thousand residents and countless visitors, I knew maybe a dozen. What were the odds that I knew the person under that blanket?

The EMTs laid a stretcher on the grass, and with practiced efficiency, moved the body onto the stretcher before lifting it onto a wheeled cart waiting nearby. Around me, a murmur went through the assembled crowd. "Make a hole!" one of the medics barked, and I was shoved sideways as everyone shuffled to give them room.

Then the cart hit a rough patch of terrain, jostling the stretcher. An arm slipped out from under the blanket to dangle for a brief second. One of the paramedics caught it and tucked it back into place, but that was enough. I recognized that arm. Or rather, I recognized the cute little turquoise owl tattoo on the inside of her wrist.

Bethany's cute little owl tattoo.

Bethany was dead.

3

I TRUDGED BACK TO Untapped Books & Café in a fog. I'd never seen a dead person before today. No one I'd known had ever died before. Even my grandparents were still alive and well—older than dirt, but surprisingly healthy.

"Where on earth have you been?" Todd bellowed as soon as I entered the alley. He was pacing, smoking a cigarette with one hand and holding his phone to his ear with the other. I guess the stench of the dumpsters didn't bother him. "No, not you," he said into the phone. "I'll call you back." He slid his phone into his back pocket. "You better have one heck of an explanation."

"It's Bethany . . ."

"Don't worry about Bethany. I've taken care of her. I warned her last time she pulled a stunt like this, disappearing in the middle of the lunch rush. Bethany doesn't work here anymore. I already left her a voicemail firing her. If you want to keep your job, you'll never mention her name again. Capisce?"

Hot tears stung my eyes, and they had nothing to do with the disgusting odor coming off the dumpsters or the smoke wafting from Todd's cigarette. It was sheer frustration. If I didn't need this job so badly, or if I had even one friend in New York outside of the bookstore, I would have told Todd where he could stuff his job. Without Untapped Books & Café, I wouldn't have any connection to this strange—and often daunting—new world of Williamsburg. "But you don't understand. Bethany . . ."

"I'm serious. Say that name again, and I'm docking your pay."

"She's dead, Todd. Bethany's dead."

"Don't even joke about that," Todd said, shaking his head. He dropped his cigarette and ground it out with his toe. "I know kids these days will say anything to get out of work, but there are some lines we don't cross."

"But I'm not joking," I insisted.

"Enough. Get back to work before I fire you, too." He jabbed a finger at the back door. "Oh, and, Odessa?"

"What?" I asked in a sharp tone. It was the closest I'd ever come to being rude to a boss before. I think New York was rubbing off on me.

"I liked your tweet earlier. Now that Bethany's fired, you're in charge of the social media accounts."

I stared at him in disbelief. It was bad enough that he wouldn't listen to me, but to order me to replace Bethany when her body literally wasn't cold yet? That was unconscionable. "I can't believe you."

"Did I stutter?" He gave me a frustrated frown, assuming I was arguing about the extra duties. "Try to post at least one thing a day on all the platforms. I'll write down the password for you later . . ." He really meant it when he said password, singular. He used the same password for everything to make it easier, and still managed to forget it half the time, so he resorted to writing it on a sticky note on his computer. He finished, ". . . so you can post on your days off."

Geez, why was I not surprised? Todd had once called me on my day off to take Huckleberry for a long walk because "he was getting restless." And no, he didn't pay me for it. "Yes, sir," I replied, knowing it wasn't worth arguing over.

I walked past him and let myself in. It felt disrespectful, to go back to work as if nothing had happened, but what else could I do? I couldn't force Todd to believe that Bethany was dead. The news would come out soon enough. In the meantime, I had a job to do.

I was sorely tempted to nudge the brick propping the door open out of the way so Todd would have no choice but to walk the long way around and go in the front entrance, but I couldn't afford for him to be any more annoyed at me than he already was. He'd probably find another unpaid job for me to do.

Inside, a dozen neglected tables of customers all clamored for attention. I had finally gotten everyone sorted and served when Kim Takahashi, one of the waitresses who normally worked the night shift, showed up, snapping her gum loudly.

Kim kept her waist-length, jet-black hair in long, braided pigtails. She wore her neon green Untapped Books & Café polo and stained waist-only apron over a black lace floor-length dress, under which were knee-high motorcycle boots. Unlike me, Kim had worked here long enough to have a name badge pinned to her apron. My apron was plain, but I could recognize it because of a

Rorschach-esque set of stains that looked like an elephant on the center pocket.

Kim wore more eyeliner in one shift than I wore in a year. And I was never as thrilled to see someone as I was to see her today. "Thank goodness you're here. Todd called you in?"

"No worries." She twisted her gum around one long, black-polished nail and pulled. "I needed the hours."

"Hey, new girl," a customer called, and I headed toward him. The man sitting at the table tucked into the corner, his back to the garish orange carnation wallpaper, was as much a fixture of Untapped Books & Café as the rope lights strung along each bookshelf or the glass brick stairs leading up to the front entrance. I hadn't noticed him earlier, but considering he only ever sat in Bethany's section, that wasn't surprising.

"Seth, right?" I had to force a friendly smile. "How's that coffee coming along?" I asked, gesturing at his empty coffee cup. Most of our regulars came for the atmosphere, free Wi-Fi, awesome sandwiches, and an impressive selection of local beers. This customer, however, sat for hours nursing free coffee refills, surfing on his laptop, and ogling Bethany while completely ignoring the rest of the staff. I wasn't sure how to break the news, so I took the coward's way out. "Bethany doesn't work here anymore."

"Oh." He frowned and looked down at his coffee cup. "That's unfortunate."

"You need anything else?" He'd find another waitress to obsess over. I crossed my fingers and hoped it wasn't me. If he was my regular, he'd drive me batty. Seth hogged a table for hours, refusing to relocate to a stool at the counter, and never ever left a tip.

He, like a lot of the New Yorkers I'd met, spoke so rapidly I had a hard time understanding him sometimes. "A million dollars in uncut diamonds, and a gluten-free donut that doesn't taste like ash?"

"Sorry, we're all out, but I can bring you a refill on that coffee."

He shook his head, placed the exact amount of his bill—three dollars even, as always—on the table without me having to write up his check, grabbed his laptop and his bag, and left. I dropped the money into my apron pocket, cleared his cup, and wiped down his table as three loud women headed toward the newly vacated seats. I gave them the rundown of the menu, and noticed out of the corner of my eye that Kim was talking to one of my tables.

I'd never worked with Kim before. As the newbie, I got the early weekday shifts that no one else wanted. The real tips came in on evenings and weekends, when the patrons ordered round after round of local IPAs and shared appetizer platters. It was instantly apparent that she was good at her job, but she got the opposite impression of me.

She pulled me aside after she'd had to fix the third order I'd bungled in the last half hour. In my defense, it was way busy and my head wasn't in the game. "Hey, Odessa, I know you're new and all, but you can't keep making mistakes like this. Table Four ordered iced tea, but they got Table Six's beer instead. Some people aren't cut out to be waitresses."

I swallowed my pride. "I've got a lot going on right now."

"Don't we all? Leave it at the door and concentrate on the job."

It was good advice, and any other day, I would have appreciated it. But I couldn't get the scene from Domino Park out of my mind.

"It looks like we're slowing down," she said. I'd been so busy juggling the small, constantly revolving crowd that I hadn't had a chance to catch my breath yet. I looked around and realized there were only three tables now, all with their drinks and food already, with no one waiting to be seated. No one sat outside in the courtyard out back since we didn't open that area until after five. "Why don't you take a break and get your head straight?"

"Good idea." I headed for the front counter, where Izzy was finishing ringing up a customer. She handed him three thick books and a receipt before wishing him a nice day. Then she turned to me. "Odessa? What's wrong? You're pale as a sheet."

"We need to talk."

"Can it wait?" Another customer approached the cash register and put a pile of children's chapter books on the counter. "Did you find everything you were looking for?" Izzy asked in her friendliest voice.

"Izzy, it's urgent," I said.

"Hold on just one second? I'll be right with you," she told the customer. Then she narrowed her eyes at me and took a step away from the counter.

I grabbed her arm and dragged her into the hall and toward the stockroom door. "You and Bethany are friends, right?"

She shrugged. "We hang out sometimes outside of work. Supsies? I heard Todd fired her for taking off in the middle of her shift. That jerk. I swear, we should all not show up for work one day. *That* would teach him a lesson."

"That's not it. I mean, yes, Todd fired Bethany, but that doesn't matter anymore. Bethany's dead."

Izzy glared at me. "That's not funny."

"I'm not joking," I insisted. "Why does everyone think I would joke about something like that? She fell off the elevated walkway at Domino Park and died."

"No. No way. Bethany's fine. We'll call her and prove it." She pulled out her phone and scrolled through her contacts, tapping Bethany's name. After a few seconds, Izzy scowled at her phone. "Straight to voicemail. But that doesn't mean nothing. She's always forgetting to charge her phone."

"I saw her. I saw Bethany. She was wearing an Untapped shirt."

"Did you see her face?"

"Well, no," I admitted. "But it was her. I know it was." It had been her, right? I was certain. At least 90 percent certain. I wanted to be wrong; I really, really did. But deep down, I knew it had been Bethany on that stretcher in the park. "She had a turquoise owl tattooed on the underside of her wrist. And she was dead."

Izzy scowled. "Lots of people have owl tattoos."

She had me there. Owl tatts were to our generation what lower back tattoos and tribal armbands were to Todd's. "Yes, but how many of them work here?"

"Excuse me, but are you going to be much longer?" a female voice asked. "I've got places to be, you know."

I poked my head back into the main bookstore and noticed a line had formed in front of the cash register. "We better get back," I said, even though my job didn't feel very important right now in the grand scheme of things.

"Bethany's fine," Izzy insisted, ignoring both me and the customers. "You'll see. You're mistaken. You've gotta be."

Without waiting for my response, she hurried back to the front counter, leaving me alone in the hall. I hoped that Izzy was right. To be fair, I'd only caught a glimpse of neon green in the background of a video and then a quick view of a fairly common tattoo on an otherwise bare arm. Something was off about that. It took me a minute to realize what it was.

Bethany always wore a gaudy, fake medical bracelet that she refused to take off. It was an old stainless-steel plate attached to a thick chain. The name engraved on it was Timothy O'Shay and, according to the bracelet, he was allergic to bullets.

Except the arm I'd seen hadn't been wearing the bracelet.

Bethany had supposedly found it at a thrift shop ages ago. I thought it was creepy and a little disrespectful, but it was also very much on-brand for Bethany to wear something like that. Maybe Izzy was right. Maybe Bethany *was* fine and my imagination had run away with me. Maybe Bethany would come waltzing through the door any minute now, laughing at Todd when he told her she was fired, donning her apron, and getting back to work.

Speaking of which, I had to get back while I still had a job. But first, I should probably update all of the social media accounts so Untapped Books & Café's followers could see what was happening today. I was about to head to Todd's office when Izzy stuck her head back into the hall. "Kim's calling you."

When I stepped out of the hall and closed the door behind me, I glanced toward the front door and held my breath for a heartbeat. On a nice spring or fall day, the front door would be propped open to let in some fresh air and invite customers inside, but in the heat of June it was closed tight to keep in what little relief the ancient air conditioner could provide. In front of the door was a security gate tucked up into the ceiling that would be rolled down after closing to lock the store up tight. A small bell was rigged to tinkle pleasantly when someone entered or left, and I stared at it, willing it to jingle, announcing Bethany's return.

Nothing happened.

Of course.

I made my way back to the café, even though waiting tables was my absolute lowest priority right now. I needed something to get my thoughts off Bethany. The mind-numbing act of serving food and drinks might be just what the doctor ordered.

Kim brushed past me. "You gonna stand around or are you gonna get back to work?" she asked, juggling a full tray in one hand and a pitcher of ice-cold lemonade in the other.

Before I could answer, she was already gone. She had a point. I headed for the window, where several plates sat, waiting for delivery. Parker poked his head out and said, "Orders are piling up."

"Yup, taking care of that right now." I checked the ticket, grabbed the plates, and lined them up along my arm to deliver them to the right table.

I'd hoped that work would serve as a distraction, but I was sorely mistaken. As the day wore on, the café was buzzing. As usual, everyone was focused on their screens. But unlike every other day, they were all watching the same thing—the viral video from Domino Park.

The rest of my shift went by in a blur. The early dinner rush was starting to slow when my replacement showed up. I happily cashed out my tips, hung up my apron, and headed for the front door.

"Odessa!" Izzy called out as I passed the cash register. "Wait a sec!"

"What are you still doing here?" I glanced at the clock on the wall behind her. The hands were enormous, mounted in the center of a numerically ordered ring of books with titles like Janet Evanovich's *One for the Money*, Charles Dickens's *A Tale of Two Cities*, *The Three Little Pigs*, and James Patterson's *Four Blind Mice* where the clock's numbers should be. When we got bored, we would grab a stepladder and swap out the books with other titles that fit the pattern. "Didn't your shift end like an hour ago?"

"I was waiting for you, dummy," she said, but I heard the affection in her voice. "Come on, let's roll."

"Where are we going?"

Izzy rolled her eyes at me. "We're going to the police station to prove to you that the woman in that horrible video isn't Bethany."

"Why not go by her place and check on her?"

A shadow crossed Izzy's expression. "I already called one of her roomies, and Bethany's not home. But she's hardly ever there."

"All right." I crossed my fingers and fervently hoped Izzy was right and I was wrong. "Let's go, then."

I'd been in the police station in Piney Island dozens of times. Well, maybe not dozens of times, but a lot. We went on elementary school field trips and to sell Girl Scout cookies. The police station was where I got my driver's license and paid my first traffic ticket. I knew the cops by name, and they knew me.

The Williamsburg precinct was *nothing* like Piney Island.

The police station was uncomfortably warm with everyone crammed in like sardines. And like the New York City subway during rush hour, I smelled something strong and unpleasant I didn't want to identify. We signed in at the front desk and were told it could be a while. There was one open seat in the cramped waiting room, but we took one look at the stained chair resting over a puddle that may or may not have been a spilled beverage, and elected to remain standing.

After an hour of waiting—long enough for Izzy to duck out and return with lattes and for us to witness two different men dragged into the station in handcuffs, blathering nonsense—a bored patrolman called our names and led us back to a small, cramped room. He told us to wait, propped the door open with a metal chair, and disappeared.

Izzy jumped up and ran her hands along the walls. "What are you doing?" I hissed. I don't know why I felt the need to keep my voice down. It wasn't like we were in a library or something.

"Looking for an observation window. I was hoping for two-way mirrors but I guess they've gone high-tech. What do you think? See-through paint? Porous walls? Or old-fashioned hidden cameras?"

"I wish." We both looked up as a plainclothes officer filled the doorway. "Captain's so stingy, we have to buy our own bullets. What makes you think he would spring for cameras, hidden or otherwise?"

The median age for police officers in Piney Island was somewhere between seventy and dead. Every once in a while, a new uniformed officer would come in, fresh from the academy and still wet behind the ears. They might stay six weeks before transferring to Shreveport or New Orleans, where the real action was to be found. As a result, I'd only ever seen cops that didn't need orthopedic shoes or used Clearasil in procedural law dramas on television.

The man standing inside the doorway was around my age, give or take a few years. He wore dark indigo jeans with an off-white button-down shirt under a gray waistcoat. His hair was buzzed almost to his scalp but his warm sable-colored eyes, flecked with gold, were framed by long, almost black lashes. He looked like he'd be more comfortable in a J.Crew commercial than behind the wheel of a police cruiser.

In other words, I wouldn't complain if he pulled me over for speeding.

"Detective Vincent Castillo," he said with a hint of a Spanish accent, closing the door behind him. He dragged the chair back to the table. One leg scraped the ground, making a sound akin to nails on a chalkboard, only worse, because it echoed painfully in the small room. "You ladies have information about the young woman whose death in Domino Park is all over YouTube?"

"Yes, sir," I said, at the same time as Izzy said, "Nope."

"Start from the beginning." The detective sat down across the table from us. He pulled out an antiquated electronic tablet and slid a stylus out of a slot on the side. "Names?"

"Isabelle Wilson," my friend said, in a much quieter voice than usual. Izzy was vivacious, friendly, and upbeat. She was the complete antithesis of what I thought New Yorkers would be like, and yet the more people I met, the more I realized that was just another misconception of the big, bad city. I'd never heard her so subdued before, and when I glanced over at her, I realized why. Her eyes were sparkling and she was all but drooling as she ogled the dapper detective.

I kicked her under the table.

"Ow!" She jumped in her seat and glared over at me. "What'dya do that for?"

I gave her a tight smile while widening my eyes, trying my

hardest to psychically remind her that we were on a mission, one that didn't involve flirting. I returned my attention to Detective Castillo. "Odessa Dean."

"Could you spell that please?"

I swallowed and forced myself to enunciate each letter. "O-d-e-s-s-a D-e-a-n."

Personally, I didn't think I had an accent, or if I did, it was barely perceptible. I certainly didn't have the sleepy Southern drawl that everyone else in my family did. And yet, since coming to Brooklyn, more often than not people had to ask me to repeat myself, or simply stared at me like I was speaking Elvish or something. In return, I found myself saying, "Huh?" more often than my nearly deaf grandpa when he left his hearing aids at home. It wasn't that I couldn't hear what people were saying as much as they talked so quickly I couldn't understand them.

"Where are you from, Odessa Dean?" he asked, and I liked the way he pronounced my name. He spoke as quickly as the other New Yorkers I'd met, but with a lyrical quality to his voice.

"Piney Island, Louisiana," I told him.

"Never heard of it."

"No one ever has. Sneeze and you'd miss it."

"And what brings you two ladies in today?"

"It's nothing," Izzy said.

I was tempted to kick her under the table again, but instead, I corrected her. "It's not nothing. We need to know what happened to Bethany."

4

Bethany?" Detective Castillo asked, cocking his head to one side. Even in the harsh, sterile lighting of the police station, his skin had a bronze glow that I couldn't seem to achieve no matter how long I stretched out on a lounger in the backyard back home.

"Our friend, Bethany Kostolus. The woman who fell off the walkway in Domino Park this morning in that viral video?" I explained.

"And what makes you think that this Bethany Kostolus is the woman from the video?" he asked.

"See? I told you so," Izzy hissed. "It's not Bethany. It can't be."

I tugged at the uncomfortable collar of my polo. "She had on one of these, didn't she? And I saw her tattoo." I clasped my hand to the underside of my left wrist, where Bethany's tattoo had been. "The cute little turquoise owl? Plus, she left work today, right before that video was shot, saying she had some business to take care of in Domino Park. Said it was a matter of life or death. She never came back."

"A matter of life and death, you say?" the detective asked. "Care to elaborate?"

I shifted uncomfortably in my seat. "That's all she told me. To be completely honest, I assumed she was exaggerating so I would cover for her while she ran an errand."

He scrawled notes with his stylus as I talked, never breaking eye contact with me. "I saw you in the park earlier, you know. You're hard to miss in that shirt. Tried to talk to you, but I lost you in the crowd. Mind explaining exactly what you were doing in Domino Park?"

"I watched that video, the flash mob proposal video, shortly after it was first posted. I saw that girl fall, and recognized the shirt as one of ours. I came running, thinking I could maybe help or something."

The detective pursed his lips in thought. "But you didn't stick around."

"I went back to work, to tell Todd."

"Todd?"

"Todd Morris, the manager at Untapped Books & Café. I figured he'd know what to do."

"And?" the detective prompted.

"And nothing. He didn't believe me. He left a voicemail firing Bethany for running out in the middle of her shift and threatened to dock my pay if I didn't get back to work." I took a deep breath. "Please, Detective, talk to us. Everyone thinks I'm bonkers, even Izzy. Just tell us that it was someone other than Bethany that you found in the park, and we'll get out of your hair."

"I'm sorry, Ms. Dean, but I can't do that."

My heart sank. I'd spent the last several hours of my shift

second-guessing myself until even I was starting to doubt what I'd seen in the park. I'd wanted to be wrong so bad I'd half convinced myself that I was.

Now, all hope of Bethany being alive—unemployed, sure, but alive—was squashed.

Beside me, Izzy made a strangled noise and I turned to her as tears flooded her eyes and began to overflow down her cheeks. I threw my arms around her and hugged her tightly. "I'm so sorry, Izzy."

"I should let you ladies have some privacy," the detective said, scooting his chair backward against the hard floor.

"No," Izzy said, sniffling and pawing at her tear-filled eyes. She pulled herself upright, then grabbed my hand and squeezed, holding on for dear life. Her eyes were red and a clump of mascara clung to her cheek, but other than that, it could have been any normal day. It was hard not to envy her. At the end of a long, busy shift, I probably looked like something that normally hid in the dumpsters behind the café. And when I cried, my eyes didn't merely glisten. I got red-nosed, with snot dripping down my upper lip. I was *not* a pretty crier. "How can we help?"

"Sorry to waste your time, ladies, but unless you have something more to offer, I don't see how the NYPD needs your help in this matter. We've pulled all the cell phone pictures and videos before and after the incident, and I'm reviewing them, along with the surveillance footage and witness statements, personally. The flash mob drew in quite a crowd, and they were all filming, which means we have a lot of angles. Several people caught her falling, but no one saw her go over the footbridge."

"Kinda convenient, wouldn't you say?" I asked. "All those witnesses, but they were distracted by the flash mob."

"I didn't even know that flash mobs were a thing anymore," Castillo mused.

"I said the same thing! Makes it all that much more suspicious, don't you think?"

He shook his head. "So far, there's no indication that Ms. Kostolus was with anyone else, and no signs of foul play. Unless something comes back in the ME report to indicate otherwise, it appears your friend's death was an unfortunate accident."

Beside me, Izzy slumped in her chair.

"What about her medical alert bracelet? Did you find that at the scene?" I asked.

"Ms. Kostolus had a medical condition I should know about?" the detective asked, sitting forward with his stylus poised over the tablet in anticipation of my response.

I shook my head. "No. It wasn't a real medical alert bracelet, just one she wore all the time." I described it, and told him the inscription. "It was like a joke."

"Not a very funny joke if you ask me," he replied.

I didn't disagree. "In any event, she never took it off, but I didn't see it on her arm when the paramedics wheeled her away. Did you find it or not?"

He looked down, tapped a few buttons, and then frowned. "Not that I know of. Didn't find a phone, either. I'm assuming Bethany owned a cell phone."

"Of course," Izzy said. "I've been calling it all day, but it goes straight to voicemail."

"A lot of people were on the scene. If she dropped her phone or bracelet, they could be anywhere. I'll send a uniform to look for them, but like I said . . ."

"I know, I know," I interrupted him, annoyed that he was so quick to jump to conclusions. Sure, I couldn't prove anything, but would it kill him to take a harder look before closing the case? "Looks like an accident. Don't you think that maybe you're relying a little too much on tech to do your job for you? Since when did police crowdsource crime scenes?"

"See here, lady," he said, and I could tell by the way a sharp edge had replaced the musical lilt in his voice that I'd hit a nerve. "There can be a hundred witnesses, and they'll all see and hear something different." He touched a finger to his temple. "Within minutes, their minds scramble the details, and by the time we interview them, they're already remembering what they *think* happened, not what really happened. But cell phone vids tell the story how it happened, not how people perceived it."

I still didn't like it. "Just because you don't have a video of someone pushing her . . ."

"Ms. Dean," the detective interrupted, placing both hands on the table palms down and leaning forward, "if it looks like a duck . . ." He let his voice trail off.

Fine. Whatever. I could take a hint.

I pushed my chair back, letting the legs squeal against the floor, picked up my messenger bag, and tugged on Izzy's shoulder. "Whatever happened to good old-fashioned police work?" I asked her, ignoring the still-seated detective.

"If you think you can do a better job, be my guest," he said with a nod of his chin. He picked up his tablet and got up to hold the door for us. "I *am* sorry about your friend, ladies. But trust me, her death was a freak accident. Nothing more."

We left the station and headed west, away from my aunt's

apartment. "Odessa, thanks for everything you've done today. I mean, you barely even knew Bethany, and yet you're going out of your way for her and everything. I can't thank you enough for that."

"I hate seeing you upset," I said, putting my arm around her shoulder.

"I'll be okay. You don't have to walk me all the way home."

"Oh, I wasn't . . ." My voice trailed off. I didn't want to sound insensitive. To be honest, I hadn't realized we were headed toward her apartment. Izzy and I had hung out several times, but I hadn't been to her apartment before. "I want to make sure you get home safe, that's all."

Izzy stopped and looked at me, her head tilted to one side as if she were a bird trying to figure out a complicated puzzle. "You weren't walking me home, were you?"

"Well, no, not really." My parents had taught me some valuable life lessons. How to fish. How to drive. How to keep a little bit of cash stashed away for a rainy day. And how to never lie unless you really, *really* had to. I saw no reason to lie to Izzy now. "I was thinking about swinging by Domino Park to take a look around. See if maybe I can find Bethany's bracelet."

"Why is this such a big deal to you? I mean, don't take this the wrong way, but you barely knew Bethany. You're so sweet but she's, well, she was a little judgmental at times. I caught her making fun of your accent one day, right after you started. I told her to cut it out before you overheard and got your feelings hurt." Izzy sighed. "I shouldn't have told you that. Bethany was a good person at heart."

"Don't worry," I assured her. "No one's perfect."

"But why are you so determined to figure out what happened to her?"

I shrugged. My mom always said that I had such an inquisitive mind. If my dad hadn't shattered his knee my senior year in high school, I would have gone to UT on a full scholarship. The world would have been my oyster. But instead, I stayed home to help Mom take care of him. Besides, even with a scholarship, college was expensive and we couldn't afford it, not with Dad out of work and everything.

There wasn't much to do in Piney Island, besides sitting on the tailgate of someone's beat-up Chevy pickup watching the sunset or trying to catch crawdads in the stream. The closest movie theater was all the way in Shreveport. We had satellite internet and cable, but it went out when it rained. And it rained pretty much always in Louisiana.

I'd gotten into listening to true crime podcasts to pass the time, and the next thing I knew, I was hooked. I couldn't get enough of them. In all the best real mysteries, little clues were hidden throughout. Clues a listener might miss if they weren't paying close enough attention. I was convinced that Bethany's missing bracelet was one of those clues.

"I have this feeling that the cops are missing something. Look around." I spread my arms wide, almost hitting a woman struggling to walk half a dozen dogs at the same time, the leashes in a hopeless tangle. "Oof," I said. She muttered something rude and gave me a nasty hand gesture, but kept walking.

A steady stream of pedestrians flowed around us, heading home from work or out to the gym. People were meeting friends, picking up dinner, going out on first dates. They were taking a jog or pushing a stroller. They were going to the park or the grocery store.

Beside us, cars sped by on Division Ave, barely noticing the bikes weaving in and out of traffic. A siren wailed in the distance. The faint smell of barbecue wafted out of a nearby restaurant.

"Yeah? What about it?" Izzy asked, tired of waiting for me to make my point.

"There's what, eight, nine million people in New York City? Almost three million of those live right here in Brooklyn. You really think the cops are gonna put any effort into investigating a death they're already convinced was just an accident?"

"You heard Detective Castillo. When the ME's report comes back . . ."

"That will be weeks from now. Months, maybe. In the meantime, if there is any evidence at Domino Park, it will be long gone by then." Then it hit me. In a few months, I'd be gone, too. As soon as Aunt Melanie returned, I was going back to Louisiana. I wasn't sure how I felt about that. I still felt like a fish out of water half the time, but the more I got to know the people of Brooklyn, the more I loved it here. It made me sad knowing I would be gone by the time the ME published an official finding about Bethany's death.

"What difference does it make if you do find Bethany's bracelet? She'll still be dead." Tears sprang into Izzy's eyes and I felt like the worst friend in the world. I was trying to help, but I was making things worse.

"You know what? You're right. How about we go get a nice glass of wine somewhere? Or maybe a whole bottle of wine? We can watch a stupid movie on Netflix. Or, aren't you always telling me you want to take me to see that local punk band you like so much?

Deep Fried Cigarettes? Maybe they're playing tonight." I pulled out my phone, but before I could unlock it, Izzy put a hand over mine.

"Raincheck? I really need to be alone right now, if that's okay."

"Of course it is!" I kicked myself. I shouldn't have been so pushy. I was doing everything all wrong, wasn't I? "Call me if you need to talk."

"I will," she promised. "See you at work tomorrow."

I frowned, trying to picture the schedule in my head. "I'm not scheduled to work tomorrow, but Todd might call me in to cover Bethany's shift." As soon as the words came out, I bit my lip. If I put my foot any further in my mouth, I'd choke on it.

If Izzy noticed my faux pas, she ignored it. "Okeydokey, then. Later."

She turned south, presumably toward her apartment, and I continued heading due west, toward the river. The sun was low enough on the horizon that I had to squint to keep from being blinded. By the time I reached Domino Park, I'd missed the gorgeous sunset over Manhattan, but the park lights were bright enough that it might as well have been the middle of the day. Heavy clouds hung on the horizon. The weather app on my phone predicted storms tonight.

It wasn't hard to locate the exact spot where Bethany had fallen, as all of the nearby landscaping was trampled down by the onlookers and paramedics. This particular spot was almost equidistant between the two closest floodlights, making it one of the darker places in the park. And since most of the surveillance cameras in the city were mounted to street lamps and traffic lights, I was in a dead spot. That must have been why the city surveillance cameras hadn't caught much.

I dropped down to my hands and knees. Using my cell phone's flashlight app, I crawled around scanning for anything that the police might have missed. If Bethany had lost her bracelet or phone down here, they were long gone by now.

Glancing up, I saw that the elevated walkway was almost directly overhead. I pocketed my phone and headed down the park. The walkway was designed by the same architects that created the popular High Line Park in Manhattan. It ran almost the entire length of Domino Park, and was constructed at least partially from original beams from the old sugar factory. I wound my way through the switchbacks of a ramp leading up to the walkway. I passed two towering metal cranes painted nearly the same shade of turquoise as Bethany's cute little owl tattoo and worked my way back down the length of the elevated path.

The walkway ran along the meandering bank of the East River. Even in the middle of the day I wouldn't be able to see from one end to the other. If I'd been posing for a selfie on a crowded day, I might capture a glimpse of some of the other people around me, as long as they were within arm's reach. There were always plenty of people around, but the walkway itself made a boring background, especially compared to the river and the illuminated Manhattan skyline. Which meant anyone taking pictures would get themselves with the skyline as the backdrop. They could have stood right next to Bethany and not gotten her in the photo.

I made my way along the walkway. As I approached the spot above where Bethany had landed, I realized I was not alone. A shadowy figure stood approximately where Bethany had been about ten hours earlier, hands clutching the rail as he stared at the water.

My shoulders stiffened and a chill ran down my spine. Was this Bethany's killer, hunting for his next victim? I froze, unsure of what to do next. There was nowhere to hide, one of the park features that up until now I had really appreciated.

"Ms. Dean. Fancy seeing you here."

My heart just about burst out of my chest.

The figure turned toward me, and I could make out his rugged features. "Detective Castillo?" To my embarrassment, my voice came out shaky.

"Did I scare you, Ms. Dean?" he asked.

"Maybe a little." Did he scare me? Does a gator scare a fish? "How'd you know it was me?"

"I recognized your neon green shirt from a block away."

I looked down at my uniform shirt. Usually I kept a spare shirt in my messenger bag, in case I wanted to go out after work without looking like a corporate tool, but I'd been running late this morning. "I haven't been home to change yet."

"They say that the killer always returns to the scene of the crime. This is the second time I've seen you here. Where were you at 10:41 a.m. this morning?"

"It must be nice to have a death on video," I said in lieu of answering. I closed the remaining few feet between us and stood next to the detective, facing the river. "At least you don't have to worry about pesky details like time of death."

"It is convenient," he agreed. "And your whereabouts?"

"At work. Ask anyone." I turned to face him, understanding dawning on me. "Detective, if Bethany's death was an accident, why are you treating me like a suspect?"

5

WHEN DETECTIVE CASTILLO didn't answer right away, I wrapped my hands around the railing and peered over at the ground below. The lawn didn't look that far away. At its highest point, the elevated walkway was barely fifteen feet off the ground. I wouldn't jump that distance for no reason, but if I had to, I could probably do it. I might break my ankles, but that would be a worst-case scenario.

So how did such a short fall kill Bethany instantly?

Bethany was several inches taller than me. The railing came up almost to my elbows, and would have been at least waist high on her. I climbed up on the bottom rail and leaned forward. The wide wire mesh that ran between the bottom of the walkway and the railing would prevent children or pets from slipping through, so the only way down was over.

"You want me to believe that a grown woman accidentally fell over this railing?" I asked, breaking the silence.

Castillo must have been contemplating the same thing. "Or she jumped."

"Or she was pushed," I insisted. I waved my arm at the Williamsburg Bridge, just a few blocks away at the end of the park. "Why jump off a fifteen-foot walkway when there's a three-hundred-foot-tall bridge right down the street?"

"Why push someone off a fifteen-foot drop when there's a three-hundred-foot drop right down the street?" he countered. "People do strange things. Chances are, she figured she wouldn't get hurt." He put his feet up on the bottom rail and leaned over as far as he could. "Ninety-nine times out of a hundred, you'd limp away from a fall like that."

Up until now, I'd just had a weird feeling gnawing away at my gut that the cops were wrong about Bethany's death. The closest I had to any evidence of foul play was that her phone and bracelet were missing. But the more I looked down onto the lush lawn not far below, the more I was convinced that whatever happened here was no mere accident. "So you agree with me?"

He turned his head and stared at the Williamsburg Bridge. It was close enough that I could hear the distant rumble of traffic. "Unless the ME's report says otherwise, Ms. Kostolus's death was an accident."

"You have got to be kidding me," I muttered.

"Wish I was." I almost missed the note of wistfulness in his voice over the sound of the wind coming off the river.

"Can't you, like, trace her phone or whatever?"

"It's turned off, probably dead by now. Last activity we had, it pinged off a cell tower consistent with our deceased's place of business."

Knowing that he at least tried to find her phone and had returned here tonight was encouraging. "Makes sense." I wondered why Bethany had dashed out on her shift like she had. "Any chance she got a call right around ten thirty?"

"She hadn't received a call for days. Without a warrant, we can't know much about her phone usage, but she wasn't using it for calls."

"Well, yeah. I mean, who actually makes calls anymore except for emergencies?" I could think of three or four messaging services I was connected to, and that wasn't counting straight texts or direct messages associated with all of the apps I used. Last time I checked, I had more replies to Yelp reviews than recent calls.

Castillo continued to stare off into the distance. I wasn't even sure if he was listening to me anymore. "Bethany was like a social media guru. She had a popular YouTube channel, and a huge following on Instagram. Wasn't there a story a few weeks ago about a YouTube star with a stalker?"

"Online stalkers are nothing new," the detective replied. "Did your friend Bethany have a problem with trolls?"

I shrugged. "Doesn't everyone?" Even the café's professional account attracted its fair share of trolls, bots, and spammers. "The internet is toxic."

Lightning cracked the sky, and I jumped. "Storm's rolling in," he observed.

"I'm thinking we might not want to be on a metal bridge when it hits," I said. New York City storms were pretty tame in comparison to the destructive tornados and flash floods back home, but when it came to lightning, I didn't mess around.

"I'll walk you down." The first drops of rain splattered at my feet, and we hurried back toward the ramp on the north end. The bridge grew slick under my cowboy boots, and I clutched the rail for support. "Can I give you a lift?" he offered when we reached the ground.

Normally, I would have turned him down. Untapped Books & Café was only a few blocks away, and it would be open for several hours still. I could probably shelter there until the storm passed, but I didn't feel like going back to work and risk running into Todd, not today. My aunt's building was probably a good fifteen- or twenty-minute walk from here, which would be miserable in the driving rain. I didn't have money for an Uber, so my options were down to huddling under the shelter of a metal walkway during an electrical storm, or taking the detective up on his offer. "Yes, thank you."

A second before we reached his car, an unmarked brown Chevy sedan that practically screamed "undercover cop," the skies opened up and a deluge rained down on us. I glanced over my shoulder. The lights of Manhattan were faint, blurry dots of color in the thick fog rolling off the river and heavy downpour. If Bethany's bracelet was still in the park, it would be washed into the river within minutes.

"Get in!" Castillo bellowed, and I realized I'd been standing in the rain like an idiot long enough to be soaked to the bone.

I slid into the front seat. "Sorry, I'm getting everything wet." Rain dripped down the bridge of my nose.

"Don't worry," he said. He slapped the side of his seat. "You can't imagine the things I've washed out of this car. Good thing it's Scotchgarded."

I shuddered. I didn't want to think about the things his car had seen. I gave him directions to my aunt's building. "Thanks for the lift," I said as he idled next to the curb. I reached for the door handle.

"Nice digs," he said, straining to see through the rain. It was coming down in sheets now. The couple of steps between the street and the front door of the lobby might as well have been a mile. The building itself used to be a warehouse. It had been gutted and rebuilt as luxury apartments, while maintaining the industrial look of the original building. The wall facing the side street was covered by a mural that incorporated old street graffiti with a newer image of the Williamsburg Bridge.

"I'm house-sitting for my aunt." I don't know why I felt the need to explain that to him. Before coming to Brooklyn, I'd looked up my aunt's building so I'd know how to get there from the bus station. The website had listed the prices for available apartments. A three-hundred-fifty-foot studio cost more in rent per month than I had paid for my car. I didn't even want to know what Aunt Melanie paid for her large two bedroom with a balcony overlooking a small garden plot. The last thing I wanted was for Detective Castillo to think I was some hoity-toity snob who could afford a place like this.

Castillo dug out his wallet, pulled out a business card, and handed it to me. I glanced down at it, running my thumb over the embossed NYPD seal. I looked back over at him. The detective was out of my league. If my league was Piney Island, Louisiana, he was the moon. And yet, he *was* giving me his number. "Call me if you think of anything else about Ms. Kostolus."

Oh. Duh. Even if I dyed my boring brown hair funky colors, guys like Castillo were *way* out of my reach. "Yeah. Sure. Will do," I mumbled. "Thanks for the lift."

I dashed through the rain and fumbled with the front door lock. After a few frustrating seconds, I was standing in the lobby dripping water all over the floor. The air conditioner was on full blast and I shivered.

I took the elevator upstairs and let myself into my aunt's apartment. When I opened the door and flipped on the lights, Rufus, my aunt's longhaired, long-tailed cat, wound himself around my legs, getting all tangled up in my long, wet skirt. He purred loudly, and meowed up at me. "Hey, Rufie," I said, bending down to scratch the top of his head. "Miss me?"

Rufus was a striking-looking cat. Most of his face was dark gray, but one cheek was bright orange and his nose, chin, and chest were white. The rest of his body alternated between the three colors everywhere except for his pure white socks. But his most remarkable feature was his fluffy coat that looked like he'd tried an at-home perm.

He was the friendliest, and most talkative, cat I'd ever met. Whenever I was home, he had to be right by my side. He was also the primary reason I was staying in Williamsburg while my aunt was out of town. Some cats were content to be left alone for long stretches of time as long as they had food and water, like a houseplant. But Rufus needed attention and when I wasn't soaked to the bone, I was happy to lavish it on him. I pried off my cowboy boots and let them drip onto the rubber shoe tray by the door.

For the record, Texas might be famous for cowboy boots, but they didn't have a monopoly on them or anything. They were worn all over the country, from Montana cattle ranches to California avocado farms. They were practical, comfortable—once properly broken in, that is—and let's be fair, cute. Sure, New Yorkers looked at me like I was a visiting alien from Mars or something when they noticed them, but I liked them.

Besides, it never occurred to me to pack a lot of shoes. Or, any shoes except the boots on my feet. They were murder on these urban streets, but they were my only option.

"Come on, little dude," I said, reaching down to pet Rufus again. "Let's get you something to eat."

Aunt Melanie's apartment looked like a flea market had exploded. From the handwoven throw rugs on the floor to the seven-foot-tall metal giraffe statue in the corner, everywhere I looked I discovered something unique and wonderful. Bookshelves lined the walls and were filled with everything from first-edition Charles Dickens to ceramic tanuki statues—a stylized Japanese raccoon-slash-dog that carried a sake bottle with him wherever he roamed.

The lighting was every bit as eclectic as the rest of her decoration. The overhead light above the front door had been replaced with a chandelier fashioned out of severed doll heads. Other lamps scattered around ranged from original lava lamps and goddess rain lamps from the sixties to a three-foot-high armadillo holding a lightsaber.

I scooped a can of food into Rufus's bowl. Once the cat started eating, I could finally get out of these sopping-wet clothes. The big bathroom was decorated with all things hippo, from a blue ceramic hippopotamus covered in hieroglyphs to a hippo planter holding a lush ivy. I stripped out of my clothes and tossed them onto the floor before turning on the shower.

When I passed the wall-to-wall mirror above a sink that looked like a hippo yawning, I caught a glimpse of myself and ground to a stop. My torso was the exact same shade of green as a bottle of

Midori. As I stared, a giggle escaped, and before long I was laughing so hard I could barely breathe. Talk about a fitting ending to one of the weirdest days of my life.

I toed aside the offending shirt and reminded myself that the next time I was gonna wear a cheaply dyed neon shirt in a downpour, I should probably wash it a few dozen times first. A puddle of green water spread across the floor. Not wanting to dye my aunt's bathroom floor, I tossed the shirt into the shower under the running water.

After wrapping one of Aunt Melanie's big fluffy towels around myself, I dashed into the kitchen to grab a roll of paper towels and used them to mop up the mess. Luckily, the shirt didn't stain the floor like it had stained my skin. I threw the towels in—what else?—a trash can shaped like a hippo.

The hot shower felt great after the freezing cold lobby downstairs, but by the time I had scrubbed most of the green dye off my skin, the water was tepid at best. I finished up and tossed my new work shirt into the tiny washing machine in a closet near the kitchen. If I needed to wash anything much larger than two days' worth of clothes, I would use the laundry room in the basement, but for small loads, it was terribly convenient.

It was early—most of the hotspots in Williamsburg didn't get interesting until midnight—but I didn't feel like going out again, even though the rain had mostly abated. Aunt Melanie didn't own a television, unless I counted the ancient cabinet TV set that had been converted into a terrarium. But I had Netflix on my laptop, and before I knew it, I'd watched half a season of *The Great British Baking Show*. When I finally drifted off, I dreamed of decadent desserts that collapsed when I got too close.

I slept until nearly ten o'clock the next morning, which was a glorious luxury. I had a missed call from Todd and a voicemail begging me to work the day shift. I don't know why Todd bothered with voicemails when he could text me instead, but that was his way. When I called back, he'd already found someone else to cover for Bethany. He also mumbled something that might have been an apology. Apparently, reliable word of her death had finally gotten to him.

Stretched out in Aunt Melanie's bed—a queen-sized mattress in a sleigh frame—I stared at the ceiling, thinking about Bethany. I didn't know why her death was eating at me so much. We were hardly what I'd call close. Maybe it was because I'd never had to deal with the death of someone I knew before, but it felt like something else. Something more. I couldn't stop the nagging voice in the back of my head screaming at me that the police had it all wrong.

Rufus jumped up on my chest and began kneading the hem of the soft T-shirt I'd worn to bed. "You wanna play, don't you?" I asked. He meowed in response. I hadn't grown up with cats, and I had no idea how much he actually understood, but he certainly acted like his vocabulary rivaled a relatively intelligent kindergartener.

I selected a feather on the end of a fishing pole out a basket of toys that sat on a repurposed nine-drawer tool chest, and Rufus proceeded to chase me all over the apartment. He leapt from the backs of couches and chairs as if the floor was lava. He twisted in midair, caught the feather, and yanked the pole out of my hand. "Nice move!" I complimented him, but he was too busy dragging his hard-won prize up to the top of the bookshelf to acknowledge my praise.

Playing with Rufus was a nice distraction, but I couldn't get Bethany out of my mind. The police weren't going to be any help. Last night's storm would have washed away any possible evidence at the park. All that remained was the one thing that the cops hadn't bothered to do. I needed to talk to Bethany's friends.

The problem was, I didn't know any of them. No, that was wrong. I knew Izzy. She could point me in the right direction. I got dressed and walked the eleven or so blocks to Untapped Books & Café.

Before coming to Williamsburg, I measured everything in miles. According to Google Maps, it was approximately point-seven-five miles from Aunt Melanie's apartment to the bookstore. But in the few short weeks I'd been here, I was already starting to think like a New Yorker, who measured distances in blocks, not mileage.

It could be worse. I could be living in Jersey, where apparently everything was measured in exits off the Turnpike.

Eleven blocks sounded like a lot, but I'd gotten used to walking everywhere. Aunt Melanie had told me I could use her bicycle—a vintage Schwinn—but to be honest, I was more than a little intimidated by Brooklyn traffic. Besides, I liked walking. It gave me time to think and a chance to watch the world around me. If I was on a bike, I'd be so nervous about being creamed by a taxi that I wouldn't get to enjoy sightseeing.

When I got to Untapped, I was surprised to see Todd manning the front desk. "Where's Izzy?" I asked.

"Sick. Not like we're short already. Her calling out is icing on the cake."

"Oh." I knew I should pound sand before Todd tried to rope me into taking over the cash register for him, but I hadn't come all the way down here to give up that easy. "You've got Bethany's home address, don't you?" Then realizing how creepy that request might sound, I hastily added, "I want to send a sympathy card to her parents."

He blinked at me. "Sure. Yeah, that's a good idea. Pick one out, and let everyone sign it. Her address is somewhere on my computer. While you're at it, post something cute on Instagram. There's a folder on my desktop of Huckleberry photos."

Unlike most bookstores these days, Untapped Books & Café didn't devote half of the real estate to the same toys, games, and junk food that customers could buy anywhere. But we did sell stationery, journals, and greeting cards. Instead of mass-produced cards, all of ours were handmade by local artisans. I selected one that seemed appropriate and circulated it around to the employees that were on shift.

Todd signed the card, along with Kim. Parker scribbled his name in the card, too. "How are you holding up?" he asked me.

"Fine, I guess," I told him. "I mean, it's sad, of course." Was it weird that I felt guilty that I wasn't torn up about Bethany's death? Or maybe my obsession with how she had died *was* my way of mourning. If we'd been closer, or known each other longer, it might have been different.

"If you need a shoulder, I'm here for you."

"Thanks, Parker. That's sweet," I told him.

"That's our Parker. Such a sweetheart. Amiright?" I turned around to see Andre Gibson, the assistant manager, leaning into the window that separated the tiny, cramped kitchen from the diners in the café. "I know it's not on the menu today, but do you have the ingredients for your yummy peanut and tofu Thai salad? Got a special order out here."

"Yeah. Gimme a sec and I'll whip it up."

As soon as Parker turned to the refrigerator and started pulling out the ingredients, Andre turned his attention to me. "How you doin', 'Dessa?"

"Same ol', same ol'," I replied. I'd met some strange and interesting characters in Williamsburg, but by far, Andre was one of my favorites. I think that was at least partially because, despite all of our differences, Andre and I shared the same weird sense of humor.

Andre had been born in those fuzzy years, too late to be Gen X and too early to be a Millennial—a Xennial? Oregon Trail Generation? Despite pushing forty, he still lived with his mother, along with his boyfriend, his younger sister, and a much younger cousin. Between student loan debts and the lack of affordable housing, my generation tended to live at home longer than those that came before us, but in New York City, it was perfectly normal— expected, even—for multiple generations to live under the same roof.

When he wasn't working at Untapped Books & Café, Andre volunteered with an at-risk youth program and he spent his lunch breaks knitting. He'd even knitted me a fun, floppy hat, but it would be months before it got cool enough to wear it, and I wouldn't be in Brooklyn that long.

"Hanging in there," I told him. I slid the card toward him. "Can you sign? It's for Bethany's family."

"Of course." He opened the card, grabbed the pen out of his apron, and started scribbling.

"What are you doing on the morning shift?" I asked. Andre

usually worked the late shift, when the tips were better. He had seniority, so he could pick when he wanted to work. Besides, as the assistant manager, he wrote the schedule and acted as supervisor after Todd went home for the day. Unlike Todd, he was an absolute pleasure to work for, and I loved working on days when he was in charge.

"I've got applicants coming in this morning I wanted to interview personally." He flapped one hand over his shoulder, toward the bookstore half of the shop. "You know how Todd gets. The last thing I need is him scaring away employees before they even start."

"In that case, good luck with that." I knew we needed a full staff, but the idea of replacing Bethany so soon was depressing. I took the greeting card back from him and slid it into the envelope. "Well, I guess I'll see you later."

"Not if I see you first," he replied with a wink. I grinned at the cheesy line that sounded like something my dad would say and waved over my shoulder as I ducked into the hall.

6

I KNOCKED ON THE door leading into Todd's office, not expecting a reply since he was manning the cash register out front. But when I pushed the door open I noticed the light was on. That was weird. Todd was a real stickler about wasting electricity, or wasting anything, really. At first, I'd been impressed, thinking that Todd was an environmentalist, but it turned out that he was just cheap. Untapped Books & Café was one of the first places in Brooklyn to stop giving out plastic straws, not because of all the room they take up in landfills, but because they cost too much. Which I guess was a step in the right direction, but it wasn't fair to people who *needed* straws.

His computer was powered on, and unlocked. That was par for the course. Todd couldn't remember his password, no matter how easy we made it, so we eventually set his computer to never lock.

I wiggled the mouse to wake the screen, and the first thing I saw was the internet browser, logged in to the store's Twitter account.

Seriously, if Todd couldn't be bothered to lock his computer, he could at least lock his door. His office was off the narrow hallway that ran the length of the building. On one end was the stockroom where we kept the extra books, cases of craft beer, and boxes of spare neon green polo shirts. On the other end was the exit to the alley. We're supposed to keep that door locked, but it's such a pain when it accidentally closes behind us when we're taking out trash or accepting deliveries that it's always propped open with a brick.

This area was supposedly off-limits to customers, but the single-person bathroom was also tucked back here. The restroom was employees-only, but when customers came in with a little kid doing the pee-pee shuffle, we always made an exception and let them use it. It was unlikely that someone would walk in off the street, make their way to Todd's office, and start posting nonsense to the official Untapped Books & Café account, but not impossible.

Just to be safe, I scrolled through the store's Twitter account. No recent spammy posts or trolls. No unusual DMs. No posts at all since my comment yesterday about Parker's hummus. Since that had been a one-day special, I knew I should post something new and fresh for today, but my heart wasn't in it. "It's always a good time for homemade Untapped lemonade!" was the best I could come up with on short notice.

True to his word, a whole folder of Huckleberry photos was on Todd's desktop, but the pictures were mostly poorly lit or fuzzy. Besides, last time I checked, the only way to post to Instagram was from the app. Resigned to using my own phone for Instagram, I logged out of my own account and made sure I could access the store's using the password written on a Post-It note that was stuck to Todd's monitor. I shook my head. What was it about old people and technology?

After another minute of searching, I found Bethany's home address on Todd's computer and wrote it on the front of the sympathy card's envelope. Knowing that Todd would probably get me to take out the trash or something if he saw me leaving, I decided to go out the back door.

I popped back into the kitchen to say goodbye to Parker and noticed two giant bowls of his famous peanut and tofu Thai salad were sitting in the window, waiting to be delivered. In addition to being delicious—and this was coming from someone who had been deeply suspicious of tofu before coming to Brooklyn and finally trying it—it was colorful. Plated on a bed of greens with big, lightly grilled chunks of marinated tofu, sprinkled with bright orange carrots and golden brown peanuts, and drizzled with a creamy sauce, the dish looked as good as it tasted.

"Hey, Parker, you gonna put this on the menu tomorrow?"

He looked up from where he was slicing pickle spears. "I could. Why?"

"I'm gonna feature it, if you don't mind," I said. I took a couple of snapshots of the colorful meal next to a bottle of Arts and Craft Lager, posted it to Instagram, and tagged it as tomorrow's chef special. That should make Todd happy, at least for a little while. I waved goodbye to Parker and slipped out the back door, careful to not disturb the brick propping the door open.

A few blocks later, I was on the subway, heading deeper into Brooklyn. Bethany's apartment was in Bedford-Stuyvesant, a neighborhood south of Williamsburg. Like Williamsburg in the nineties, Bed-Stuy was undergoing gentrification and the previous generations of residents were being pushed out to make room for young urban professionals. Rents rose steeply as more people searched for apartments in the neighborhoods closest to Manhattan.

Quiet, tree-lined streets greeted me as I emerged from the subway station, the shade providing welcome relief to what was promising to be a scorcher of a day. In contrast to Williamsburg's industrial chic, Bed-Stuy was made up of tall, narrow brownstones crammed together in long rows of alternating colors and complementary architectural accents that broke up the sea of conformity. Bethany's apartment looked like a single-family four-story home until I mounted three brick steps and reached the front door—a metal, reinforced security door disguised as an ordinary wooden entry door—and noticed a buzzer panel with eight different buttons.

I rang the buzzer for Unit C and a woman's musical voice answered, "Yes?"

"Hi. I'm a friend of Bethany's. Can I come up?"

Without any answer, there was a buzz and a click as the front door unlocked. I pulled it open, noting that it was a lot heavier than it looked. Inside was a narrow hallway with two doors on either side—two had those peel-and-stick letters they sold at the hardware store marking them as A and B; the other two doors were unlabeled. I saw a steep staircase at the end of the hall. I mounted the stairs and found Unit C on the second floor.

A woman stood in the doorway, one hand clutching the door. She was tall and thin with lovely brown skin and heavy, shadowed bags under her eyes. Her dark hair was short and tightly curled.

She had sharp cheekbones and high arched brows. "How did you know Bethany?" she asked, eyeing me suspiciously.

"I worked at Untapped Books & Café with her," I told her. "I'm Odessa, the new girl."

She nodded and opened the door wider. "Bethany told me about you. She said you had a mad thick accent, but I thought she was exaggerating. Guess she wasn't. Come on in." I followed her into a long, narrow room. "I'm Cherise. We've got two more roommates, but they're not home right now."

"You've got four people living here?" I asked in astonishment, looking around at the tiny space. The brownstone had originally been a single-family home, but had since been subdivided into individual apartments. Bethany and her roommates split an apartment that couldn't have been much larger than five hundred square feet. I still had a hard time wrapping my head around the typical living arrangement in New York, which was apparently stacking people in a tiny space like cordwood until the building burst at its seams.

"Yup. It's way better than my last apartment. We had three people living in a studio, with only one single bathroom per floor. We all share the kitchen downstairs here, but at least we have our own bathroom," she explained, and I shuddered. Back home in Piney Island, I'd converted my parents' garage into my private living area. I had to go into the main house to cook or use the restroom, but I was sharing with family, not strangers. Bethany and Cherise's apartment made me appreciate Aunt Melanie's palatial apartment even more.

I handed her the envelope with the card inside. "A couple of the folks at work signed this. Do you think you could get it to Bethany's family?"

Cherise frowned. "Bethany didn't have a family, not really. I guess *we* were her family. Well, us, and her friends from work."

"I'm sorry for your loss." I didn't know what else to say. "Have the police been by yet?"

"What for? Bethany's death was an accident. At least that's what the guy who called to notify me said. I'm listed as her emergency contact," Cherise explained.

It was just as I'd expected. I knew they were overwhelmed, but if the police wouldn't investigate her death, who would? "What if it wasn't?"

"What do you mean?" Cherise asked, eyes growing wide. "Why would anyone want to hurt her? Sure, she wasn't the most popular person in the house. She wasn't even the most popular person in the apartment, truth be told. She monopolized the kitchen for her YouTube soap-making videos, and left a mess behind that could qualify for federal relief. She never had rent on time, and refused to share her Netflix password. I mean, she meant well but to be honest, the best thing about rooming with Bethany was that she was hardly ever at home."

"Oh?" I asked, ears perking up. I remembered Izzy telling me something similar, but it hadn't struck me as important until now. "Where did she spend all of her time?"

"She had a boyfriend in Astoria. Stayed at his place most days."

Bethany had a boyfriend? I knew almost nothing about her. "Do you have his address?"

"Maybe." She scrolled through the contacts on her phone. "I got a first name, Marco, and a phone number."

"I'll take whatever you've got." I gave her my phone number, and she texted me the contact file. "Did Bethany have any enemies?"

"You're kidding, right?" Cherise laughed. "She might have been a pain in the butt sometimes, but she wasn't the kind of person who had *enemies*. Unless you count those folks at the bank. They were always calling about her student loans. She sent them money when she could and the calls would stop for a week or two, but then they'd start up again."

"Did Bethany owe a lot?" I asked.

"She graduated from Princeton," Cherise explained.

Most days I regretted not going to college. In my imagination, college made everything better. I'd have a better job and could afford to move out of my parents' house. I could get a car that didn't have rust spots larger than my fist. But at least I didn't have crippling student loan debt hanging around my neck while working for less than minimum wage side by side with folks like me without any college at all.

"Well, thanks for your time and for her boyfriend's contact info. Sorry about Bethany."

"You wouldn't happen to be in the market for an apartment, would you?" she asked.

Inside I cringed. It was a nice enough neighborhood, but I couldn't imagine stepping over three roommates all the time. "I'm good, but if I hear someone's looking, I'll let you know."

I'd passed a cute little park on my way to Cherise and Bethany's apartment, so I headed back to it and claimed an empty bench. I pulled up the MTA app to see how to get to Astoria from here. It was only eight miles, less as the crow flies, but the way the tangled subway lines were laid out, I'd have to take a train to Manhattan and then back out to Queens, an hour-and-a-half-long trip. Still, at $2.75, it beat the $40 fare the Uber app estimated.

And that was assuming that Bethany's boyfriend would speak to me.

I dialed his number, and it went to voicemail. I *hated* leaving voicemails. Just last night I was discussing with Detective Castillo about how no one ever called anyone anymore, and now here I was, calling a total stranger. Irony much? My number would pop up as unknown and he'd ignore it, just like I would if the tables were turned. "Hi, my name's Odessa. I'm a friend of Bethany's. I'm trying to reach Marco. Can you call me back, please?" As soon as I hung up, I started composing a text message to Marco, but before I could type half of it, he called me back. "Hello? Marco?"

"You said you're a friend of Beth's?" he asked, without bothering with a greeting.

"I worked with her at Untapped Books & Café," I explained. "Do you have a minute to chat?"

"What about?" I heard a heavy sigh on the other end of the line. "Look, if she wants to pick up her stuff, she can do it herself. She doesn't have to send her little squad to do her dirty work like she did last time."

Alarm bells went off in my head. Pick up her stuff? Dirty work? I closed my eyes and took a deep breath. He didn't know. "I don't think you understand . . ."

"No, *you* don't understand. I think I've been perfectly reasonable but there's only so much I can . . ."

I broke in, talking over him for a second before he stopped to listen. "Marco, you've got it all wrong. We need to talk, in person preferably. Can I meet you somewhere?"

"Look here, I'm at work. I don't have time for this nonsense."

"I'll meet you after you get off," I offered. "Tell me where and when."

The pause was long enough that I was afraid he had hung up on me, but instead, he sighed heavily, and said, "Fine. Whatever. I've got a break coming up." I was about to interject and tell him it would take a while for me to get all the way out to Astoria, but then he continued, "Do you know the taco place in Domino Park?"

I exhaled a sigh of relief. It might be poor manners to break the news of Bethany's death to Marco so near to the spot where she died, but it beat schlepping all the way out to Astoria. "I'll be there in fifteen." I had to look down and check my outfit. "I'll be the petite brunette in the white tank top and purple skirt."

"I'll be the giant in the orange safety vest," he said, and disconnected.

Giant? I wondered as I hurried toward the nearest subway entrance. If I caught the train just right, I might make it with time to spare. I got lucky, and a train pulled up to the platform a few seconds after I did. I made it to the taco stand before Marco.

I hated arranging to meet strangers in public spaces. Sure, it was safer than the alternative, but trying to find someone in a crowded place when I had no idea what they looked like was nerve-racking. Fortunately, I recognized Marco from his description the second he approached. He wasn't kidding about being a giant. He was closer to seven feet tall than anyone I'd ever met before, and was wearing a blazing orange vest with a yellow hard hat tucked under his massive arm.

"Marco?" I asked, hurrying up to him. I looked up. And up.

Bethany was taller than me, but unless she wore the world's tallest heels, she would need a stepladder to give Marco a hug.

"You must be Odessa," he said, his voice a deep bass. He had bleached blond hair that looked odd against his warm olive-tinted skin, especially in contrast to a dark beard that crept down his neck, the bushy curls looking uncomfortably warm on a hot summer day. His hand swallowed mine when I offered to shake. "I've only got a few minutes. Why don't you grab a table while I place my order? Get you something?"

"Thanks, but I'm good." Even as I declined, my stomach grumbled loudly. I shouldn't have skipped breakfast. After we were done here, I'd swing by the café and use my employee discount to get a break on one of Parker's delicious creations.

"You vegan? Vegetarian?"

I shook my head. I'd never met a single vegetarian before coming to Williamsburg. When Izzy told me she was a vegan, I'd had to Google the difference. Apparently, vegetarians could eat eggs and dairy, but vegans didn't eat any meat or animal by-products at all. Not even yeast or gelatin. Believe me, when I found out what was in gelatin, I briefly considered a vegan diet myself. Ground-up cows' hooves did *not* sound appetizing.

"I'll be right back," Marco said.

I found two empty seats at a long community table and claimed them before someone else could snatch them. I took the seat that faced the elevated walkway that Bethany had fallen from, which meant my back was to the Williamsburg Bridge. As I waited, I watched a stream of people flow over the walkway. No one seemed to care that just a day ago, someone had died in this very park.

"I didn't know what you like, so I got you one chicken and one veggie," Marco said when he returned, placing two wrapped tacos in front of me, and six in front of him. That was awful nice of him. He didn't even know me, and he'd bought me lunch. He unwrapped the first one and looked at me expectantly. "What's Beth playing at this time?" he asked before taking a huge bite.

I waited for him to swallow before saying, "I don't know how to break this to you, but Bethany passed away yesterday."

He stared at me with a blank expression. "Huh?" I repeated myself, this time more carefully. I knew my accent got thicker when I was stressed, but I didn't think I was that hard to understand. "I heard you the first time," he said, blinking at me. "But I don't believe it. I *can't* believe it."

"I'm so very sorry for your loss." Somehow it sounded even worse than when I'd said those same words to Cherise earlier.

"You're mistaken," Marco said.

"I wish I was," I said. Why did no one believe me? Didn't I look trustworthy?

Marco pushed back his chair and stood up. "Look here, I know Beth's mad because I dumped her, but this is just cruel."

I stood, too, and was dwarfed by him. "I'm telling the truth. Hold on half a second and I'll prove it." I googled Domino Park news, and an article popped up with a candid shot of Bethany that looked like it had been pulled off her Instagram. The article was titled "Local Woman Plunges to Her Death in Domino Park" and included a link to the viral flash mob proposal video, which now had millions of views. "Look familiar?" I shoved my phone toward his face. He stared at the article.

He shook his head. "No. That can't be her. That's not my Beth."

"I'm afraid it is. If you want, I can put you in touch with the cop who has her case. Or you can call her roomie, Cherise. She's the one who gave me your number."

"Cop? Case? How did it happen?"

"She fell," I said.

"She fell?"

"She fell off the walkway," I said, gesturing toward the elevated walkway over Marco's shoulder. Even from this angle, it didn't look that high. "The cops are calling it an accident, but they're wrong. Bethany was murdered, and I'm gonna prove it."

7

Odessa Dean @OdessaWaiting · June 25
Summer in the bayou: unbearable. Worst in the world. Doesn't
get any hotter than this.
Summer in NYC: hold my beer
#1000degrees #melting

WHAT?" THE EXPRESSION on his face was abject shock, which
morphed into pain. He stood, his shoulders hunched and his face
averted. "I have to go."

"Wait," I pleaded with him. "I need to ask you some questions."

"What's wrong with you?" He smacked his huge hands on the
table and looked at me, tears streaming down his face. "You tell
me my girlfriend's dead. That she's been *murdered*. You drop this
bomb on me and expect me to, what? Stick around and chat?"

"But you broke up . . ."

Marco's face twisted into anger. "Not that it's any of your business, but I love Beth. Always have. Always will. Yes, she cheated
on me and broke my heart but I never in a million years thought
that we wouldn't have a chance to set things straight."

"I'm so sorry for your . . ."

"Save it," he snapped. "Gotta bounce." Then he stormed off in the opposite direction.

Not that I blamed him.

He was distraught, and I did sort of spring everything on him. But what's an easy way to break the news to someone that a person they cared about was dead? "Hi. Nice weather we're having. Your ex got murdered yesterday," certainly wasn't it.

" 'Scuse me. You gonna just sit there all day or what?" A stranger loomed over me, a tray of tacos in his hand. His lips were pursed and his eyebrows knitted together.

I looked around. There were no empty seats. Someone had already taken Marco's spot, and I hadn't even noticed. I unwrapped one of the tacos he'd bought for me and took a bite. The stranger made an annoyed sound in the back of his throat and moved on, searching for someone else he could intimidate into vacating a spot for him.

When I'd first come to New York, I was taken aback by the gall of some people. People are rude in the South, too, but it's subtle. A passive-aggressive wave here. Neglecting to offer someone sweet tea when they came to call. Backhanded compliments like, "Well, aren't you just as cute as you wanna be?" when what they actually meant was, "You didn't fall too far from the ugly tree."

New Yorkers are no better or worse than the folks I grew up with in Louisiana. They were just more overt, and nine times out of ten, they were reacting to something they perceived as rude. Like when I'd bumped into the dog walker last night. Sure, she'd flipped me off and said some nasty things about my parentage, but in her mind, I'd started it. Even the food truck driver who'd almost run me over was reacting because I'd gotten in his way. Sitting at a crowded eatery, taking up space at a community table but not eating was, at least by Brooklyn standards, a rude act. A stranger calling me out on it wasn't.

And in an overpopulated metropolis like New York City, taking up too much space was the biggest crime of them all.

I scarfed down both tacos—delicious, by the way. I was used to crunchy-shelled tacos that were stuffed with way too much lettuce and cheese with a hint of flavored crumbles that might be beef. The tacos served in Domino Park were on a whole 'nother level. The soft corn tortillas were made by hand daily onsite, and were filled with fresh, yummy ingredients that didn't need to be drowned in hot sauce to be palatable.

When I was done, I gathered my trash, plus Marco's leftovers, and moved away from the table. My spot was snatched up before I'd taken two steps away from it. As I walked away, I could hear someone else arguing that they were waiting for my seat, but the one who was now occupying it had the classic schoolyard defense of "you snooze, you lose" on their side.

It was getting hot, and after enjoying the delightful tacos, I was thirsty. But I didn't want to brave the long lines at the counter for just a bottle of overpriced water, so I headed for the park exit instead.

Summer in Louisiana was rough. Sometimes I would rather don a full-body chicken suit and jump in the boiling vat of water at the Crawdad Shack than walk across the black tar parking lot to my car. Humidity hovered around 125 percent, if such a thing were possible, and it could be a hundred degrees in the shade.

And it couldn't hold a candle to New York City in June.

It wasn't as hot, at least not according to my weather app, nor

OLIVIA BLACKE

as humid. But Williamsburg offered no shade. The sun reflected off the windows and sidewalks and metal and cars, trapping heat between the towering buildings and turning the city into a shimmering oven. Summer was short but brutal, with limited working air conditioners and rolling brownouts as the city's aging power grid could not keep up with demand.

And the smell.

I couldn't even begin to describe the smell.

Imagine eight and a half million unwashed people squeezed into an elevator for a three-day weekend. Now imagine that the elevator didn't have a bathroom or a fan, and it was a gazillion degrees. New York in the summer kinda smells like that. Only worse.

Between the smell and the sun beating down on me, I was getting a headache. I headed back toward Aunt Melanie's apartment building, hoping that the long walk would give me time to figure out what I needed to do next. It always seemed so easy in the true crime podcasts I liked to listen to. Everyone the amateur detective interviewed would drop a hint, and they'd stumble across clue after clue until they had all the puzzle pieces. I was starting to think it wasn't quite as simple as they made it seem.

By the time I got halfway home, I was drenched in sweat. All thoughts of Bethany's death were replaced with fantasies of diving into the pool on the rooftop deck of my aunt's building and staying under the water until I grew gills. Now *that* sounded like a viable plan.

The apartment lobby was all steel and marble with darkly tinted floor-to-ceiling windows. The temperature was set to a few degrees above iceberg. Last night, soaked from the rainstorm, it had been miserable. But coming in out of the heat of the day, it was pure paradise.

In one corner was a pair of wingback chairs, a lamp, and a potted plant that nearly brushed the eleven-foot-high ceiling. Along the back wall ran a bank of mailboxes. Guarding it all was a long, low desk. The concierge desk was staffed from eight to seven, and would accept anything from packages to pizza for the residents. The concierge today was an older African American gentleman who always looked at me like he knew I didn't belong.

I waved at him and summoned enough energy for a half-hearted smile. "Afternoon, Earl."

"Miss Odessa," he replied, his expression never changing. Then he sniffed and I felt self-conscious. After a thirteen-block walk home from the park under a blazing sun, I doubted I smelled like a bed of roses. More like a bed of rose fertilizer. "You have a visitor."

"I do?" I glanced around. We were the only two people in the lobby.

"I sent them upstairs to wait," he explained, with the barest hint of a smile. I was glad he found me amusing.

"Thanks, Earl."

"You're welcome, Miss Odessa."

I took the elevator upstairs to the fifth floor. When the door opened, the first thing I saw was Izzy, sitting on top of a large hard-sided suitcase that looked to be held together with duct tape and prayers. Her nose was buried in her phone, but when she heard the door swoosh open, she looked up. "I was just about to text you."

"Been waiting long?" I stepped out and the door closed behind me. Along with the big suitcase she also had a duffel bag stuffed to bulging, a backpack, and one of those enormous crinkly laundry totes. "You, um, going somewhere?"

"They're fumigating my place, so I was hoping I could crash here for a day or two."

"That's an awful lot of luggage for a day or two," I said.

"Oh, you know how it is." Izzy stood and ran her hand through her short, artificially orange hair. It had a touch of wave to it and barely came to the tops of her ears. She grunted as she picked up her duffel bag and slung the strap over her shoulder. "You never know what you'll need."

"Glad to see you're doing better." I flipped through the keys on my keyring, letting them clank against each other. "You seemed pretty upset last night, and Todd said you called in sick this morning."

"Well, I'm not exactly in a partying mood, but the last thing Bethany would want would be for me to sit around moping and feeling sorry for myself. So, um, would you mind opening the door? This bag is getting awful heavy awful fast."

"I'd love to help, but Aunt Melanie was adamant about me not having any visitors." We stared at each other, the long awkward pause stretching out between us. "I mean, if it was my place, of course I'd invite you in, but it's not . . ."

Izzy grinned. "Don't worry about it. Your aunt won't be back for months. She'll never know I was here."

"Sorry, but I promised."

"And I a hundred percent understand. If I had any other options, anything at all . . ."

"I hear that Bethany's old apartment has an opening," I said, then quickly bit my lip. Talk about insensitive. I unlocked the door and waved her inside.

Izzy put her bag down and started to explore the living room. "Yowza, this place is enormous," she said, wandering slowly past my aunt's collection of knickknacks and bizarre decorations, taking it all in. "Bethany's roomies are cool, but Bed-Stuy?" she asked, thumbing through the books on the shelf. "No thank you. That commute would drive me up the wall."

"What commute? It's ten, fifteen minutes on the train, tops, to Untapped. I used to drive longer than that to get to the Crawdad Shack back home, but that was only because my parents' house is on the far side of town by the railroad tracks and if I timed it wrong, I had to wait for the train to pass so I could get to work."

Izzy giggled. "Sometimes I forget that you're not from here, and then you whip out some story about life in the bayou."

She forgot, even for one second, that I was an outsider? That I utterly didn't belong? That I was a proverbial fish out of water in Williamsburg? "I think that might be the nicest thing anyone's said to me since I got here, and that's counting the time you pointed out that I'd accidentally tucked the hem of my skirt into my underpants."

"What are friends for?" Izzy asked with a grin.

She had a point. My aunt would surely find out, and there was no telling how she'd react, but Izzy was my friend. And she needed my help.

I liked to think of myself as a good person. I respected crosswalks. I never shoplifted or littered. Back home I volunteered at the old folks' home. I ate my vegetables and recycled. I most certainly did not turn my back on a friend in need. "Just for a night or two?" I asked.

"Maybe three. Help me with my suitcases? I mean, sure, it's a real swanky building and all, but I can't leave my stuff out in the hall where just anyone could walk off with it."

"True." I grabbed the large wheeled suitcase and dragged it inside. Frankly, I wasn't concerned that one of the neighbors would steal something. The building had concierge trash collection, and if anything, bags left in the hall were liable to be whisked away and dropped down the incinerator chute. Especially a beat-up old suitcase or a plastic tote filled to the brim with miscellany.

The cat chose that moment to make an appearance, ignoring me completely in favor of winding his way around Izzy's legs. She dumped her backpack onto the growing heap of luggage we'd dragged inside and scooped him up, rubbing her face into his fur as he purred so loud that I could hear him from halfway across the room. "And who's this cutie patootie?" she asked, her voice muffled by his fluffy body.

"That's Rufus. My aunt's cat. Don't let him fool you. He's not starving to death no matter what he says."

"Gotcha," Izzy said, giving Rufus another big squeeze before putting him back down. "Aren't you the most perfect kitty in the whole wide world?"

"I had no idea you liked cats so much. Do you have one of your own?"

Izzy shrugged. "Can't afford a pet deposit. Besides, there's lots of feral cats in my building, and some of them are real friendly. They wander in and out through the broken windows in the basement. Keeps the rats at bay."

I shuddered. I wasn't afraid of rats, per se. I was used to nutria, the giant rodents that infested Louisiana parks and waterways. They grew up to twenty pounds and resembled a nightmarish cross between a beaver and a rat, with giant buckteeth and a long, snakelike tail. I just didn't like the idea of rats in my house. Or nutria, for that matter.

"Wouldn't it be easier to have the landlord fix the windows?" I asked.

"Landlord? I live in an old abandoned public school, along with a few dozen other people. I shower in the gym locker room, and make food in a galley kitchen. I share a science classroom with another girl and an articulated skeleton we call Mandy Funny-bones. We don't exactly pay rent."

And I thought Bethany's living situation had been rough.

"You're a squatter?" I'd heard of squatters, people who take over otherwise unused buildings and made them their own. In New York, they had the same legal rights as paying tenants under certain circumstances. It wasn't exactly the same as being homeless, but close enough in my sheltered opinion.

"Yup." Her brow furrowed. "I'm hoping the fumigators do their job and leave, but if one of them is a stickler and reports back to the city that people are living there, we're all screwed."

"If they are sending out fumigators, then someone cares about the building, at least a little, right?"

"City-owned property has to be maintained, even derelict schoolhouses," she said with an unconcerned air.

I don't know how she did it. I didn't expect I'd ever be rich, but so far I'd always known where I was gonna sleep that night, and I didn't miss a lot of meals, even when money was tight. "What will you do if they board the doors and windows up tight?"

"I'll figure something out. Always do." She looked around.

"Which room's mine?" Izzy jiggled the handle of the closest door. It didn't open.

"Technically, it's a two bedroom, but Aunt Melanie converted one room into an art studio. It's locked, and she didn't leave the key," I explained.

"No problem. Couch is fine, I'm sure."

"You can have the bedroom," I told her without hesitation, good old Southern manners rearing their head. Izzy was my guest, and more importantly, she was my friend. Guests don't sleep on the couch.

"Nope. Wouldn't think of it." She stretched out on the couch, her feet propped up on one arm. "Comfy. You had lunch yet? My treat."

"I'm good." Maybe I should have mentioned that Bethany's ex-boyfriend had bought me tacos, but then I'd have to admit that I was sticking my nose where it didn't belong. "Seriously though, the bedroom's all yours. Hey, I was heading to the pool to try to cool down, if you want to join me."

"You're kidding me? This place has a pool? I mean, my building has a pool, too, but it's just the southeast corner of the cafeteria where the floor caved in and rainwater puddles there after a storm."

"I'm not sure I can beat that," I said, trying not to cringe. "But on Wednesdays there's a Mommy and Me class that meets up at the pool, and those mothers are savage."

"I'll bet. Give me a second to change." Izzy rifled through her suitcase, came up with a scrap of cloth, and disappeared into the bathroom.

I went into the bedroom and changed into my favorite suit. It was a cheery orange plaid with a vintage-inspired cap-sleeved top and high-waisted bikini bottoms.

Izzy let out a wolf whistle when I emerged. In contrast to my classic swimsuit, she was wearing an itty-bitty white string bikini. I realized for the first time that she had a sentence tattooed in flowing script on her ribcage.

"Back atcha," I said, taking a bow.

I was feeling cute and confident, until Izzy gave me a concerned look and asked, "Um, Odessa, do you have, like, a low-key skin condition or something I should know about?"

"No." I contorted my arm so I could feel the back of my exposed shoulders. "Am I having a breakout? Ugh. Bacne is the absolute worst."

"You're *green*."

"I'm what?" Then I remembered. Neon shirt. Caught out in a downpour. Green-dyed skin. "I thought I'd gotten it all." I was more than half tempted to let it wash off in the pool, but if I had spots that hadn't faded after last night's epic shower session, it wasn't going away without a fight. "Help me scrub it off?"

"Sure." We headed to the bathroom, and I dropped the shoulders of my suit while clutching one arm around the front to prevent a wardrobe malfunction. "This stuff is stubborn," she commented. Maybe I should have given her a Brillo pad and bleach instead of a washcloth and mild soap. "What on earth happened to you?"

"It's dye from an Untapped uniform shirt."

"Ugh. I despise those shirts. I mean, neon green isn't flattering on anyone, except maybe a frog. Or a turtle. You have really nice shoulder blades, you know. Have you ever considered getting a tattoo?"

"Never thought about it before." Tattoos looked great, on other people. I couldn't imagine one on me, though. "Besides, I can't think of anything I like well enough to permanently etch on my skin."

"Fair enough. Although a bunch of us were talking about getting matching owl tattoos." She cupped the underside of her left wrist. "As a tribute to Bethany."

"That's sweet," I said, wondering why no one had included me in that discussion. I guess between being the new girl and not having any tattoos already, they thought I wouldn't be interested. And to be fair, they were right. I'd never even been in a tattoo parlor before. Back home, they were in the sketchy part of Shreveport. Here, they were everywhere. "Maybe I can come along, just to watch?"

"Of course." She finished scrubbing my back, rinsed off the washcloth, and draped it across the sink. "All done here."

"Thanks a bunch. Come on, let's go hit the pool. Don't worry about towels, they have them up there," I told her, leading the way up to the roof.

8

Dizzy Izzy @IsabelleWilliamsburg · June 25
after much contemplation, i've decided i'm done adulting 4 the
day. i'll be poolside working on my vitamin D deficiency. send
sunblock. #metime #dontforgetthesunblock #thestruggleisreal

THE ROOFTOP POOL deck was a lush oasis compared to the scorching
city below. My aunt's building wasn't particularly tall. Unlike
nearby Manhattan, with a few towering exceptions, most of the
real estate in Williamsburg was in the three- to five-story range,
which put us well above street level but not dizzyingly so.

On a clear day, I had a view of the Manhattan skyline from the
rooftop. Not as magnificent as the view from Domino Park, but it
was pretty good. Once night fell, the not-so-distant lights from the
skyscrapers dominated the sky. But on a hot, humid day like today,
everything was hazy and gray.

The rooftop deck sported several leafy green plants, colorful
beach umbrellas, two large grills, and of course, the pool. It was a
few feet shy of Olympic-sized, a long oval with a thatched tiki hut
on one end and comfortable lounge chairs arranged around the

sparkling water. There was even a small bathroom—not much bigger than a porta potty, but cleaner—so residents didn't have to go back to their units, dripping wet, to use the restroom. We had the place to ourselves, as most of the building residents were at work in the middle of a weekday. The water was cold, but only five feet deep. Unlike the pools back home, I didn't even have to check for gators or water moccasins before diving beneath the glassy surface.

"This is amazing," Izzy said, levering herself up on the side of the pool. "Is that a bar?" she asked, pointing at the tiki hut.

"Weekends after five it is," I told her. I took a deep breath and slid under the water. I surfaced every few kicks for a quick breath of air before submerging again. I reached the far end of the pool, flipped, and headed back.

"Where'd you learn to swim like that?" she asked when I surfaced next to her, holding on to the edge while my legs floated behind me.

"Dunno. Never did really learn how to swim like the athletes do, just picked it up from hanging out at the lake back home." Most of the lakes in Louisiana weren't entirely safe to swim in, unless you *liked* being gator bait, but the way I saw it was that plenty of people went swimming in the ocean all the time, alongside tons of critters a lot more dangerous than gators.

"We should throw a party or something. It would be a riot!"

"I don't know about that," I said, chewing on my bottom lip. "I'm not supposed to have visitors, remember? Besides, I don't know anyone to invite."

"You know me. And the rest of the crew at Untapped. Parker. Andre. Kim and the rest of the night crew. Even Todd, if you're feeling charitable."

"The timing doesn't feel right. Isn't it a little, you know, insensitive? I mean, Bethany's been gone what, a day? We should be in mourning, not arranging a pool party."

"Odessa, you're a genius." Izzy pushed off the lip of the pool and splashed into the deep end, treading water to stay afloat. "We host a memorial service. Poolside. BYOB. A wake."

"Good idea, but still . . ."

"Don't fret, I've got this," Izzy declared. "We'll keep it small, just a few of her closest friends. I'll take care of everything."

My aunt was gonna kill me.

Then again, Izzy's idea wasn't the worst I'd ever heard. We could celebrate Bethany's life. And, it wouldn't hurt to gather all of Bethany's friends in one place. What better way to get more information about her death? The more I considered it, the more I realized it was a great opportunity to interrogate everyone Bethany knew in the city. "We'll have to reserve the pool, and we might have to bribe Earl the concierge, so he doesn't rat us out to Aunt Melanie."

"Consider it done," Izzy agreed. "This place is the actual bomb. I mean your aunt's bathroom alone is bigger than my last two apartments. I can't believe she doesn't have a roommate or seven."

I dipped my head under the water to avoid Izzy's next question, but I knew what she was thinking. This building wasn't cheap. I didn't want her thinking that I was loaded just because my aunt could afford a place like this. When I couldn't hold my breath any longer, I popped up.

Izzy continued chatting as if I hadn't disappeared for a little over a minute. She was telling me a horror story about some apartment she used to rent in Manhattan's Alphabet City. For two grand a month, she got a ninety-nine-square-foot hovel in the basement. It had its own bathroom—a minor miracle in that neighborhood—and its own kitchen, although the appliances never worked. She had two tiny windows that peeked into a court-yard and provided a handy-dandy way for burglars to break in every other week or so. She spent more money replacing the secu-rity bars than ever got stolen from her, so after a while she stopped bothering.

I could imagine living in a tiny studio apartment barely large enough for a single full-sized bed, but with roomies? Especially if I had to share with two people I'd met on Craigslist. What was it that Cherise had told me? Bethany's most redeeming quality was that she was never home, because she spent most nights at her boyfriend's house.

What had I learned in the park today? Taking up too much space in Brooklyn was the biggest crime of them all.

I needed to talk to Marco again and find out how long ago they had broken up. If I was squeezed into a tiny living space with a complete slob who never paid her rent on time, and I had just found out that she was going from part-time to full-time resident, I'd be pretty upset. Not murder-someone upset, but upset none-theless. I needed to interview the other roommates to see how they'd felt about these new circumstances.

"We should invite Bethany's roommates to the wake," I sug-gested, interrupting Izzy's description of a rat the size of a loaf of bread dragging a whole bag of groceries out the front door while she was busy putting her other purchases away.

"There you go again with another of your fabulous ideas. Of course we should invite them."

"And her boyfriend, too." Sure, he was the ex at the time of her death, but two birds with one stone, right? I'd rather not have to traipse all the way out to Astoria to talk to him again.

"Yes! Wait a second. I thought they broke up?"

"Why did they break up, anyway? What happened?" I should have known that Izzy would have all the answers. She was easy to talk to, so people told her everything.

"Bethany was terribly upset about the whole thing. Her man, Marco, read some thirsty DMs on her phone and dumped her. She swore she would never cheat on him, but apparently, he didn't believe her. It's tragic, like Romeo-and-Juliet tragic."

"Uh-huh." Star-crossed lovers never ended well. "You don't think . . ." My voice trailed off. It was difficult to imagine, but I saw three distinct possibilities. It was an accident, it was a murder, or it was something much too horrible to contemplate. "I mean, if she was upset over the breakup? That maybe she jumped? On purpose?"

"No," Izzy said, her voice firm. "No way. Bethany would never do something like that. Especially over a guy. She and Marco had broken up half a dozen times before, and they always ended up back together. Bethany even confided in me that she had a sure-fire plan to get him back."

"Oh yeah? She didn't happen to share the details, did she?"

Izzy frowned. "Well, no. But knowing Bethany, it was going to be extra." Something glittered in the corner of her eye. It could have been pool water, but I didn't think it was.

Time to change the subject.

"Got any plans for tonight?"

Izzy climbed out of the pool and stretched out on one of the lounge chairs. "It's too stinkin' hot to do anything." She sat up a bit so she could look at me. "I noticed the sewing machine on your aunt's table." I hadn't thought of it before, but having enough space for a full-sized table in the living room was a luxury most New Yorkers couldn't afford. "Maybe you could teach me to sew something later? Then I can teach you how to make my famous vegan pesto pasta. You'll love it."

I wasn't so sure about vegan pasta, as I normally dumped the entire contents of the cheese shaker on top of my spaghetti, but I was willing to try anything once. "Deal." Refreshed, I got out of the pool and led Izzy to the stack of towels in a basket near the door that led back into the building, dripping as I walked. We dried off and left our towels in a bin.

A pool that not only provided towels but also washed and dried them after use was a perk even better than the hallway trash collection, in my opinion. Then again, the bougie building was probably trying to keep residents from hanging beach towels on their balconies to dry. It might hurt their image.

Dressed and hair as dry as my thick hair was going to get with just a vigorous toweling off, I started setting up my sewing supplies. "Back home, I hoard fabric. It's so expensive, I try to only buy it on sale." It wasn't fair. Buying a few yards of fabric was more expensive than getting ready-made clothes at Walmart, but they bought in bulk. Besides, *my* creations fit me perfectly, and didn't fall apart the first time I wore them. "But I didn't bring any cloth with me, so I'm gonna let you in on a little secret."

"Oh yeah?"

"Come on. We're going shopping."

Williamsburg was many things. It offered a wide selection of exotic foods. It boasted some of the greatest artists and art galleries I'd ever seen. Practically every block had a live music venue, a coffee shop, and a holistic spa. There was something for everyone, from jogging clubs to escape rooms. But one thing that Williamsburg had in spades, above all else, was killer thrift stores.

Only they didn't call them thrift stores here. They had second-hand stores, upcycled boutiques, and consignment shops. The granddaddy of them all was Brooklyn Flea, but it was only open on the weekends.

Luckily, smaller thrift stores were everywhere, and I led Izzy to one of my favorites. As I opened the door, my senses were assaulted by the sparkly glass jewelry in a display case under the cash register, strange pipe music wafting out from tiny speakers, and that underlying scent of age that never fully goes away no matter how many times you wash something. Better still was the twinge of anticipation, not knowing what hidden gems I might discover today.

I made a beeline for the racks of clothes in the back, but got distracted by a pair of six-inch shiny red patent leather platform shoes. I reached out and caressed one of the buckles before turning the shoe over. As luck would have it, they were two sizes too small. "Drat," I said, picking up its mate. "Maybe if I stretched them out?"

Izzy took them from me and placed them back on the shelf. "Eyes on the prize, Odessa. Besides, you're the only person I know who can pull off cowboy boots and not make it look like you're trying to be ironic or something. You don't need those platforms."

"You're right," I grudgingly admitted. "But if the shoe-size fairy visits me tonight and shrinks my feet, I'm coming back for these."

"Deal. Now, what are we looking for?"

"Look for colors or material that catch your eye. Don't worry about what it is, just that there's plenty of it. If you shop up a size, it's easier to repurpose and make a unique garment of your own." For Izzy, that would be easy. Between a high metabolism and her vegan diet, she could probably shop in the kids' section.

I didn't envy her, though. Sure, there were more cute choices for a size two than a size sixteen, but I liked being curvaceous. I ate relatively healthy—choosing water over soda and a side salad over French fries *most* of the time—but I wasn't interested in crash diets or starving myself to death just to fit in a smaller size. I was moderately active without spending money I couldn't afford on a gym membership. I'd much rather be comfortable in my own skin than worry about a few extra pounds.

Being a bit curvier than average—whatever that was—made it more difficult to find the perfect fabric for myself at a second-hand store, but sometimes the shopping deities were in a generous mood. Today was one of those days.

I spotted the dress—it was pink roses on a field of silvery gray—at the end of the row and snatched it up, hugging it against my body. The fabric was silky soft and there were yards of material in the full dress. I looked at the price tag and said a little prayer of gratitude. It was marked down to fifteen bucks. It would cost me maybe five or six times that just to buy the fabric wholesale, assuming I could ever find something this lush at a local hobby store.

"Hey, that's mine. I saw it first."

"Huh?" I looked down and saw a woman in a wheelchair, several dresses already draped across her lap, glaring up at me. If I had to guess, she was a decade or so older than me, younger than Todd but likely closer to his age than mine.

"You heard me. That's my dress." The expression on her face was anything but friendly.

I clutched the dress closer to my body, even knowing that I was wrinkling it. "I don't see your name on it." I know, I know. I sounded like a petulant third-grader. But this dress really *did* have my name all over it. In my head, I was already deconstructing it, taking apart each seam, and removing each button with the careful hands of a surgeon. I already had the perfect pattern picked out for it. It would be a long, simple sundress with enough material left over to make a matching shawl.

It was the kind of dress to wear on a first date. The perfect dress. And I wasn't going to let it go.

"Hand it over. You don't gotta be a jerk," the woman in the wheelchair ordered, holding out her hand. I noticed she had on fingerless gloves, like a bicyclist might wear for a long ride. Her outfit was black from head to toe. Black shoes. Black tights. A black tank top. Even her hair was dyed black.

"Be reasonable," I said. "Do you even wear pink? Besides, I had it first."

She narrowed her eyes at me and dropped her hand so she could inch closer to me with her chair. "Seriously? You wanna go? You think you can steal that dress from me? Gonna take my purse, too? My wallet? Maybe you want my chair?"

"Nobody's stealing anything from anyone," I said. I glanced down at the dress. It was perfect. But was it worth getting into a fight over? "You know what? You're right."

I smoothed the fabric in my hand before holding the dress out toward her. It was hard to judge with any real accuracy since she was seated and I was standing, but she was probably taller than me, and several dress sizes smaller. No way would the dress, *my* dress, fit her. It would be as flattering as a wet paper sack. "Do me a favor? If it doesn't fit, let me have a shot at it?"

The woman snatched the dress and let it fall in a crumpled pile on top of the other dresses in her lap. "Good thing I don't need it to fit. I just need to chop it up into little tiny squares," she gloated.

"You *what*?" I stared at her, appalled. Sure, I'd been planning on repurposing it, too, but as a gorgeous dress that I would wear. Not as confetti.

Izzy reappeared, her arms laden down with an eye-searing mishmash of colors and patterns. "Help me narrow this down, will ya?" She studied my face. "What's wrong? Looks like you're about to blow a gasket or something."

I shook my head. "It's not important."

The woman in the wheelchair laughed and I had to bite my tongue to keep from saying something rude I would regret later.

"Hey, I know you," Izzy said.

"I doubt it," she replied.

"No, I never forget a face. You're that girl on YouTube that makes the all-natural soaps. Bethany showed me one of your vids one time. I think you were making aloe vera soap that day."

The woman snorted, and a grin split her face. "Bethany? That hack. I always knew she secretly watched my vids. That's how she stole my ideas. I'm gonna crucify her."

"Too late for that," I said, without thinking. "Someone already beat you to it. Bethany's dead."

9

Odessa Dean @OdessaWaiting · June 25
U call it a defect, I call it a 1-of-a-kind creation #sewing
#homemade #crafty

WAIT, SHE'S WHAT?" the woman in the wheelchair asked, her glee-ful expression disappearing in the span of a heartbeat. "You're talking about a different Bethany."

"Maybe you're right." I was still salty over losing the dress and her talking bad about Bethany, but something about the woman's crestfallen face tugged at my heartstrings. I hoped we were talking about two different people, but how many people in Williamsburg were named Bethany and made homemade soap videos on You-Tube?

Don't answer that.

Probably about as many women our age running around New York with cute little owl tattoos.

"Bethany Kostolus passed away yesterday," Izzy clarified.

The woman in the wheelchair started to cry, tears running

down her face. "No, that can't be." She shook her head and used the dress, *my* dress, to dab at her eyes. "No way."

"I'm sorry, but it's true." Izzy shifted the clothes she was carrying so they were tucked under one arm. She used her free hand to touch the other woman's shoulder. "It was an accident, very sudden. We're all still trying to process it." She gave me a sideways glance. "I'm sorry for your loss. Were you two close?"

She sniffled. "You could say that."

"Oof," Izzy said.

"Hey, we're planning a memorial-service-slash-pool-party for her. A wake of sorts, if you will," I said. "Maybe you'd like to come?"

"That would be nice," she said, bobbing her head several times. "A poolside memorial service. Bethany would have liked that."

"We thought the same thing," Izzy said.

The woman in the wheelchair shifted the clothes on her lap and dug out her purse. She scribbled down something on a piece of paper and handed it to Izzy. "You'll call me with details? I'm Jenny Green, by the way."

"Izzy Wilson. And this is Odessa Dean. We worked with Bethany at Untapped Books & Café."

Jenny sniffled. "Good to meet you. Wish it had been under better circumstances."

"Same," Izzy said. "I'll text you when we know more."

Jenny wrenched one wheel around so she was poised to head to the counter with her purchases. Then she paused and gave a half-turn back toward us. "Odessa, sorry about the dress." She held it out to me.

"You keep it," I said, feeling ashamed that I'd almost picked a fight over a silly dress.

"I insist." She was still holding it at arm's length. The roses had shiny thread woven into them that I hadn't noticed earlier, and it sparkled in the cheap overhead lights.

"Thanks," I said, snatching it before she could change her mind. "Look forward to seeing you at the service." She gave me a curt nod before spinning back around and heading away.

"I don't get it," I said, as soon as she was out of earshot.

"You don't get what?" Izzy asked. She draped her finds along the top of a clothes rack, a garish orange-checkered pinafore next to a yellow-and-blue-striped track suit next to a romper with purple stars on a field of gold.

"One second, Jenny was acting like she hated Bethany's guts, and the next she was crying her eyes out like they were besties."

"Oh, that." She held a sheer white blouse up to the light before hanging it back on the rack. "They're frenemies."

"Huh? I thought frenemies were friends in public but enemies in private."

"In this case, it's the other way around. Reverse frenemies?" Izzy suggested.

"Or Jenny was pretending to be upset when we told her about Bethany because she was hiding something." I looked down at the gorgeous dress in my hands. But would Jenny have given up her claim on the dress unless she was genuinely distressed?

"We'll know the tea if she shows up to the memorial service. What do you think about this?" She held up a green lace blouse.

"Lace is a pain to sew." I forced myself to give her my full attention. I couldn't go around suspecting everyone in Williamsburg of murder. I'd drive myself batty. "Same goes for anything too stretchy, mesh, or really thick. Start out simple, with cotton or a cotton blend. What are you looking to make?"

"I was thinking maybe those big loose pants that almost look like a skirt. You know what I'm talking about?"

"Sure do. Palazzo pants. Good choice. They're easy." I rifled through the clothes that she'd collected. Izzy was a woman of varied tastes. "Do you want something cutesy or something fun?"

"Nothing basic," she replied.

"Well, then, let's mix it up a little." I draped the orange-checkered pinafore and a simple dress covered in bold yellow daisies next to each other. I left a gap between them, then laid out the purple and gold romper next to a blue and lilac tie-dyed maxi skirt. Finally, I matched a red and white Hawaiian print muumuu with a pair of loose cotton pants that were covered in bold, primary-colored American traditional tattoos like screaming eagles, huge red roses, snakes interwound with skulls, and daggers piercing hearts. "Pick the combo you like the best. We'll do one leg in one pattern, and the other leg in the second. It will look amazeballs, much cuter than anything you can find in the stores and tons more affordable."

"Not the orange check." She hummed to herself for a minute. "I like the tie-dye a lot, but that third set is lit."

"Help me put the rest of this back, and we'll get the tattoos and Aloha dress." We carried our selections to the front counter. Izzy insisted on paying for everything, even my new material. "You don't have to do that," I told her. "You're making dinner, remember?"

"And you're letting me crash at your place for free. Least I can do."

When we got to the building, Izzy went out of her way to flirt with Earl, even though he was old enough to be her grandpa. I think he liked the attention, because he was nicer to her than he'd ever been to me before. Upstairs, I showed her where the washer and dryer were, and advised her to wash the clothes before we ripped them apart and reused them. Sure, she could have washed them when we were done, but I never knew what might be on second-hand clothes.

Once the laundry was started, she took my key—Aunt Melanie had only left me one set—and a few reusable canvas grocery bags, and headed to the market. I pulled out my laptop, made myself comfortable on the couch, and pulled up Bethany's YouTube channel.

I'd never had an urge to make my own soaps or lotions before, but Bethany made it look so easy. I was half tempted to text Izzy and ask her to grab some lye and shea butter while she was out. In addition to learning how to combine essential oils into the soap-making process, I also found out that Bethany talked a metric ton's worth of smack about Jenny in her videos.

So of course I had to check out some of Jenny's vids, and the next thing I knew, I'd gotten sucked into the black hole called YouTube. In the first video, I was greeted with a cheery, upbeat tune that I just *knew* was gonna be stuck in my head as Jenny—dressed in cute cotton-candy colors—greeted me with a friendly, "Hello again! So happy to see you guys!"

Granted, I'd just met her the once, but that Jenny hadn't exactly been warm. Or welcoming. Or particularly nice. Maybe Jenny was the evil twin?

"Okay, today, we're gonna make"—she held a dramatic pause—"soap! Surprise! Just kidding, of *course* we're making soap today. Unlike that hack *Bethany*, we're gonna experiment with colors and scents instead of using cheesy molds that *someone* found on eBay."

Now *that* was more like the Jenny I'd been expecting. Frankly, I couldn't see why they were such bitter rivals. Both were in the same general market, sure, but they were different enough that they weren't direct competitors.

Bethany's soap-making videos were popular, but her real hustle was selling her soaps in her Etsy store. Her claim to fame was her funny shapes. From flamingos to raunchy bachelorette party favors, she made just about everything. She had an entire line of nerdy soaps including a TARDIS, a *Firefly*-class spaceship, and Thor's hammer.

Jenny, on the other hand, concentrated on teaching people how to make soap with simple, natural ingredients. She demonstrated how to make colorful soaps without using artificial dyes and how to infuse soap with essential oils. She had more web traffic than Bethany, but didn't sell as much direct to the public.

I thought it was weird that anyone would buy their soaps after watching the detailed tutorials, but I guess some people didn't have the time or energy to make their own. Someone who wanted a wide selection of fun, funky shapes shopped with Bethany. Those who wanted more natural ingredients bought from Jenny, who always packaged her soaps in pretty scraps of cloth instead of plastic before mailing them out to her buyers.

Just thinking about the near fate of my perfect thrift store find, I shuddered. It would have been a crime to cut the fabulous dress up to make fancy tissue paper.

Between all of the snarky jabs they aimed at each other in the videos and the comments section, it was hard to imagine the two of them being in the same room as each other, much less singing "Kumbaya" around a campfire. Jenny had sure talked a good game before doing a one-eighty. Comparing the sullen Jenny I'd met at the thrift store to the perky Jenny in the videos, I knew she was an expert at pretending to be someone she was not. Was she acting when she was mad or when she was distraught? Could Jenny be so competitive that she would want Bethany out of the way, permanently?

That was ridiculous. Wasn't it?

What kind of sicko would murder someone over a YouTube feud?

I was so engrossed in the videos, no time at all seemed to pass before Izzy burst back into the apartment. "I'm back!" she announced. She kicked the door closed behind her and lugged her grocery bags to the counter.

Unlike the rest of the apartment, Aunt Melanie's kitchen was bland. Modern. Basic. It had long, gray granite countertops and shiny steel appliances with a subway tile backsplash. At least the dishes were clunky, mismatched, and brightly colored. Even the drinking glasses were of uneven thickness with visible bubbles, as if they were someone's first attempt. I wouldn't be surprised if my aunt had made all of her dishware. But she hadn't bothered putting her unique stamp on the rest of the kitchen, other than a row of funky cookie jars lining the island bar.

Although, judging by the basket overflowing with takeout menus and the drawer filled with packets of soy sauce and individual ketchup servings, Aunt Melanie ordered out. A lot.

While Izzy worked on dinner, I took a break to feed Rufus before returning to YouTube. There were an awful lot of videos to review, especially since I was alternating between Bethany's and Jenny's channels. The videos and comments began to all blur together.

"What are you watching those for?" Izzy asked, peering over my shoulder. She had a dishcloth draped over one arm and a smear of green on her cheek that I could only hope was pesto.

"Seeing if I can find any clues," I admitted.

"Come on, Odessa. You couldn't possibly think that Jenny killed Bethany. I mean, you heard her, they were buddies. Besides, and don't take this the wrong way, but do you know how hard it would be for a person in a wheelchair to hoist a grown adult woman up and over a waist-high railing?"

"It's not unmanageable."

"No, and neither is monkeys flying out of the refrigerator, but it's low-key impossible."

"Or, that's just what Jenny wants us to think," I argued.

Izzy shifted the dish towel from her arm to over her shoulder before sitting down on the low coffee table across from the couch. She had to nudge her suitcase out of the way to make room. My aunt's apartment was huge by New York standards, but almost every inch of it was filled with eye-catching tchotchkes or oversized sculptures.

"Why are you doing this, Odessa?"

"I told you, there might be clues in—"

She interrupted me. "No, I mean this. Obsessing over Bethany's death like it was some kind of a murder or something."

"Because I think it was."

"It's not fair. Bethany was young. Bright. Talented. She wasn't supposed to die in a senseless accident, but that's all it was. An accident."

"You're wrong. What about the mysterious meeting she attended in the park? She said it was a matter of life and death."

"Bethany exaggerated. All the time. You've seen her videos." She waved a hand at my laptop where, even now, Bethany demonstrated how to make unique molds out of other objects for one-of-a-kind soaps. "She lived for attention," Izzy said.

"And her bracelet? She never took that silly thing off."

"Maybe she gave it to someone. Or maybe the clasp broke a week ago, but no one had noticed yet."

"Please. I've barely known her a week," I pointed out.

"Exactly. Don't take this the wrong way, Odessa, but you didn't even really know Bethany and it's a little sus how you're fixated on her death. I think maybe this memorial service will help you, too. Help you accept that she's gone."

"Maybe you're right," I said, closing my laptop and setting it aside. I wasn't sure I believed her, but I couldn't get her to come around and she wasn't going to leave me in peace until I acquiesced.

"Of *course* I'm right," Izzy replied with an impish grin. "Aren't I always?"

Ignoring that last question, I asked, "How long until dinner is ready?"

"The zucchini has to marinate in my secret sauce in the fridge a bit to soak up the flavor."

"In that case, your clothes should be dry by now." Even in the tiny dryer, it didn't take long to dry three articles of clothing. Personally, I preferred to line dry when possible, or spread all my wet clothes out in the bathroom to drip dry, but the electric dryer was more expedient. "Go grab them and I'll show you how to take them apart so you can reuse the cloth."

I grabbed my sewing kit and handed her a pair of scissors. She laid the clothing out on the table, and I advised her to cut the seams off, since it was quicker and easier. While she worked on that, I took a seam ripper and carefully removed all of the delicate seams on my silvery dress.

Sewing was meditative for me, from carefully removing each stich of a seam to the whoosh of the sewing machine and repetitive motion of the needle. Then there was the sense of accomplishment when something that had only existed in my mind previously was now tangible in my hands. Plus, for the bonus round, I got new, personally tailored clothes out of the deal.

All in all, it was a win.

Izzy had finished deconstructing her items and I was almost done with all but the collar of mine when I heard a knock on the door. My heart sank. "You didn't invite anyone over, did you?" I asked.

She shook her head. "Nope. You?"

The downstairs buzzer had never chimed. If it had been a delivery, they would have left it downstairs with the other packages.

Which meant whoever was on the other side of the door was either a neighbor or the concierge, come to check up on me and report back to my aunt. I was in so much trouble.

There was another knock. This one was louder, sharper, and was followed by the announcement, "NYPD. Open up."

10

IZZY AND I looked at each other with panic in our eyes.

I've always been a law-abiding citizen, more or less. As a slightly-below-average-height, curvaceous brunette, I didn't exactly appear very threatening, except maybe to a chipmunk. Even so, when I was driving and saw flashing lights appear in the rearview mirror, my anxiety shot through the roof. But that didn't hold a candle to the feeling of the NYPD pounding on the door demanding to be let in.

"What should we do?" I whispered to Izzy. She shrugged.

The apartment was built to muffle as much sound as possible. It was hard enough living elbow to elbow with a bunch of strangers without having to hear them every time they cleared their throats. The walls were thick enough that unless they were watching an action movie, set off their fire alarm, or were listening to music with a lot of bass at top volume, I barely noticed them.

Until they walked past the front door.

Even with a big draft blocker tacked to the bottom of the door, I could see a thin line of light all the way around it, and voices traveled easily from the hall into the living room. I could hear every little tiny noise as people walked from the elevator to their apartments, chatting away on their phones or dog collars rattling. Which meant whoever was on the other side of the door right now could hear me, too.

"Ms. Dean, I know you're in there. Open the door," the voice demanded, rapping again.

The concierge had a copy of the key. I found that out when, on my second day, I'd managed to leave my key in the apartment—the door automatically locked behind me—and had to beg Earl to let me back inside. If I didn't open the door, the cops could do what I had and borrow a key from the concierge. I knew they needed a warrant to enter a private home, but who actually owned an apartment? The landlord? Or the niece of a resident who was letting Izzy stay here against her aunt's express orders?

I approached the door and jumped when he banged on it again. "Who's there?"

"It's Detective Vincent Castillo, NYPD," he replied, and I felt my heartbeat return to normal.

It still took me a minute to fumble all of the locks open. "Yes?" I asked once I had the door open.

Without waiting to be invited, he brushed past me. "Bad time?"

"We were just making supper," Izzy said. While I was answering the door, she had abandoned the material she was reclaiming and had moved into the kitchen, where she was filling a pot with water.

"Ms. Wilson, I wasn't expecting to see you here."

"Izzy is fine," she said with a flirty grin before moving the pot from the sink to the back burner of the stove. She lit it, and the rhythmic clicks fell silent as she adjusted the gas.

"What's up with the home visit?" I asked. My voice came out shaky. I knew I had no reason to feel guilty, but I'd never had a cop in my house before, and it was nerve-racking.

"I wanted to follow up with you." He focused his full attention on me, resting one hand on the granite counter, angled so he could see the door, the kitchen, and me all at the same time. That was quite a talent.

Like yesterday, the detective wore fitted jeans, a button-down shirt with the sleeves rolled up in deference to the heat wave that had arrived in the wake of last night's storm, and a slim waistcoat. The color combination was different today—black, cobalt blue, and more black, respectively—but it was the same basic outfit.

And he made it look good.

Dayum good.

I swallowed the sudden lump that had formed in my throat. I needed water. Or maybe tequila. "Can I get you something to drink?" I offered.

"I got some beer while I was out. Not quite the selection we have at the café, but it's better than nothing," Izzy added.

"I'm good, thanks," Detective Castillo said. He turned to me. "Results came back from the ME."

"They did?" I had expected them to take weeks. Months, maybe. "So fast?"

"In light of the issues you raised, I had her pushed to the top of the list. A young, healthy woman like Ms. Kostolus dying from such a short fall, well, it bore taking a closer look."

"And?" I asked, barely able to bear the suspense any longer.

"Her injuries were consistent with a fall." He paused for a beat, watching my crestfallen face. "It's not what you wanted to hear, but your friend's death was an accident. I'm sorry for your loss."

"Wait, that's it? You're closing the case, just like that?"

"I understand your frustration, Ms. Dean. It's hard to accept when a loved one passes unexpectedly. I have to admit, you had me half believing there was something to it, but all evidence says otherwise. There is nothing suspicious about Ms. Kostolus's death. You need to let it go, and find another way to honor your friend."

"Thank you." I might have been disappointed in the results, but I hadn't forgotten my manners.

Izzy, on the other hand, took hospitality to the next level when she asked, "Why don't you stay for dinner? We're having vegan pesto pasta, spicy zucchini salad, and fresh baked bread. Way too much for just the two of us."

"Sounds delightful, but I have to get back to the station. Ladies," he said, with a nod. Forgetting that he'd given me his card last night, he left one on the counter and let himself out. The door clicked locked behind him.

I waited until I heard the elevator ding, and then counted to three to make sure the elevator doors closed before turning to Izzy. "What were you thinking?"

"That he's cute. And employed. And he doesn't wear a wedding ring."

I rolled my eyes. Sure, I'd had similar thoughts last night, but I hadn't actually acted on them. "He's a cop," I said.

"I know, right? Where do you keep the strainer?"

"Top right cupboard."

"Thanks." She pulled out the strainer and set it in the sink. The water was boiling in earnest now, and angel hair pasta danced in the pot. She paused to stir it occasionally in between slicing bread, combining other ingredients in a large bowl, and assembling the peanut and sriracha zucchini salad. "This is almost ready. Do you mind setting the table?"

Aunt Melanie's table was currently occupied by my sewing machine and our projects. "We might be better off eating off the bar," I suggested as I started moving my aunt's collection of colorful cookie jars out of the way, and used a damp cloth to wipe down the island counter.

As I pulled mismatched bowls and plates out of the cupboard, my mind wandered back to Bethany. It was one thing for Izzy to want to believe her friend's death was an accident. And one over-worked NYPD detective. But the medical examiner, too?

I could almost believe them. It was three against one, after all. But there was still the matter of her missing bracelet. Bethany didn't take it off, not ever. I thought it was weird, bordering on tacky, but she took it as seriously as any real medical alert bracelet.

Sure, it could have fallen off.

Except medical alert bracelets were more rugged than ordinary jewelry. As a waitress, I knew better than just about anyone how difficult it was to work in a restaurant, even a tiny café. I couldn't even begin to calculate how many uniforms I'd ruined working in the service industry. Stains. Spills. Burns. Cuts. Between sliding heavy trays on and off my arm all day, washing my hands dozens of times a day, and juggling multiple orders at a time, it was a minor miracle my hands and arms weren't maimed by now.

If Bethany's bracelet was going to fall off, it would have done so a long time ago. It would have gotten snagged a gazillion times, but it had held fast. It was hard to believe that something with the tenacity of a cockroach, or maybe Britney Spears, would break and disappear on the same day as Bethany *accidentally* went over a waist-high rail, dropped over the edge, and mysteriously died on impact despite only having fallen fifteen feet. It wasn't just unlikely. It was downright suspicious.

Despite Izzy's logic, Detective Castillo's assurances, and the ME's expertise, I had to trust my gut. Her death was no accident. I knew that in my bones. Bethany deserved justice. Someone killed her, and they weren't going to get away with it.

Not on my watch.

Even if I had zero proof that she had been murdered.

"Odessa?" Izzy asked, and I could tell from her tone of voice that it wasn't the first time she'd called my name.

"Huh?"

"Man, you were really off in la-la land, weren't you? Dinner's ready. Pass me those plates, will ya?"

THE NEXT MORNING, I woke up with a crick in my neck. Dinner had been great, delicious as advertised. The pasta was tender and creamy, and the zucchini salad had just the right amount of kick. Afterward, Izzy tried to convince me to go out with her, but I felt like narping around, so I stayed home and finished the season of *The Great British Baking Show* I'd started the other night. She got home sometime around four in the morning and despite her efforts to tiptoe around in the dark, kept knocking into the furniture, even kicking the edge of the couch I was snoozing on in her effort to be stealthy.

I could hear Izzy's snores through the closed bedroom door, long and rhythmic with an occasional loud rattle. Despite my discomfort last night, I was glad I had insisted that Izzy get the bedroom. After listening to some of her housing horror stories, I don't think she'd had a room to herself for years, if ever.

The only problem was that all of my clothes were in the bedroom. I know, I know. I should have planned ahead and set out my clothes for the day last night, but after the baking show finale, I'd gotten sucked into a new podcast and by the time I was ready to go to bed, Rufus was curled up on my stomach purring in his sleep and I hadn't had the heart to wake him. Which meant now I had to wake Izzy up or wear yesterday's clothes all over again. At least my new uniform shirt was still in the laundry closet.

Luckily, Izzy didn't stir at all when I slipped into the bedroom and grabbed clothes more or less at random. I guess a lifetime parade of roommates made it easy to sleep through anything. After a quick shower and breakfast—organic wheat cereal soaked in unsweetened almond milk—I headed off to work. To be completely honest, I would have preferred something colorful and loaded with extra sugar like Froot Loops or Lucky Charms with a cold bowl of whole milk, but if someone saw me smuggling that yummy sugariness into Williamsburg, they'd take away my MetroCard.

I left the keys on the hook by the front door and let the door automatically lock behind me. I wasn't sure how this was going to work out, two people with only one set of keys, but it was only for a few days. We would have to figure it out as we went.

The walk down to the waterfront was pleasant and gave me plenty of time to think. In a few hours, these same streets would be sweltering. And to think, just a few days ago, it had been bearable all day long, until the thunderstorm that seemed to drag this heat wave in its wake came to town the night that Bethany died.

It had been so pretty that morning. The temperature held steady in the low eighties without a cloud in the sky. It had been a great day to be outdoors, soaking in a little sun while taking advantage of the slight breeze coming off the river.

If I was being honest with myself, I'd probably have to acknowledge that Bethany wasn't exactly known for being prompt. Or reliable. Her sneaking out of work in the middle of the shift was totally on-brand. When it came to her own YouTube channel or her Etsy soap shop, she was 100 percent. But at the café? She was a solid sixty. On a good day.

With such a perfect day outside, who's to say that Bethany didn't just ditch work to go out and enjoy it?

Sure, she *said* it was a matter of life or death, but she could have said that just to get me to cover for her while she flittered around the park. I had no idea if she had actually met anyone at Domino Park that day, or if so, who it had been. According to Detective Castillo, she'd been alone in all the photos. But one thing I'd learned was that in New York City, no one was ever truly alone.

I pulled my phone out of my messenger bag and pulled up Instagram. I was still logged in to the Untapped Books & Café account, but I wasn't planning on posting anything so I left it like that. I searched for Domino Park, and was taken aback by the sheer number of photos that had been uploaded this morning alone, and all of them were model-quality.

Don't get me wrong, I've got a killer selfie game. I knew my exact best angle and lighting. I could flash a smile that would blind an unsuspecting camera. But I didn't have anything on these posers. Literally.

Perfect makeup. Perfect hair, despite the breeze. Perfect clothes. Perfect dogs on perfect leashes with perfect doggy grins. In other words, what was that word I was looking for? Oh yeah. Perfect.

And to top it off, there were scores of photos. I was still scrolling back the forty-odd hours between now and Bethany's death when I arrived at the doorstep of Untapped Books & Café. Absorbed in my phone screen, I pushed the door open with my elbow. I'm sure the little bell tinkled, but I heard it so many times a day that I'd gotten pretty good at blocking it out now. I wish I could say the same for Todd's salty voice. "It's about time, Odessa. I was starting to think you were dead, too."

11

Untapped Books & Café @untappedwilliamsburg · June 26
NYT bestselling author @RealGeoffreyTate at Untapped Books
& Café today only! Reading @ 11, signing to follow. LIMITED
SEATING!! #bestseller #thriller #Williamsburg

I GLANCED DOWN AT my phone display, my thumb still scrolling through perfectly staged Instagram shots. "What are you talking about? I'm early, boss," I protested. "My shift doesn't start for another five minutes."

"Yeah, well, Izzy is a no-show and I need your help."

Uh-oh. When I'd left the apartment, Izzy was still sound asleep. I wondered if she'd forgotten to set an alarm, or if Todd had changed the schedule without bothering to tell anyone. Either scenario was equally likely. "Let me give her a buzz."

"No time for that. We've got *New York Times* bestseller Geoffrey Tate coming in for a reading in"—he glanced at the huge clock on the wall—"less than an hour. And nothing's set up. I need you to move the display tables and endcaps into the back room, and bring out the chairs. Set a couple rows up along that wall, and make sure you get a desk for Mr. Tate."

"Wouldn't it be easier to arrange the café area?" I asked, looking around the already cramped bookstore. A big-name author like Tate was bound to draw a huge crowd. Come to think of it, the store was already unusually crowded for this time of day. "We could seat more people that way."

"What? And shut down the café for half the day? Are you nuts?" He shook his head and muttered something under his breath.

"'Scuse me? I didn't quite catch that last bit," I said, with a forced grin on my face.

"Never mind. Get to work."

Like most of the odd jobs I got stuck with around here, it was dirty, dusty work. The ancient air conditioner did a valiant job of taking the edge off the worst of the heat, but when the temperature was creeping toward ninety outside and I was lugging furniture all over the bookstore, it might as well have been a cricket spitting into the wind for all the good it did. Finally, after what felt like a week, I'd squeezed every spare chair we had into the sliver of space I'd managed to clear.

Normally, business didn't pick up until later in the day, with a small peak around lunch and then a swell that started at four and grew until closing. Today was the exception, as people lined up against the wall, waiting for their favorite thriller writer to take the proverbial stage. The line snaked through the store, out the front door, and down the sidewalk. We couldn't accommodate even half of them without opening up the café area, and then the audience wouldn't be able to see anything because of where I'd had to set up the signing table.

"Excuse me, miss? You work here?"

I took a beat and let myself roll my eyes skyward. Do I work here? Nope. I just enjoy wearing florescent green polo shirts and rearranging bookstores in gazillion-degree weather. Then I fixed a polite smile on my face and turned around to greet the customer. "How can I—"

My voice lurched to a halt like the J train with a trainee conductor.

I've never met a famous person before. Once upon a time, Margot Robbie came into the Crawdad Shack, but as luck would have it, it was my day off. Then there was that time that Fall Out Boy's tour bus broke down on the highway right outside of town and the band and all the roadies were stuck at the gas station for most of the day, but I'd been in Dallas on a field trip. There weren't that many chances to rub elbows with the rich and recognizable in Piney Island, Louisiana.

The same can't be said for Williamsburg, apparently.

Obviously, I knew that Geoffrey Tate was scheduled to appear at Untapped Books & Café to read a bit out of his latest bestselling novel and sign some books afterward. I'd spent the last hour prepping for his arrival. I just didn't think, not in my wildest imagination, that I would have a chance to look him in the eye. If I was very lucky, I'd hoped that I would catch a glimpse of him from afar. And here he was, talking to *me*.

"Um, well, er . . ." I realized I was stumbling over my words, but in my surprise, I'd forgotten the question.

"I'll take that as a yes. Geoffrey Tate." He extended his hand to me. Tate looked exactly like his author picture on the back of his book jackets on the display I'd just set up, give or take a few gray hairs. He looked like he belonged on a lowrider motorcycle on the open road, wearing a red bandanna instead of a helmet. He looked like someone who would be cast in the movie version of one of his own thrillers—rough, tumble, and fit. He probably ate a lot of kale.

Behind me, I heard cell phone cameras clicking and the familiar chirps of people posting to their favorite sites. "Odessa Dean," I managed to mumble, and shook his hand hastily. "How can I help you, sir?"

"What a lovely name. Odessa, would you be a dear and fetch me a pumpkin spice latte?"

"Huh?" I liked pumpkin spice lattes as well as the next twenty-something female. I was only human. I would never have imagined a man quite as . . . weathered . . . as Geoffrey Tate would touch a pumpkin spice latte with a ten-foot pole. I pictured him as a black-coffee man, or better yet, whiskey, neat, disguised in a coffee mug. "I mean, it's June." I wiped the sweat off my forehead before it could trickle into my eyes. "I don't think they make PSLs for a few months still."

"Oh. I was hoping, what with this being Williamsburg and all, there would be pumpkin spice lattes year round."

"Don't I wish?" Then a thought struck me, and I remembered what I'd learned when I was memorizing all the trivia about craft beer so I wouldn't sound like a blathering idiot when I was serving them. "There's kinda a joke, you know, that craft beers are the new pumpkin spice lattes. We have a great selection, if you'd like to try one."

He grinned at me. "It's been a while since I've had a beer before noon, but I am awful thirsty, and when in Brooklyn . . ."

"So what do you like?" I wished I'd taken the time to scan the cooler before his arrival. The last thing I wanted to do was oversell the virtues of Williamsburg After Dark Porter just to find out we only had Pale As Underground in stock.

"Surprise me."

He wandered away to organize the desk I'd set up for him and I scurried off toward the café. "Parker, quick," I said, dashing to the kitchen window. "What's the best beer we've got right now?"

"I'm partial to Pour Williamsburg," he replied. I noticed that his hairnet was askew and his workstation was even more chaotic than usual. I guess the extra crowd was keeping him hopping, too.

"Thanks. I owe you one." I nabbed a bottle of Pour Williamsburg Pale Ale from the cooler, along with a bottle of water. I carried both out to Tate's desk, set them down, and popped the top off using the bottle opener I kept on a string. I'd learned the hard way that if I didn't keep a close eye on bottle openers, they grew legs and skittered away. "I think you'll like this one. It's got a smooth finish."

Once he was settled, I helped Todd and Andre, who'd come in early for the occasion, wrangle the line of fans in a more-or-less orderly fashion to their seats. As I'd suspected, we had seats for less than a quarter of the swelling crowd. The rest had to stand wherever they found room, even if the stacks hid Tate from view. I'm fairly certain that we'd exceeded the fire marshal's limit by double, but I certainly wasn't going to be the one to call them and tattle.

"Odessa, you're needed in the café," Todd said, pulling me aside. I couldn't help but notice he had a chair saved for himself right up front.

"But I won't be able to hear anything from the café," I argued.

"So? I'm not paying you to stand around and fawn over famous authors. Get to work. Chop-chop."

He didn't pay me to do a lot of the things I did around here. He didn't pay me to lug the trash out to the dumpsters, walk Huckleberry, or stock the bookshelves. He didn't pay me to set up the bookstore for author appearances, or to manage the social media accounts, either. Speaking of which . . . I took out my phone and snapped a couple of pictures, but all I could see was the backs of the audience's heads.

I pushed my way through the crowd. "Excuse me! Coming through! Make way, please!" They parted as reluctantly as the first few rows at a general admission concert, but eventually I was able to squeeze through. "I'd like to get a few pictures, if you're all right with that," I explained to Tate as I moved behind him.

"Sure, of course." Tate stood and turned to face me. He scooped a handful of his books in one arm and gestured at the crowd behind him with the other. They cheered loudly.

The problem was, I was having a hard time getting everything in one picture. I was too dang short. Right now, Tate blocked out the crowd. "Do you mind?" I pulled his chair back as far as I could against the wall and climbed up onto it. My cowboy boots, even with worn soles, were slippery against the plastic and for a second I wavered, trying to catch my balance.

Tate reached his free hand up to steady me and I clutched it for dear life until I knew I wasn't going to fall. I let go, remembering too late that my hands were as dirty and sweaty as the rest of me. "Thanks," I told him.

"Anything for a pretty lady," he replied, and I tell you what, I almost lost my balance again.

He got back into position, posing with the rambunctious readers behind him and books on display like a proud peacock. I took a few quick shots, jumped down, and dusted off the chair before returning it to Tate. I reviewed the photos on my screen. "Yeah, these are great." I held them out so he could take a peek.

"Love 'em. Tag me when you post, will ya?"

"Of course." I couldn't hide my grin. Tate was such a nice, down-to-earth guy, not at all what I'd expected.

I took a second to post the best picture to all of our accounts—Instagram, Twitter, and even Facebook—with the caption of "Geoffrey Tate with his loyal fans at Untapped Books & Café! If you couldn't make it, swing by later for signed books while supplies last!" I tagged Tate, and watched the accounts' traffic spike.

Making a path through the crowd was easy this time. They were eager to part so I could leave, each of them taking a shuffling step forward as I passed to jockey for a better position. Sure, I was going to miss the reading, but I'd actually gotten to talk to the man. To hold his hand, even for an instant. From now on, I could tell everyone the story of how Geoffrey Tate saved my life.

That thought was like a punch to the gut. Big flipping deal. I'd almost fallen off a chair, onto a carpeted floor. Two feet away. The worst that could have happened was I would have been embarrassed in front of a bunch of strangers I'd never met before and I'd never have to see again. Sure, someone would inevitably record it and post it on YouTube or something for all the world to laugh at, but ten seconds later, the clip would be forgotten, replaced by something more dramatic or more demeaning.

For that one second when I was off balance, I caught a brief glimpse of what Bethany had felt when she went over that walkway. Out of pure instinct, I had grabbed thin air, and if Tate's hand hadn't been there, I don't know what I would have done. Fallen, probably. Humiliated myself, certainly.

So why hadn't Bethany grabbed hold of the railing?

The only possible explanation was that she'd gone over backward. Which meant she'd been pushed. One hundred percent. No doubt in my mind. She had to have tried to grab hold of something. Her attacker, maybe?

"Earth to Odessa," Parker said, and I blinked at him, trying to come back to the real world. "You were really out of it for a minute."

I gave myself a mental shake. "Sorry." I stuffed my messenger bag into the cabinet that doubled as an employee locker. "It must be a madhouse out there."

"Nah. Everyone's just here to see that Tate guy. It was busy before, and afterward we'll probably get slammed. But right now, the most challenging order up is an everything bagel. But seriously, are you okay?"

"Ducky," I assured him. I glanced out of the window. Kim was working the tables, along with another person I didn't recognize. Three servers was a little excessive for a Wednesday morning. Either Todd had screwed up the schedule or expected a huge rush after Geoffrey Tate finished signing autographs. "Who's that?"

"New girl," he replied. He pulled the long sleeves down over his arms and turned to the fryer. Despite the soaring temperature in the kitchen, the cooks didn't have the luxury of wearing ugly green polos, not if they wanted to have a single square inch of their arms unscarred or unburnt at the end of the day. Even with the long sleeves, Parker's arms looked like he'd lost a fight with a wood chipper or two.

I was New Girl for my first week at the café, too. Apparently, the turnover was so high that no one bothered learning anyone's name until they survived at least five shifts, and waiters had to make it past the three-month mark to get their own personalized name tag. Back home, we didn't have that problem. If someone was lucky enough to get a job—any job—they didn't up and quit without good reason. I'd been slinging seafood at the Crawdad Shack ever since I was seventeen, and if I'd stayed in Piney Island this summer, I'd probably be doing it right now. Knowing I'd be back in a few months, I'd even kept the name tag.

Then again, it wasn't like they were going to ever replace me with someone else named Odessa.

Waitressing in Williamsburg wasn't that different than waiting tables anywhere else. Long, hot shifts. Aching feet. Burnt arms. Greasy hair. Grumpy customers. But at the end of the day, having amazing coworkers like Parker and Izzy and working in an energetic environment made it all worthwhile. And the tips didn't hurt, either—when people were generous enough to leave one.

Thinking of Izzy reminded me that I needed to call her. After retrieving my apron from its hook and tying the belt around my waist, I pulled my phone out and clicked on her contact. Right before it was about to go to voicemail, she answered with a sleepy, "Hello?"

"Hey, it's me." I know, I know, it was an inane thing to say. In the age of caller ID, I certainly didn't need to announce myself. "You were supposed to be at work like two hours ago."

"Huh?" She paused, then exclaimed, "You've got to be kidding!" I heard her fumble around and realized she was still in Aunt Melanie's feather-soft bed. "Why didn't you wake me?"

"I didn't know you were on the schedule," I told her. I'd asked Todd to email the schedule out once a week, but he was old-school and preferred to post it on the wall near the bathroom instead. I think he liked that it was easier for him to change it on a whim that way. "Didn't you set an alarm?"

"I did," she said. I could hear a suitcase zipper opening, followed by a muttered curse. "I can't believe I overslept today of all days. And Geoffrey Tate's coming in!"

"He's here. Reading just started. If you hurry, you might catch the end of it, but you'll have to come in the back way. No way you're getting in the front door. Place is packed to the gills."

She yelped as I presumed she tripped over something sharp and heavy. My aunt's collection of oversized sculptures was impressive, but the first time I spent the night in her room, I almost broke a toe stumbling around in the dark trying to get to the restroom. I must have lost a quart of blood after getting my leg sliced by a four-foot-high realistic chimpanzee statue. Note to self—if I'm ever lucky enough to get my own Williamsburg apartment, fill it with pillows. Or go minimalist. No giant metal statues for me, no way.

Izzy disconnected. I hoped she'd hung up instead of tripping and breaking her phone, but in Aunt Melanie's apartment, the latter was much more likely.

I put my phone away and headed into the café. I waved at Kim, who tilted her head in a half-hearted nod. I guess she still didn't think I was worthy to wear an apron. I was determined to prove her wrong. Even if I burned all the skin off my forearm and got a loud group of seven drunks crammed into a four top, I was gonna smile and get every order exactly right. I was gonna get refills out on time and not let food sit in the window. I was gonna upsell, upsell, upsell. And if I noticed we were running low on coffee, I'd start a new pot. In other words, I was gonna be the best waitress this rinky-dink café had ever seen.

"Hey, you're the new girl, right?" I asked, as soon as I noticed the new waitress didn't have her hands full.

She had long blonde hair twisted into dreadlocks and wore no makeup except for pink eyeshadow. Unlike myself, the new girl was tall and willowy. She had to be almost six feet tall, and had narrow hips, a teeny tiny waist, and legs that a supermodel would envy. She blinked down at me. "You must be Odessa," she said with a hint of a foreign accent I couldn't quite place. "I visited Odessa once."

"You're from Texas?" I asked, surprised. I never would have guessed it. Texans had a unique drawl all of their own, about a hundred times thicker than mine. Odessa was a town out in the oil fields. I'd asked my parents once why they'd named me after such a dry, barren place. Maybe they'd met there? Or had a romantic date there? But alas, it turned out that they'd never even been within a hundred miles of Odessa. They just liked the sound of it.

"Odessa, Ukraine," she clarified.

"So you're what, Russian?"

"Slovakian," she corrected me. "And you're from here?"

Man, I could really get used to people mistaking me for a local. "Not quite. I'm from Louisiana, about fifteen hundred miles south of here." One thousand, four hundred and thirty-two miles to be precise, but who's counting? "You've been here long?"

"I just started today," she replied. Her voice was lyrical but her expression was blank, with a touch of disdain maybe.

"I knew *that*. I meant how long have you been in Brooklyn?"

"A few years," she said. "It's nice."

"It is," I agreed. "Would you like a hand with your tables? Maybe split them up, or I can help you run drinks?"

"Everyone has their food," she said, punctuating it with a sniff. "Maybe the waitress in black needs your help."

I glanced over at Kim, who appeared to be playing a game on her cell phone and chewing bubblegum. Parker was right. No one seemed to be ordering much. I didn't even see any beer bottles on the tables. I guess people were more interested in getting a book signed by Geoffrey Tate than the daily special. "Yeah, alrighty, then. Well, let me know if that changes. Good meetin' you."

She turned around and walked away. She moved like a dancer or a figure skater, all grace and poise. She'd gotten three steps before I realized I still didn't know what to call her. "Sorry, I didn't get your name."

"Hana," she said, without turning around. She flipped her long dreadlocks over her shoulder as she glided toward her tables.

With nothing else to do, I returned to my review of the Instagram posts from Domino Park. Plenty of people uploaded pictures *after* Bethany fell, and I wanted to scroll past them, but I forced myself to look at each of them, carefully ignoring the central figure in each photo and concentrating instead on the crowd. I kept scrolling until timestamps were earlier than ten thirty. Bethany was still in the café with me at the time.

Out of the hundreds of photos I examined, not a single person jumped out at me. All of the faces began to blur together after a while, but I didn't recognize anyone. Detective Castillo was right about one thing—even with dozens and dozens of camera phones snapping away, none of the photos showed so much as a glimpse of Bethany before she fell, or anyone else I knew.

The photos were useless.

12

Odessa Dean @OddessaWaiting · June 26
Always meet your heroes. Always. #GeoffreyTate

THE TABLES WERE taken care of, and from the bursts of laughter coming from the bookstore, Tate was a hit. I really wished I could hear his reading. Then I realized that I could. There was nothing for me to do here. I headed back toward the bookstore side of the shop. Even the steps separating the café from the bookstore were crammed with people, but I managed to squeeze myself into an opening. There are perks to being petite. I couldn't see anything except the backs of the people standing in front of me, but I could hear Tate's deep voice as he painted a chase scene through the bowels of a cruise ship.

"Hey? What did I tell you?"

I stifled a groan. Maybe if we all pitched in, we could buy a bell to hang around Todd's neck so he wouldn't always be sneaking up on us. "What's up?" Around us, we got several angry shushes and more than a few glares. I didn't blame them. They'd come to hear

Tate, not me and Todd. I made my way back toward the café, with Todd in tow. "Can I help you with something?"

"Yeah. Do something with Huckleberry. It's too crowded and he's getting underfoot."

"What do you want me to do?" I asked, confused. I guess I could lock him in Todd's office, but that seemed mean. Technically, he wasn't allowed back in the café area since we served food. That didn't leave a lot of options when the bookstore was this crowded.

"I don't know. Why do I have to do all the thinking around here? Take him on a walk or something."

"It might be hard to get through that crowd," I pointed out.

He pursed his lips. "Your generation doesn't know hardship. I remember having to log off the internet because my mom needed to use the landline. Now *that's* hardship. Do you understand what I'm trying to tell you?"

"That you're old?" one of the customers asked, visibly annoyed that Todd was talking over Tate.

"What's a landline?" his friend asked, snickering.

Todd did *not* appreciate that. His nostrils flared and his eyebrows knitted together as he turned his back on the customers. "Take care of the dog. Now. Don't make me ask you again."

"Yes, sir."

I found Huckleberry snoozing in the narrow hallway that ran the length of the store. I guess that was Todd's definition of being in the way. "Come on, buddy," I said, in my most encouraging voice. "Wanna go for a walkie? Maybe go to the park?" He lifted his head and looked at me before flopping back down.

In my experience, Huckleberry was as independent as a cat,

and twice as stubborn. If he wanted to do something, he did it. If he didn't want to, he didn't. No amount of cajoling would make him change his mind. Even when he was wearing a leash, he had a mind of his own and weighed almost as much as I did, so it would be more accurate to say I let Huckleberry take me for a walk, not the other way around.

"Hold up, I'll be right back." Avoiding the crowd, I slipped along the hall and emerged right next to the kitchen. "Hey, Parker, got any returns this morning?"

"Just this bacon and egg on brioche sandwich," he said, waving toward a plate sitting on the far edge of the counter, right next to the walk-in. Whenever a customer returned a perfectly good, untouched meal, it was up for grabs for the rest of the staff. "He said he ordered turkey bacon substitution, but that wasn't on his ticket." Parker shrugged. He was easygoing. Someone could probably call his mother names, and he'd let it roll off his back.

I don't think I'd ever seen him flustered, much less close to losing his temper. And in a kitchen, that was saying something. I mean, I think I'm pretty upbeat and I tried to not let anything get to me, but between the stress of waitressing and the attitude of a few of the customers, I'd spent a break or two in my life crying in the bathroom. It came with the territory.

Not Parker, though. He was as cool as the cucumbers he was currently slicing into thin strips and arranging in between layers of damp paper towels.

"Mind if I take the bacon?"

"Help yourself," he said. "Might as well take the rest of it, too, instead of letting it go to waste."

He had a point. Sure, I'd had a bowl of cereal for breakfast and the eggs were now room temperature, but the day I turned down anything on brioche bread was the day they played "Amazing Grace" at my grave.

"Thanks." I separated the bacon and gulped down the rest of the sandwich as I returned to Huckleberry.

"Got something for you," I told him, holding out one of the strips of bacon. He rolled to his feet and lunged for it. "Not so fast." I broke off half a piece and tossed it to him. "You'll get the rest if you cooperate." I turned and headed toward the back door. Huckleberry loped after me. Most days, he was as big and slow as a Zamboni, but when bacon was involved, he was a souped-up 1964 ½ Mustang.

I clipped the leash to his collar. I'm not sure why I bothered. Usually, when Huckleberry needed to do his business, he'd let himself out of the shop and wander back in later, sometimes waiting by the front door until a customer let him back inside. He was at least as street smart as I was, probably more so. But the last thing I wanted was a ticket for an unleashed dog, especially when he wasn't even my dog. "Good boy."

We went out back, past the overflowing dumpster. Once, when I was ten or so, my parents planned a summer retreat to Galveston, Texas. When we got there, the stench coming off the warm waters of the Gulf of Mexico was enough to make a nun curse. My dad explained the fetid, pungent aroma came from rotting seaweed suffocating all the ocean life. Personally, I thought the devil had farted.

That smell was bad, bad enough to keep us from ever going to the beach despite driving five hours. The reek of the dumpster behind Untapped Books & Café was worse. Three times as bad, easy. And the temperature was still climbing, so the trash still had a few hours to bake in the blazing sun to reach peak ripeness. When the trash collectors came by tomorrow, I hoped they were wearing hazmat suits.

A thought hit me. When I'd searched for Bethany's missing cell phone and bracelet, I'd looked under the bushes and in the rocky and grassy areas. I'd looked around benches and checked the elevated walkway. But I hadn't thought to check the nearby garbage cans. I mean, why would I? Public trash cans, especially those at a popular park, were beyond nasty. They were filled with all sorts of sharp, filthy objects that I didn't even want to begin to think about.

The Williamsburg of today was a different world than it had been thirty years ago. I'd heard that once upon a time, before being revitalized and repurposed, the huge warehouses that were now microbreweries and high-end apartment buildings were used for more nefarious enterprises. Nowadays, the drug of choice for most of the residents of Williamsburg was overpriced—but delicious!—coffee beans grown in the mountains of South America, but that didn't mean that the streets were miraculously clean. There were still drug users in New York City, and a public park in the middle of the night would be rife with them.

After all, my sleepy hometown of Piney Island was "safe." Family-friendly. It was one of those towns where a girl could walk home alone at night. The majority of the emergency calls that the local cops responded to involved a possum in someone's crawlspace or attic. And even in rural Louisiana, drugs were a problem. They weren't common, exactly, but I knew which people and houses to steer clear of, and what late-night party spots to avoid.

A late-night hangout in Williamsburg was a posh nightclub with a cover charge, dress code, and red velvet ropes protected by a scowling bouncer. Inside, they served overpriced drinks and played music so loud I couldn't hear myself think. The hot spots in Piney Island were more low-key, leaning instead toward the parking lot of the high school, the playground at the end of the community park, or a circle of old stumps ringing a dirt pit that was used for huge bonfires in the summer. From hanging out at the ends of dead-end roads to climbing into rickety deer stands to watch the lightning bugs, Piney Island nightlife wasn't exactly hopping.

Even so, a wave of homesickness washed over me. But I loved Williamsburg. I wasn't looking forward to my aunt's return at the end of the summer, bringing my time in New York to an end. Sure, I missed my parents. I even missed my old job. But I wasn't ready to think about going back. Not yet.

To my surprise, I found myself at the gates of the Domino Park dog run. I looked down at Huckleberry, who gave me a sly doggy grin. While I'd been ruminating, he'd led me across several busy intersections, right into the heart of the park. Part of me had been on the lookout for traffic, but one thing I'd learned early was that crosswalks and traffic signals meant little to New Yorkers—drivers and pedestrians alike. I was just as likely to be hit by a car while in a designated crosswalk, on the sidewalk, or, as had happened a few days ago, up on a curb as I was jaywalking into a busy street during rush hour.

On the far end of Domino Park, in the shadow of the Williamsburg Bridge, there was a small fenced-off area where dogs could roam freely off leash. There were benches for the human companions, water fountains, and plenty of trash cans. The dogs could run around on the turf or play King of the Hill on the stone risers in the center. Most of the dogs (and their people) were polite and well behaved, because any out-of-control dog would be quickly ejected by the other dog owners.

I hadn't thought of New York as dog-friendly before coming here. To be honest, I'd thought it was kinda cruel, keeping a dog in the city. In my imagination, dogs were cooped up in tiny apartments all day, only walked on bare concrete sidewalks in the early morning and late evening by people who were hardly ever home.

On the contrary, New Yorkers *loved* their dogs. They took them everywhere they could. Even the little courtyard behind Untapped Books & Café not only allowed but actively encouraged dogs—as long as they were leashed and well behaved. We put out little water bowls for them and kept a tub of doggie treats for the waitstaff to give out to them. On top of all the businesses that welcomed dogs, there were lots of parks, dog runs, doggie daycares, and doggie spas.

I was starting to see that New York dogs had it a lot better than the mutts back home, which were hardly ever leashed, rarely fenced, and certainly never invited out to dinner with the family.

Huckleberry took his time, sniffing every inch of the perimeter of the dog run. It wasn't a large area, maybe the size of a five-car parking lot. Right now, only four dogs other than Huckleberry were enjoying the ability to stretch their legs. As the day grew hotter, the small lawn would be abandoned as everyone sought air-conditioned spaces, but in the early morning and late evening, it would be packed nose-to-tail.

I kept half an eye on Huckleberry, even knowing he wouldn't

cause any trouble. He was the largest dog in the run today, which wasn't unusual. New York dogs tended toward teacup size. On the other hand, Huckleberry probably tipped the scales at almost a hundred pounds of fur and drool. He didn't have a fancy collar like the other dogs at the park, and could seriously use a trip to the groomer, but what he lacked in fashion and hygiene, he more than made up for with his gentle personality and friendly demeanor.

As I watched him ignore a miniature Chihuahua who was trying to pick a fight with Huckleberry's long foofy tail, I noticed a park employee let himself into the dog run, pushing a large cart. He pulled the trash bag out of one of the bins inside the run, tied it up, and tossed it into his cart. Then he replaced the bag with an empty one and rolled his squeaky cart to the other bin.

I intercepted him. "How often do you take out the trash?" I asked him.

"Every hour," he told me, giving me a quick once-over.

"Once an hour? That seems excessive." I'd expected once or twice a day. The park was technically only open from sunup to sundown, but that still meant twenty or so bags of garbage from this dog run alone every day. No wonder New York had a garbage crisis.

He shrugged. "Why're you so interested, anyway? It's just dog poop."

"I was here with my friend the other day, and she lost her bracelet. An old family heirloom," I said, cringing a little as I heard myself bend the truth. I probably should have just told him about the missing cell phone. It was more believable. "We looked all over for it, but never thought to check the trash cans." Rookie mistake. "When was the last time the garbage trucks came by?"

He pushed back his ball cap and scratched his temple. He was wearing thick leather gloves, despite the heat, and had to use the back of his hand to avoid getting anything unpleasant on his face. "Sunday night, I think. They should be coming by soon, come to think of it."

Uh-oh. Bethany was killed on Monday morning. If I had any chance of finding her bracelet or phone, it had to be before the trucks came. "Any chance I could take a look?"

"Through the garbage?" he asked, and his tone indicated that I sounded as off-kilter as I felt.

"Yes. Please."

"You're joking, right?"

I shook my head. "Dead serious."

He glanced skyward, as if praying for divine patience. "Follow me."

I whistled for Huckleberry, and he trotted back over to me and sat by my side, panting a little. I was glad that he was feeling cooperative. If he'd been in one of his stubborn moods, I could never have caught him, much less dragged him out of the park before he was ready to go. I clipped the leash onto his collar and followed the maintenance man.

He led the way to a golf cart that had been modified to tow the handcart he'd been pushing. He snapped the cart into place, then told me, "Hop in."

I got into the passenger side. Huckleberry gave me a questioning look before slowly climbing into the small space. His back half squeezed into the area by my feet while his elbows and head rested in my lap. I stroked his ears as the maintenance man drove, reassuring Huckleberry that he was, indeed, the Very Best Boy.

We arrived at a fenced-in yard that housed several metal sheds, each the size of a four-pack of shipping containers arranged in a cube. Seagulls circled overhead, and roosted on the shed roofs. I peered into the first shed and saw enormous piles of something that looked like dirty sand. I tried to imagine why the city was storing piles of dirt in the middle of prime real estate.

The path that ran along the East River that separated Brooklyn from Manhattan had a railing to keep people off the enormous boulders—not sand—that lined the bank. As far as I knew, the closest sandy beach was Coney Island. "What's with all the sand?"

"Not sand, salt," he replied. At my bewildered expression, he added, "For treating the roads in winter?"

"Oh. Of course," I said, feeling a little sheepish. I'd only been in New York a short while, and in that time it had gone from uncomfortably hot to unbearably so. Being from the South, sometimes I forgot that the rest of the country had more than two seasons. In Louisiana, we had summer and football season. We might get a rogue ice storm every couple of years, and once we got a whole quarter-inch of snow. It was enough to close schools for two days.

New Yorkers didn't even blink at a quarter-inch of snow. Like much of the northeastern United States, New York could be slammed with nor'easters that would drop over two feet of snow in a single storm. I couldn't fathom what two feet of snow would look like, much less how the city managed to clear the maze of roads and sidewalks. I guess that was where the mounds of salt came into play.

Then all thoughts of snow and ice and salt fled as my guide slid open the door on the next shed and the smell hit me like a physical force. I thought the dumpsters behind Untapped smelled bad, but that was child's play compared to this. The piles of bags were taller than my head in spots, and it would take me two hours with a skidsteer to load it all onto a truck. I wondered how many trucks it would take to haul all of this away, and then realized with a start that this was only three days' worth of garbage.

13

.₀₀₀₀₀₀₀₀₀₀₀₀₀₀₀₀₀₀₀₀₀₀₀₀₀₀₀₀₀₀₀₀₀₀₀₀.

Odessa Dean @OdessaWaiting · June 26
Recycle, y'all
Thanks 4 coming to my TED talk
#recycle #recycle #recycle #goals

.₀₀₀₀₀₀₀₀₀₀₀₀₀₀₀₀₀₀₀₀₀₀₀₀₀₀₀₀₀₀₀₀₀₀.

YIKES! YOU HAVE got to be kidding me," I said, staring at the mountain of waste. There was more garbage in this one shed than I'd ever seen in my entire life. I made a promise to myself then and there that not only would I up my recycling game, but I'd somehow convince Todd to implement a stricter recycling program at Untapped Books & Café—I was finding bottles in the trash bin all the time—and also to invest in a compost bin. So much food waste got tossed in the garbage that could be repurposed to fertilize community gardens, or keep what little green space we had in New York healthy and lush.

Hashtag goals.

The maintenance worker handed me a disposable mask and a pair of rubber gloves. I put them on. "If you're serious, you've probably got an hour, maybe two, before the trucks arrive."

"This can't all be from Domino Park," I said, overwhelmed by the sheer volume.

"Nah. This is a shared facility. We normally utilize that bin." He pointed at the far corner. As my eyes adjusted to the dim lighting, I realized that there was some attempt to contain the chaos, and there were giant metal bins like dumpsters, only taller and with no lids, lined up in rows. Only most of the bins were overflowing and workers had begun tossing bags of garbage any which way, not caring where they landed. "But when it gets this full, it's not hardly worth making a path back there and we do what we have to." To emphasize his point, he tossed the bags he'd collected from the dog park on top of a nearby pile of black trash bags.

I took a deep breath, steeling myself for the task at hand.

Big mistake.

Even through the mask, the stench overwhelmed my lungs. For a moment, I forgot how to breathe. I doubled over, coughing. He clapped me on the back hard enough to leave a bruise. "You get used to the smell after a while," he assured me. I hacked up what felt like a chunk of bronchial tube. I *never* wanted to get used to this smell. "If you want my advice, go buy your friend a new bracelet."

"Thanks," I told him, once I caught my breath. I was more than half-tempted to take his advice and walk away, but I couldn't give up now. If I could find Bethany's bracelet or phone in the trash, maybe I could convince Detective Castillo to reopen the case. Her cell phone could tell me who she'd talked to that morning, along with a trove of data I couldn't find otherwise. For that matter, the bracelet probably had the killer's fingerprints all over it. Bethany's prank medical alert bracelet could end up solving her own murder. "This one has sentimental value."

I took a step deeper into the shed, and Huckleberry whined. I looked down at him. "You don't have to come with me. Just don't go too far, all right?" I wasn't worried about him wandering off. He was too lazy to go far. I didn't want him getting underfoot, so I looped his leash through an opening on a post outside the door. Huckleberry lay down in the shade with a sigh and watched as I retreated back inside.

The next hour of my life felt like a year. People always said an impossible task was like looking for a needle in a haystack, but that was child's play compared to this. It was more like looking for one specific piece of hay in a whole barn full of haystacks.

As daunting as the task was, it wasn't impossible. Sure, I had a literal ton of garbage to sift through, but I didn't have to go through it all. If the trucks had last come to empty all the garbage in the shed on Sunday night, then the bags on the very bottom would have been from Monday morning, around the time of Bethany's death at 10:41 a.m.

Luckily, the taco bar didn't open until eleven, which made it easy to build a timeline. I dug down to the bottom of the bin, tossing bags over the lip of the container, until just a thin layer of garbage bags was left. I opened up one bag and saw taco wrappers. This was collected too late, and from the other side of the park. I tied the top closed again and threw it out of the bin.

The next bag I checked was more promising. It was full of empty water bottles—didn't anyone bother recycling?—and miscellaneous trash from cigarette butts to tiny bags of doggie doo. No bracelet, though. No phone, either. The next three bags were more of the same—lots of garbage but nothing interesting.

Right as I had reached the bottom of the bin and was considering rechecking some of the bags I'd chucked over the edge, I heard a deep voice saying, "What on earth do you think you're doing?"

I looked up from where I was crouching, surrounded by the bags I'd already combed through with no luck. "Oh, hey," I said, smiling up at him. I could only see part of his face from this angle. Even if I'd been standing up straight, the lip of the bin was at chin height. Being vertically challenged put me at a definite disadvantage.

"I asked you what you're doing," he repeated.

"My friend lost her . . ."

He cut me off. "You know what? I don't care. Get out of there so I can do my job."

"Yeah, of course." I stood and wiped the grimy gloves on the hem of my polo, realizing for the first time that I had ruined yet another uniform shirt. Oops. At least it was my newest one, the one I hadn't had time to tailor yet.

When I'd first pulled myself up and over into the bin, there had been a pile of garbage bags threatening to shift and suffocate me. But as I worked my way down, I kept tossing the discards over the side until I was perched on bare metal. And by bare metal, I mean the dirtiest surface I'd ever seen in my life. The problem was, now the top of the bin looked extremely far away. I grabbed the lip and tried to heft myself up, but I'd never been especially good at chin-ups.

"Can I get a hand?" I asked meekly, hoping the garbage collector would take pity on me.

Instead of reaching inside, he shuffled away. Great. What was I going to do now? Wait until they brought in the next load of garbage so I could build up enough bags to get out?

Then I heard a chain rattling and a loud screech of metal as one of the short sides of the bin swung open, revealing a broad-shouldered, muscular man in a bright yellow T-shirt covered by an orange reflective safety vest. I noticed he wasn't wearing a mask. He scowled at me. "Scram."

"Thank you so very much," I said, hurrying over to the opening as quickly as I dared, mindful of the slippery metal beneath my cowboy boots.

He grunted in response. "Made one heck of a mess here, lady," he pointed out as I stepped down onto the concrete floor.

He had a point. I'd tossed all of the bags from the bin to the floor, and a few looked like they'd burst on the way. But to be completely fair, the rest of the shed wasn't much better. Bags were piled up haphazardly, bins were overflowing, and a river of green-ish brown slime oozed slowly toward the front door. "Sorry. You want me to clean it up, or . . ."

He cut me off once again. "Get lost before I call the cops."

I wasn't sure that rummaging through garbage was a criminal offense, but his warning had the intended effect. I hurried outside, freed Huckleberry's leash, and gave it a tug. "Come on, boy, let's go home."

Hey, that was new.

I was starting to think of Williamsburg as home. Not only that, but even Untapped Books & Café felt like home now. If I felt this connected to Brooklyn after just a few weeks, I couldn't imagine what it would be like at the end of the summer.

Huckleberry was enjoying the shade, and the smell didn't seem to bother him. Come to think about it, I didn't notice it as much anymore, either. Even as I removed the mask and peeled off the gloves, the stench had dropped from overpowering to merely annoying. I guess people really could get used to anything. "Let's get going." I tugged the leash harder this time, and Huckleberry reluctantly got to his feet, stretched, wove between the large garbage trucks that had appeared while I was inside, and followed me out the front gates.

I was exhausted. I was hot. I couldn't even begin to contemplate how disgustingly filthy I was. But most of all, I was emptyhanded. All that was for nothing since I didn't have a bracelet or phone to show for it.

I trudged back toward the bookstore, Huckleberry trailing behind me. When I first met the unofficial mascot of Untapped Books & Café, I'd mistakenly assumed that the big, goofy retriever mix was named after Huck Finn. I figured, with it being a bookstore and all, that his name was influenced by classic American literature. I'd overestimated the intellectual acuity of my coworkers. Turns out, he was actually named after the old fifties cartoon character Huckleberry Hound.

One guess as to which of my coworkers used to watch old cartoon reruns, back in the days before Cartoon Network existed, when hapless kids had the choice between Saturday morning cartoons and Nickelodeon—if they were lucky enough to have cable. Seriously, I don't know how anyone survived before YouTube and Netflix. No wonder Todd turned out so weird.

When we reached the alley, I was pleasantly surprised that I couldn't smell the garbage. At first, I thought that while I'd been gone the trucks must have come by, but as I got closer I realized that the dumpsters were every bit as full as when I'd left to walk Huckleberry, if not more so.

On the plus side, if I had managed to blow out my olfactory receptors then this morning wasn't a complete waste. Sure, food would never taste the same, but on the positive side, I wouldn't cringe every time I entered an underground subway station. See? Silver lining.

"Holy smokes, what is that stench?" I heard Todd exclaim as he stepped out the back door.

I looked down at myself for the first time. My polo was covered in so much muck, it was no longer green. My skirt was beyond salvaging. That was no biggie, I'd make a new one. My boots—my favorite pair—were so dirty I couldn't even see the snakeskin pattern anymore. The exposed skin on my arms and legs was coated in something—several somethings to be precise—that alternated between sticky and slimy. And unless I was hallucinating, a line of ants was crawling up my left leg.

Todd stared at me, mouth agape for a moment before he had to cover his nose and mouth with his hand. He took a step backward. "What on earth happened to you? No, I don't want to know. Go home and get cleaned up." He shoved the brick away from the door frame with his foot and closed the heavy door behind him. I heard it click into place.

"I guess we know when we're not wanted, don't we?" I said, looking down at Huckleberry. He whined in response. "I hear you, boy."

I banged my fist on the back door.

A minute passed, then came Todd's muffled voice. "Go away."

"You gotta at least let Huckleberry in," I pleaded with him.

"Not if he smells half as bad as you do."

I hadn't noticed any bad smells on him, but right now I doubted if I could smell a corpse flower in full bloom. I'd kept Huckleberry from the worst of the garbage, but that wasn't saying much, to be fair. "Fine, I'll take him home and bathe him, but Izzy's got my keys and my phone's still in my apron."

At least, I hoped it was. It wasn't in my pocket. If it had fallen out while I was rooting through the trash, well, it was gone now.

Usually, at the start of my shift, I would toss my messenger bag into a designated cabinet in the kitchen where employees could leave their belongings. All of the skirts I designed had pockets, but they were hard to get to when I was wearing a waitress apron, so I usually transferred my phone to one of the apron pouches, next to my pad of paper and a handful of pens.

I don't know how every place runs, since I've only ever waited tables at two restaurants. But at both places I'd worked, it was the server's job to provide pens along with the check. If just one table an hour kept the pen, at the end of my shift I would be empty-handed. I collected free pens anytime I saw them, but still ended up buying them in bulk every few weeks, which came out of my own pocket. Considering I made *less* than minimum wage, that expense bit into my food budget.

In other words, people who stole pens from restaurants were not on Santa's "Nice" list.

Right now, I wasn't worried about my cheap bulk pens. I wasn't worried about my order pad. I could live without my messenger bag, which contained my (mostly empty) wallet. But I needed my phone, and my apartment keys.

I banged on the door again.

"Todd, I tell you what, if you don't let me in this very minute,

I'm coming around front and walking through the whole shop until I get my phone and keys."

"Hold your horses," came his muffled reply. "I'm coming, I'm
coming." The door opened a crack and Todd's hand appeared,
clutching my cell phone. I took it from him. Then he lobbed my
keyring at me. It landed on the pavement. The door slammed
again, and this time I could hear the bolt being thrown. As if I
couldn't take a hint.

The walk home was long and hot. On the plus side, I didn't
have to worry about crowded sidewalks since everyone was more
than happy to give me a wide berth. Every half block or so, Huckleberry would lie down on a patch of grass or in a spot of shade, and
I had to cajole him for several minutes before he would get to his
feet again. Not that I blamed him. The next bench I passed might
be as far as I went.

As luck would have it, there were few benches between the
bookstore and my aunt's apartment. Benches had gone the way of
payphones and paper checks. It seemed odd to me that even bus
stops didn't have benches in them, but according to Izzy, it was part
of a citywide initiative to keep the homeless population from adding
an "undesirable" element to otherwise nice neighborhoods. That
sounded like malarkey to me. I wasn't sure what the best solution to
the homeless problem was, but taking their ability to sit down on a
clean, comfortable surface seemed needlessly cruel to me.

After what felt like a hike across Death Valley, we reached the
door to my aunt's building. I looked down at Huckleberry. "You be
a good boy. Think invisible thoughts."

I pulled the door, and cringed when it opened easily. The front door was only unlocked when the concierge was on duty. Maybe I'd get lucky and he'd be on a break.

I wasn't lucky.

"For heaven's sake, what the devil is that smell?" Earl's familiar voice greeted me before my eyes could adjust. The lobby was well lit, but after the searing sun reflecting off the buildings and the sidewalks, I couldn't see a thing. I needed to invest in sunglasses, even if it was just a cheap pair I bought off one of the corner vendors that catered to the tourists.

"Hey, Earl," I said, hoping that the casual greeting would deflect suspicion off of me. Like maybe he'd think it was someone else in the lobby that smelled like a ripe dumpster.

"Don't 'Hey, Earl' me, Miss Odessa," he said, rising from his seat. "And what's that you got with you? A dog? You know well as I do you ain't got no dog registered to your apartment, and no way is that mutt under twenty pounds."

Frankly, I don't get the arbitrary twenty-pound-dog limit. In my experience, small dogs were more inclined to bark at every little sound they heard and drive their neighbors absolutely up the wall in close quarters. It's not like a twenty-pound dog was less inclined than a twenty-one-pound dog to tear up the carpet or scratch at the front door. But what did I know? Rufus was the closest I'd ever come to having a pet, and he was a cat.

"It's just for an hour or so," I explained, urging Huckleberry toward the elevator. But the big dog got one blast of cold air from the air conditioner, collapsed onto the freezing marble floor, and was now doing his best impersonation of an immovable object. I bent down, put my arms under his front armpits, and started dragging him across the lobby.

I got him halfway into the elevator, and then came around and pushed on his back end until he reluctantly crawled the rest of the way in under his own power. I hit the button for the fifth floor. As the elevator whirred to life, Huckleberry's ears perked up. Then the doors opened and he looked at me, abject confusion on his face.

How on earth was I supposed to explain an elevator to a dog? He got in a room. The door closed. The doors opened again, but now he was in a completely different place from where he started, like magic. "Come on, Huck. Almost home," I assured him.

He followed me reluctantly, tail tucked between his legs. Between his failing eyesight and the overwhelming stench of garbage clinging to both of us that probably clogged his nose, too, I couldn't fault him for being confused. "It's all right," I told him, scratching his big head right in front of his left ear. He leaned into my hand as I fumbled the keys into the lock with my other hand. "No one's gonna hurt you, buddy. You're gonna be fine."

I opened the door, and Rufus launched himself at us.

14

Odessa Dean @OdessaWaiting · June 26
I'd rather be doing literally ANYTHING else, but life had other
plans today. I can't even. #adulting

I GRABBED FOR RUFUS, but I was too exhausted, too slow, and too
surprised to be effective. The turbocharged ball of fur and claws
that was my aunt's normally sweet-natured cat latched on to the
back of Huckleberry's neck, yowling at the top of his lungs. The
big dog twisted away from me, ripping the leash out of my hand as
he tried to rid himself of the cat by turning in a tight circle and
attacking his own tail.

I reached for Rufus again, and this time, instead of missing, I
accidentally grabbed his ear. He hissed and swatted at me. I jerked
my hand back, but not before his nails raked down my arm, causing *me* to yelp. Between the cat's battle cries, the dog's hysterical
barking, and my own yell of pain, I was starting to see why apartments had such strict pet policies.

Luckily it was the middle of a weekday and no one came out
to investigate the ruckus, or worse, call the cops. Technically, both

Rufus and Huckleberry were my responsibility, but I had no idea if either of them had tags or were current on their shots. The last thing I needed was animal control taking them both into custody. Then it would be a competition who killed me first—my aunt, or the entire staff of Untapped Books & Café.

"Stop!" I yelled, to no avail. I managed to hook an arm under Rufus's midsection and pull him free. Hissing and thrashing, he sank his teeth into the soft tissue of my upper arm. Freed from the demon cat, Huckleberry took off like a shot. Moving quicker than I'd ever seen him go before, he dashed toward the elevator and pawed frantically at the closed door.

Knowing that Huckleberry had nowhere to go, I wrestled Rufus into the apartment. I carried him into the bedroom and closed the door behind me before he could escape. One down, one to go. Huckleberry growled at me when I approached, showing a snarl that would have been impressive if he hadn't lost most of his teeth years ago. I grabbed him by the collar and dragged him inside. He broke free as soon as we were across the threshold, but I managed to corral him into the bathroom and slammed the door shut.

Rufus meowed plaintively from the bedroom. Huckleberry barked angrily from the bathroom. And my sense of smell chose that moment to flip back into the on position. I caught a whiff of myself and almost cried.

All in all, not one of my better days.

Instead of giving in and feeling sorry for myself, I gave myself a stern pep talk as I stripped down to bare skin in the middle of the kitchen. I stuffed all of my clothes, including my bra, into the trash can pulled the bag out, and tied it shut. That bra had cost me forty-five dollars. It was my favorite—purple with pink, white, and blue polka dots.

Anyone who wears a bra knows how hard it is to find a cute one that fits.

It was *not* easy to watch it go into the trash.

Then I remembered that my cell phone was still in my skirt pocket. I opened the trash bag, dug out my filthy skirt, retrieved my cell phone, and tied it all back up again. I carried the bag—and my boots—to the sliding balcony door. It was one thing to throw out a bra, it was an entirely different matter to give up on a pair of broken-in cowboy boots without a fight. Careful to keep as much of my unclothed body as possible hidden from the outside world, I pushed the garbage bag and boots out onto the balcony, where I could deal with them later.

I pulled a mixing bowl out of the cabinet and filled it with cool water from the sink faucet. I didn't have any dog food in the house—obviously—but I found a few slices of chicken cold cuts in the crisper that were about to go bad. I retrieved those, along with a handful of baby carrots, and made my way to the bathroom.

Huckleberry was a good-natured dog. I had no idea what his life was like before he wandered into the bookstore, hungry and alone, but ever since he'd made Untapped his home, he tolerated a constant flow of strangers, delicious smells wafting from the kitchen that he wasn't allowed to eat, and more importantly, he put up with Todd. He was a good dog with a big heart, and when I opened the door to the bathroom, he thumped his tail on the floor and gave me an enormous doggy grin as if I was his favorite person on the entire planet.

I liked to think that meant he forgave me, but in my heart of hearts, I knew he could smell the chicken in my hand.

I put the chicken and carrots on the sink, as far back as I could, then set the bowl of water on the floor. When I straightened, the chicken had disappeared, and Huckleberry was still grinning at me with an expression of complete innocence, which would have been easier to believe if he didn't have a baby carrot stuck in the gap between his only remaining canine and the next tooth back. "You've got to be kidding me. That chicken was meant as a bribe, you know."

Huckleberry might not be the oldest dog on the planet, but there was dirt younger than he was. I hadn't expected him to be able to jump up and reach all the way to the back of the counter to gulp down all that chicken in apparently one bite. I wouldn't underestimate him again.

Then again, I was pretty sure I was forgiven now, which was a good thing considering what came next. But before I could give him a bath, I needed to take care of a few things myself. My swimsuit was still hanging up on the towel rack from yesterday, and I stepped into it. Yes, it's silly, but I felt a lot more comfortable wearing a swimsuit than nothing at all, even when I was home alone.

Next, I washed the cat scratches and bite off with soap and hot water. The cuts were shallower than I thought, and the bite hadn't broken the skin. After patting my arm dry, I considered putting some antibacterial cream on the scratches, but it would just wash off in a minute anyway, so I left them to breathe for now.

Blissfully unaware of what was in store for him, I pulled the last two clean towels out from under the sink. I *really* needed to do laundry soon. I started the shower and got it to a comfortable temperature. Then I started to worry that this wouldn't work. The shower had a fixed head, not one of those retractable wands. Would that be enough water pressure to clean a dog as big and furry as Huckleberry?

Or maybe I could draw a bath and convince him to jump in and splash around. But then how would I get the soap on him? For that matter, what would be better, bar soap or shampoo?

If he didn't stink so infernally bad—and me right along with him—I would have considered giving up on the whole idea and dragging him to the groomer. But I was broke, and besides, my wallet was still at the café. I could figure this out. How hard could it be?

Convincing Huckleberry to jump into the bathtub was easy.

The first time.

As soon as the water hit him, he yelped like I'd poked him in the eyeball with a sharp stick, and knocked me over in his ungraceful attempt to escape. He huddled in the corner of the bathroom, shivering and giving me pitiful "Why?" eyes while whining incessantly.

"Oh, come on, don't be such a big baby. It's just water," I told him. I tried pulling on his leash, but he didn't budge. I had to push him from behind to get him to go anywhere near the tub, but I couldn't for the life of me convince him to get inside, and I couldn't lift him up over the lip.

Frustrated and running out of ideas, I turned the shower off. No use wasting water, right?

As soon as the water stopped flowing, Huckleberry jumped into the bathtub and started licking the drain. "You're kidding. It's that easy?" I grinned and reached for the knob. As soon as I twisted it into the on position, Huckleberry yipped and leapt out of the tub. This time I avoided getting bowled over, barely.

"This is gonna take all day, isn't it?" I turned off the water. Huckleberry sprang into the tub. I kept one hand on his collar, and with the other, I grabbed the mixing bowl I'd put down on the floor for drinking water and dumped it over his big, stinky head. Huckleberry grinned at me. Feeling encouraged, I left him in the tub as I filled up the mixing bowl in the sink with lukewarm water.

I ran back and forth between the tub and the sink several times until he was sopping wet. Then I dumped half a bottle of my favorite shampoo on him and rubbed it into his matted fur. Maybe I should have sprung for a professional groomer. He needed a haircut and I was certainly not prepared for that.

"Odessa, I'm home!" Izzy called out, and I leapt to my feet. I had my hand on the doorknob, about to warn her to not open the bedroom door, but I was too late. She let out a shriek. Eager to investigate, Huckleberry—still lathered up with shampoo—climbed out of the tub, skittered across the floor, and squeezed past me into the living room.

"What on earth?" Izzy exclaimed, as the big dog ran full tilt to greet her, hit the tile, and slid into the kitchen. Rufus, who had been hiding on top of the fridge, thought that Huckleberry was aiming for him. He yowled and leapt to the kitchen counter, knocking a bag of nacho cheese chips to the floor. Ignoring the cat, Huckleberry rushed toward the chips and began vacuuming them up in giant noisy mouthfuls.

"I'd ask how your day was, but I'm not sure I want to know," Izzy said. She bent down and grabbed Huckleberry's leash in one hand while trying to pry the nearly empty bag of chips out of his mouth with the other.

"Pretty much like this," I confirmed.

She handed me the leash, then her eyes started watering and she pinched her nose. "For the love of Pete, what is that smell?"

I gave her a lopsided grin. "That would be me. Come on, Huckleberry. Let's finish up your bath so I can take a shower."

"Anything I can do to help?" Izzy asked. I was impressed that she hadn't run out of the apartment yet.

"I've been showering myself for a couple of years now. I think I can handle it," I quipped. To be honest, I wouldn't have minded a hand in the bathroom. It sure would speed up the process. I'd tried getting water from the bathtub tap, but Huckleberry had bolted again, so I went back to shuttling water from the sink. However, I wasn't about to lock Izzy up in a tiny room with me with the way I was smelling right now. *I* didn't even want to be in the same room as me. "Unless you have an idea of how to get all this matted fur off him?"

"I'll see what I can come up with," she replied, still pinching her nose.

It took twice as long to get all the shampoo off Huckleberry as it had to get him wet and lathered up in the first place, but when the job was finally done, I felt an enormous sense of accomplishment. I dried him off as good as I could, then poked my head out of the bathroom. "Where's Rufus?"

"Hiding under the bed," Izzy replied.

"Good. Can you close the bedroom door? I'm gonna let Huckleberry out."

"No problem."

"Thanks. Oh, and don't feed him anything. He's already had half a pound of chicken and all those nacho chips." Secure in the knowledge that the dog was in good hands and the cat was locked up in another room, I took a long, hot shower. I washed my hair three times, and used both soap and body wash on a loofah sponge, which was still tinted green from the shirt-staining debacle. When I was convinced that I was as clean as I was ever going to be without going through one of those decontamination showers at the CDC, I dried off with a stack of hand towels.

I seriously needed to do laundry.

I came out of the bathroom wearing my aunt's robe to find Izzy sitting in the middle of the kitchen floor surrounded by piles of orangey fluff, holding the leash of an overweight poodle. "What in heavens happened here?" I asked.

Izzy held up a pair of electric clippers, then went back to finish buzzing Huckleberry's flank. "A little help? He doesn't like it when I mess with his toes."

"Sure thing." I grabbed a jar of almond butter from the cabinet and a big spoon out of the drawer. I wasn't sure if dogs liked almond butter as well as they liked peanut butter, but it was all we had. I sat down on the floor in front of him. "Oh, who's a pretty boy?" I crooned. I fed him small bites of almond butter as Izzy finished up shaving his paws.

While she worked, Izzy told me, "I can't believe you cut out while Geoffrey Tate was still reading. He's so funny and smart and handsome, not that I need to tell you that. He asked about you, you know?"

"He did?" That surprised me.

"You made quite an impression on him," she told me. "I've got a personalized, autographed copy of his latest book for you in my bag. Here, help me turn Huckleberry around so I can get that last paw."

Once Izzy was finished, Huckleberry looked like a completely different dog. Instead of matted and dusty, his fur was soft and smelled like my favorite lilac shampoo. Without all of the hair obscuring his face, I could see his eyes clearly and I realized he wasn't half-blind after all. He'd just had a hard time seeing out of all of that matted fur. His tail looked a little weird shaved, but it would grow back. And best of all, he had to be a thousand degrees cooler now.

"He looks amazing. Where'd you get the clippers?"

Izzy ran her fingers through her own short hair, flipping it over to show the hair above her right ear was buzzed almost down to the skin. "You think I can afford to go to the barber every couple of weeks?" she asked with a grin. "By the way, your phone has been ringing off the hook ever since I got home."

"Thanks." I got up and checked it. Fifteen missed calls, all from my aunt. No voicemails. "Uh-oh. Busted."

I'm a pull-the-Band-Aid-off-quick kind of woman. I never understood people who avoided bad news when they could get it over with and get on with their day. So instead of hesitating or making up some kind of excuse to talk to her later, I called my aunt back.

"Odessa, sweetheart. So good to hear from you," she said by way of a greeting. I knew from the excess molasses in her voice that I was in trouble, big time.

"I can explain," I replied. Maybe not the best way to open the conversation, but it was the truth. "By the way, Rufus is doing great. He misses his mommy, but he's eating and playing and behaving himself." I left out the part where he had bit and scratched me because, really, that wasn't his fault.

"Uh-huh. Good to hear." She fell silent.

"About the roommate, it's just for a couple of days. Two, three at the most. She's a friend. I trust her. And the dog isn't staying, I swear. I needed to give him a bath and I'm taking him back home right now, as soon as we get off the phone. Yes, the cops stopped by, but that was a totally unrelated matter."

There was a long pause, and I wondered if we'd gotten disconnected. Thanks to the miracle of cell phones, talking to someone in Nice—or was she in Paris this week?—was as easy as talking to someone in the same room, except without the benefit of their facial expressions.

"Aunt Melanie, are you still there?"

"A roommate, Odessa? The cops? And a *dog*? I'm so disappointed in you." I could almost hear her shaking her head on the other end of the connection. "I thought I was very clear about not having friends over. Some of my collection is irreplaceable, and if it got knocked over or broken . . ."

"I understand, and we're being careful. Izzy's building is being fumigated and she needs a place is stay. You don't want her living on the street, do you?"

"Well of course not, dear, but don't you think . . ."

"What, that any of her other friends are staying in a huge apartment all to themselves? I met someone the other day that has three roommates living in a space about the size of your bathroom. One of my friends lives in an abandoned school and has to shower in the gym locker room. Or maybe I should have turned her away and found out later she's sleeping in the park? Sure, it's not like she's gonna freeze to death this time of year, but what park benches remain in Williamsburg are specifically designed to be too uncomfortable for anyone to sleep on."

"Odessa," Aunt Melanie cut me off, "you've always had such a big heart. It's just for a few days, right?"

"Right," I told her.

She sighed. Aunt Melanie couldn't have turned Izzy away any more than I could. "I only wish you would have asked first."

"I know. I should have."

"Why were the police there?"

"Detective Castillo was just following up on something that had happened at work." All right, that wasn't exactly the full truth, but if I told my aunt that one of my coworkers had been murdered, she'd tell my mom, and I'd be yanked back to Louisiana before I could count to five.

"Now about the dog . . ."

"It's the shop dog at Untapped Books & Café. We just finished his bath and I'm taking him back the minute we hang up."

"Rufus doesn't like dogs." *Now* she tells me. "He had a bad experience when he was a kitten."

"Don't worry, Aunt Melanie. He's in your bedroom with the door shut. When I get home tonight I'll give him lots of treats and extra playtime."

"No harm, no foul, I guess."

I glanced down at the red marks on my arm. Huckleberry had escaped unscathed. He might have been terrified, but Rufus's claws couldn't gain any traction though his thick, matted coat. "Exactly. I'm sorry if I worried you . . ." I paused and thought. "Wait a minute. If you didn't know about Izzy, and you didn't know about the cops or the dog, why *did* you call me more than a dozen times and not leave a single message?"

"Earl the concierge called, told me I needed to talk to my dear, sweet niece. Refused to tell me why, but said it was a matter of some urgency."

I narrowed my eyes. Rat Fink Earl. I knew it. "So nice of him," I said between clenched teeth.

"He's just doing his job. I've got to get back to my friends, but please do at least try to stay out of trouble."

"I will. Love you, Aunt Melanie."

"Love you, too. Oh, and, Odessa? There's a spare set of keys in the junk drawer. Make sure you get them back when your friend moves out. They're very expensive to replace." She hung up before I could thank her.

15

Dizzy Izzy @IsabelleWilliamsburg · June 26
busted! #sorrynotsorry

THAT WENT WELL," Izzy said hesitantly.

"Better than can be expected," I agreed.

"Do you want me to leave? I know I kinda pushed my way in here and didn't give you much of a choice. I'm sure I can find someone to crash with until it's safe to go back home."

I shook my head. "No way. Like I told my aunt, there's more than enough space here, and she gave us her blessing, so you might as well stay." I rummaged through the junk drawer in the kitchen. I think there's a law somewhere that everyone needed a miscellaneous drawer somewhere in their house to store everything from matches to string to box cutters to spare keys that didn't fit anything anymore. Aunt Melanie was no exception. I found the keys. They were on a keyring along with a big fuzzy piece of fur.

I tossed it to her.

Izzy caught it in one hand, and then almost dropped it again. "Eww, what's this supposed to be?"

"I think maybe it's supposed to be a kitten? Anyway, it's your key for the duration so we don't have to keep playing do-si-do with the door."

"Thanks, Aunt Melanie," Izzy said.

"I better get Huckleberry back to the shop before Rufus has a heart attack." The dog in question was stretched out on the cool kitchen tile, snoring softly. With his new haircut, he was probably comfortable for the first time all summer, and I had no idea how I was going to convince him to walk all the way back to Untapped in the heat, especially after forcing a senior dog into more exercise in one day than he'd had in months. I'd call an Uber but most of them didn't allow dogs. "Do we know anyone with a car?"

"I don't even know anyone with a driver's license," Izzy said. I think of all of the culture shocks I'd had in Brooklyn, that was the biggest. Less than a quarter of eight and half million plus New Yorkers had a driver's license, and most of them were over forty and living outside of Manhattan. Why bother learning to drive when they can take a bus, train, or Uber anyplace they couldn't bike or walk? "Oh wait. I think Parker has a van."

"Perfect. Do you have his number?"

She gave it to me and I texted him. It's Odessa. Got a sec?

A few seconds later, my phone beeped. Sup?

Big favor. Need car 2 drag Huckleberry 2 UB&C.

Addy? I typed in my address. Meet U 5 min.

Thx.

I slipped my phone into my pocket. "Parker's on his way. Thanks for the suggestion." I changed out of the robe into real clothes and pulled my wet hair back into a ponytail. With my only pair of shoes out on the balcony, I borrowed a pair of flip-flops from Aunt Melanie's closet. I hoped she wouldn't mind.

Huckleberry's leash was still damp—I'd tried to wash the stench of garbage off it—but I clipped it to his collar and cajoled him to his feet. As stubborn as Huckleberry could be, it could easily take a lot longer than five minutes to get to the lobby, but luck was on my side and he ambled slowly behind me without much resistance.

I waved at Earl on our way out. I couldn't resist telling him, "Melanie sends her love," in my sweetest voice, to make sure *he* knew that *I* knew he'd dimed me out.

Parker was standing on the sidewalk, and waved as soon as we emerged. Huckleberry barked in greeting and ambled over to greet him. Parker stood next to a bicycle, but it was nothing like my aunt's old Schwinn. It had a standard front wheel and handlebars, and a normal seat, but the back was two smaller tires instead of one, and set on a wide base that supported a wooden box set into a metal frame. The cargo box itself was maybe two feet wide and three feet long, big enough to haul a couple of toddlers or maybe a mini-fridge.

"Nice building," he noted.

"Thanks. It's my aunt's." I circled the bike. Not exactly what I was expecting. "Is it safe?"

"I've hauled over three hundred pounds before," Parker said, patting the seat affectionately. "I wouldn't recommend it on hills, but it does the job."

"I mean is it safe for Huckleberry?" I asked.

"Are you kidding? This is as spunky as I've ever seen him. He'll be fine." Parker patted the dog's head. Huckleberry was sitting patiently on the sidewalk, his lolling tongue and thumping tail the only signs of movement. "Although I barely recognized him. You sure this is the same dog?"

"He just needed a bath and a haircut. Give me a hand getting him in the cart?"

It took both of us pushing and pulling to lift the overweight dog up over the lip and get him settled into the cart. Parker did most of the work, but he was small for a man—only a few inches taller than me or Todd—and not much stronger than I was. Then again, waitressing was better for arm strength than a gym membership, and a lot cheaper. Once we finally got Huckleberry inside, he circled three times and curled into a ball with plenty of room to spare.

Parker brushed dog hair off his arms—shaving Huckleberry would help with the shedding, but stubborn tufts of fur clung to him still—and I noticed up close how many cuts and scrapes he had, crisscrossing from his elbows to the palms of his hands. "Don't those hurt?" I asked, running my thumb over the underside of his arm. It felt almost like braille.

"Nah," he said, going perfectly still for a moment. "Comes with the territory. I hardly feel it anymore." He pulled his arm away. "I was about to swing by the shop and check on my bees anyway, and you weren't far out of the way. When it's hot like this, I worry about them." He climbed onto the bike, then slid forward to the very tip of the seat. "Well, what are you waiting for? Hop on."

"I don't know. I haven't ridden on the back of a bike since I was twelve." I left my main concern unsaid. Parker had a big heart. He was an amazing cook. A genuine nice guy that I was proud to call a friend. But he wasn't exactly The Rock, and I was no bag of bones. Between Huckleberry and me, I wasn't sure he could manage the cargo.

"If it makes you feel better, you can ride on the handlebars," he said with a grin. "Get on. Don't worry. I'm a safe driver." He flipped a switch and the bike whirred to life.

"That thing's electric?" I asked. I hadn't noticed any batteries or mechanical parts, but then again, I hadn't examined it with a magnifying glass.

"Sure is. Come on, Odessa. Trust me." I climbed onto the bike, scooting as far back onto the seat as I could manage so Parker had a little room, with my flip-flops propped up on the metal frame. "Hold on to my waist," he instructed.

For the first few blocks, I was nervous that I was going to fall off or Huckleberry was going to freak out and jump out of the cart. But once I relaxed, I started to enjoy the ride. Too soon we arrived at the shop. Parker hopped the curb and came to a halt on the sidewalk.

I clambered off as gracefully as I could—which, considering I was in a long, billowy skirt and had to get off the bike without falling or kicking Parker, wasn't very graceful at all—and went to check on Huckleberry. He was sitting up, his chin resting on the edge of the cargo box, ears perked as he sniffed the wind. When I went to lift him out, he whined. "Aww, you want to go for a longer ride, don't you, boy?" I turned my attention to Parker, who was lifting the dog's backside. "I don't blame him. That was fun."

"Uh-huh," he grunted. Together we lifted Huckleberry up and

out of the cart and deposited him on the sidewalk. He stood on his back legs and propped his forelegs on the cart, as if begging to be let back inside. "Told ya."

Parker opened the front door and gestured me to go first. Andre looked up from the stool behind the cash register. Unlike Todd, when Andre was managing the store, he actually worked, whether it was serving, checking out customers, or doing grunt work like stock and inventory. He even ran the kitchen when necessary. His culinary imagination was limited to peanut butter and jelly, but he could follow a recipe with the best of 'em.

"Whoa, hold up. You can't bring a dog in here," he told me with a frown. "Odessa, you know better."

I unclipped Huckleberry's leash and he flopped down in his usual spot, right in the middle of the main walkway so that anyone entering or leaving Untapped Books & Café would have to step over or around him. I liked to think it was his passive-aggressive plea for attention. "Seriously?"

"Shoot, is that Huckleberry?" Andre came around the desk and squatted down next to him, running a hand along his flank. "What the what did you do to him?"

"Duh. It's called a bath and a haircut." I grinned. "Maybe you should try it sometime." I was joking, and he knew it. Andre kept his hair clipped close to his head, arranged in neat waves. He shaved religiously, leaving only a neatly trimmed goatee. Even his nails were manicured, something I had to admit I sometimes neglected. And by sometimes, I mean always.

"You should talk, girlfriend. No offense, but you're a little . . . ripe." He waved his hand delicately in front of his nose as if he were a turn-of-the-century royal lady with a lace handkerchief instead of a turn-of-the-millennium broad-shouldered black man with an exercise tracker on his arm.

I sniffed myself and caught a faint odor of garbage. I guess my shower hadn't been quite as successful as I thought it was. "Yeah, well, it's been one of those days."

"Tell me about it." He paused. "No, seriously. Tell me about it. I'm all ears."

I shook my head, "You wouldn't believe me if I told you."

"'Scuse me, I need to go check on the hives," Parker said, squeezing past me.

"Question," I said, moving to the side so he could pass. "Aren't you worried that the bees are gonna bother people?" They'd been right over my head the whole time I worked at Untapped Books & Café, and they'd never buzzed at me, but if they stung someone, they would certainly complain.

"Are you kidding? The neighbors love them. My bees pollinate every flowerbed and community garden within two miles. That's like most of Williamsburg. If it weren't for my bees, all of the beer and veggies we serve in the café would come from Jersey or something instead of right here in Brooklyn. Take our most popular beer, Pour Williamsburg. They use coriander, grown on the rooftop garden next door and pollinated by my bees, to give it that little extra flavor. Then they bottle it right here and deliver it out of the back of a minivan. That's what makes eating local so special. The whole of Brooklyn can get involved."

"I hadn't thought about it that way," I admitted.

"Plus, I sell my excess comb to candle makers and soap makers and other artisans in Williamsburg willing to pay top dollar for local beeswax. They actually pay more for the raw honeycomb they render themselves, which is great for me. Along with the raw honey, which is awesome for combating allergies, I can make a tidy profit," Parker added.

I was curious to know how honey was connected to allergies, but something else he said caught my attention more. "You ever sell beeswax to Bethany?"

"Sure. All the time. She is . . . was one of my best customers. I gave her a break because she was a friend and always bought in bulk. She mentioned me on her YouTube channel once and I was flooded with orders for months. Couldn't hardly keep up with demand."

I must not have watched that episode yet, but it was nice to see the two of them scratching each other's backs. He supplied cheap wax and she gave him free advertising. If that didn't say everything about the new world economy, I didn't know what did. I liked to imagine a world where every transaction worked that way. Then a thought sparked. "You ever sell beeswax to a woman named Jenny Green?"

He smiled. "Jenny. Talk about a character. She's as abrasive as sandpaper on the outside and gooey as honey on the inside."

"Yeah, that's her," I agreed. "How'd you meet her?"

"Bethany introduced us, I think. Bought from me a couple of times, not as often or in as big of quantities as Bethany, though." He frowned. "Guess I'll have more stock for the farmers market now. Hey, I could talk about bees all day, but I'm losing light."

"Oh! I'm sorry." I hadn't considered that my questions were keeping him from doing his job. "Some other time?"

"If you stick around, I can give you a lift home and you can ask me all the questions you can think of," Parker offered.

I didn't know a polite way of telling him I'd gotten the information I needed already. "Thanks, but it's a nice night for a walk."

"Then I'll see you later."

"Later," I agreed. He made his way toward the front and I ducked into the kitchen. Despite it being a Wednesday night, the café was packed. Between overpopulation and the fact that few people under forty worked Monday through Friday, nine to five anymore, there wasn't a lot of fluctuation between the crowd on Saturday night versus the crowd on a Tuesday night.

"You workin' tonight?" Silvia, the night shift cook, asked as soon as she saw me lurking in the doorway. Her dark hair was tucked up in a hairnet, and her apron was covered in unidentifiable splatters and stains. The grill was sizzling, the fry oil was popping, and the toaster dinged. The music piped in over the speakers, which was just background noise during the day, was cranked up to compete with the dozens of conversations happening at the tables right now.

The vibe at night was more friendly neighborhood bar than the daytime lunch-counter feel. It was more exciting and the tips were better, but I was satisfied on the day shift, because I knew all of the customers and most of them were sober. "Just popping in to grab my bag," I replied.

I could survive without my wallet for a few hours, if I had to, but I was already starting to feel itchy without it. What if I wanted to stop and get an iced coffee on the way home? Sure, I could use the app on my phone, but what if the network was down or I decided to order something at one of the food trucks that only took cash? What would I do then?

I waited until Silvia moved over to the small walk-in refrigerator before ducking under the counter and opening the employee cabinet so I wouldn't be in her way. Like most of the employees at Untapped, Silvia was incredibly nice, but if I got between her and her food prep, she was likely to donkey kick me without so much as an "excuse me."

The cabinet was stuffed so full the door barely closed. That was my fault. I shouldn't have left my bulky messenger bag here when I left earlier. I removed a couple of purses and a backpack before I could reach my bag. As I dragged it toward me, I noticed something behind it—a waitress's apron.

That was weird.

We were supposed to hang our aprons on the hooks in the hall. We didn't have assigned hooks exactly, but there were always enough hooks that we didn't have to fight for space, so I'd pretty much used the same hook every day since I'd started here. So why was an apron shoved into the back of the employee cabinet?

I grabbed it and pulled it out, but even without reading the name tag I knew whose apron this was. Bethany's. When she skipped out of her shift, she'd tossed me her apron. I had my hands full, so I'd stuffed it back in the cabinet instead of hanging it up like I should have, and then promptly forgot about it.

I felt something hard in the pocket. Her cell phone.

I smacked my forehead. I'd spent the morning going through how many bags of garbage when her cell phone was here the whole time. And worse yet, *I'd* been the one to put it here. Sure, her bracelet was still missing, but her cell phone could tell me more than a bracelet she'd bought at a thrift store ages ago ever could.

"¿Como?" Silvia asked. In my limited understanding of Spanish, "como" meant "how" or sometimes "why," but Silvia seemed to use it as a catch-all when she was busy. She nudged the pile of purses on the floor with her foot. "Either vámonos or grab a hair-net and get to work."

"Sorry," I said, wrapping up Bethany's apron so the contents of her pockets wouldn't fall out and make even more of a mess. I dropped it into my messenger bag, then shoved all of the purses and the backpack into the cabinet. "I'm getting out of your way right now."

I scooted out of the kitchen as quick as I could before Silvia could press me into service.

I waved at Andre on my way out, but he was ringing up customers and didn't notice me. Huckleberry did, though, and lifted his head to lick my palm when I bent over to give him ear scratches. He whined when I stood up and stepped over him. "Sorry, boy. I'd love to take you home with me, but Rufus would probably kill both of us. You're safer here." As if understanding me, he sighed and plopped his head back onto the floor.

The night was warm, but not skin-searingly hot like it had been all day. A cool breeze off the river blew down the street, and I was glad my hair was up in a ponytail, or it would be blowing everywhere. Sidewalk cafés overflowed into the street. I passed a noisy crowd stumbling between bars, a pair of blissful lovers holding hands, and a lady trying in vain to convince her labradoodle to finish up their business so they could go inside and watch television. It was a perfect evening, but I wasn't paying attention to any of that.

I must have checked inside my messenger bag half a dozen times between Untapped and my aunt's apartment, to assure myself that Bethany's apron was still inside. I was debating between turning her cell phone in at the police station or taking it home, charging it, and checking out the recent activity myself.

What would the police do with it? Drop it in an evidence box and let it rot? Did they even have an evidence box for Bethany? Detective Castillo had said they weren't opening a case. So what did they do with her effects? According to her roommate Cherise, Bethany didn't have any family. So who was listed as her next of kin?

Then it hit me. I wouldn't know who her next of kin was unless I looked through her phone contacts. I wasn't being nosy. I was being helpful. If I thought about it that way, it was the least I could do. As the person who found her phone, I was practically obligated to go through it, right?

Right.

I had a responsibility to Bethany to snoop through her phone.

Yeah, sure.

As hard as I tried to justify it, I had a nagging feeling in the back of my head that it was the wrong thing to do. So I compromised. I'd take it home and charge it, and maybe glance through it to see if anything popped out before taking it to the station tomorrow. That was only fair.

Satisfied with my decision, I let myself into the lobby of the apartment building. Good thing Earl had gone home for the evening. The last thing I needed was him deflating my buoyant mood. Today hadn't exactly been a total success, but I'd found Bethany's cell phone, hadn't I?

"Ms. Dean?" The now-familiar voice stopped me in my tracks, and I looked around to see Detective Vincent Castillo lounging on one of the lobby's wingback chairs. He uncrossed his legs and stood to greet me.

After his last visit, when he'd announced in no uncertain terms that Bethany's death was officially an accident, I figured I'd never see him again. But his presence here meant maybe he'd changed his mind. Maybe he was here to give me some good news, or at least tell me that he'd formally reopened the investigation.

I was never a big believer in fate. I didn't check my horoscope. I thought signs and déjà vu and alien abductions were a bunch of malarkey. But even I had to admit there had to be some higher power at work here. I'd spent the last eleven blocks waffling between turning Bethany's phone in to the police or trying to crack it open myself, only to get home and find one of NYPD's officers waiting for me.

I flipped open the top of my messenger bag and laid a hand on Bethany's stained apron. "Detective Castillo, just the person I wanted to see."

Then the elevator dinged and Izzy strode into the lobby. She was wearing a skirt that stopped a good six inches above her knees, high-heeled sandals, and a crop-top that showed off an awful lot of smooth, tan skin. Her orange hair was combed over to one side, and she wore a bright red lipstick that screamed for attention. Her gaze landed on the detective, and her eyes positively sparkled. "Vince! Hope I haven't kept you waiting long."

He grinned at her as his eyes flicked up and down, taking in her outfit. Compared to my long hippy skirt, oversized T-shirt, and borrowed flip-flops, she was a knockout. "Not at all."

Her attention drifted to me. "Odessa, glad you're home. I left you a note. Salad and pizza in the fridge. Help yourself. And don't wait up." She winked at me.

"Ms. Dean," Detective Castillo said, nodding at me.

"Detective," I said, returning the nod. He held the front door for Izzy, and together they disappeared out into the night.

I closed my eyes and counted back from ten, concentrating on my breathing. It wasn't like I was dating Castillo or anything. I mean, I knew he was out of my league. I just hadn't realized that Izzy might be into him. Then again, I hadn't said anything to her, either.

I was just surprised, I told myself. Not disappointed. Happy for Izzy, even. And, on the bright side, now I had the apartment all to myself tonight. I could finish up my new silver sundress and then start a new true crime podcast. Sounded like a perfect evening.

16

THE NEXT MORNING, I woke determined to have a fabulous day. I wasn't scheduled to work, so I had time to do whatever I wanted. Too bad I couldn't use some of that freedom to sleep in late, but the living room windows faced east, and the flimsy privacy curtains did little to block out the early morning light.

I sat up and stretched. Aunt Melanie's couch wasn't half as comfortable as her bed. Izzy had come home either very late last night or very early this morning and was now peacefully snoring on the giant mattress. In the room with blackout curtains. It was just for a few days, I reminded myself.

There was a warm weight on my feet, and I tried to move without disturbing Rufus, who was curled up at the end of the couch. No luck. He stood and stretched before coming over and demanding to be petted. "I hope this means we're friends again, Rufie," I said, but I wasn't sure he could hear me over his loud, rumbling purrs.

I got up to fix him breakfast. My feet tingled where he'd fallen asleep on them, and I had to shake off the pins and needles. I selected the last can of cat food from the cabinet—I needed to remedy that sooner rather than later—scooped it into his bowl, and dropped the spoon into the sink. That's when I noticed the sink was empty. Even the dishes I had forgotten to wash last night after dinner had been cleaned, dried, and put away.

Izzy snored. She also apparently went out on dates with someone I was harboring a secret crush on. The optimal word here being secret. I hadn't told her I thought Detective Castillo was attractive. How would she have known? Besides, I reminded myself, I only had a little over two months left here in Williamsburg. The last thing I wanted to do was get tangled up in a romance. If I looked at it that way, she'd helped me dodge a bullet. Along with her cooking, buying groceries, and cleaning—even when I was the one who'd left the mess—Izzy was turning out to be the ideal roommate.

I set a pot of coffee to brew and decided I could probably use another shower or two to get the stench of yesterday's adventures off of me. Then I remembered we didn't have any clean towels, and I didn't want to dry off with hand towels again. It worked in theory, but my hair was too long and thick to air dry. Using a hand towel on it yesterday hadn't helped at all.

Two mesh bags hung in the tiny closet that held the washer and dryer. The bag that held my dirty clothes was half-full, but the other one that held soiled towels and other household linens was empty. That didn't make any sense. I could have sworn it was almost full. In my haste to meet Parker outside yesterday, I knew I'd left a pile of dog towels in the bathroom, but I didn't remember seeing them last night when I got home.

Sure enough, I checked and the towels were gone. I peeked into the cabinet under the sink, and lo and behold—freshly laundered towels. And they were fluffy and folded, not stiff and hastily rolled up like they were after I did laundry. Either we'd gotten a visit from the laundry fairy last night, or Izzy had washed, dried, and folded all of the towels, along with doing the dishes. Talk about a perfect roommate.

Knowing that the coffee ought to have brewed by now, I headed back to the kitchen to pour myself a cup. I'd heard stories of people who couldn't drink coffee after noon, who thought drinking coffee in the shower was weird, and even some rare creatures who didn't drink coffee at all. I didn't have time for that kind of negativity in my life, so I poured myself a mug and headed back to the bathroom to shower.

On the way, something caught my eye, followed by a dull thud against the window.

There was movement outside of the living room window. A lot of movement. The thin curtains ensured that no one looking in would see much while still letting in natural light. They were opaque enough that I couldn't see out clearly, but something was raising a ruckus right outside the glass. It was enough to draw Rufus's focus, and I could see his silhouette on the other side of the curtain and his tail twitching like a metronome on this side.

"What's got your attention, Rufie?" I asked, drawing back the curtain and then stifling a shriek as a seagull collided with the sliding glass door leading to the balcony.

At least thirty enormous seagulls clustered around the door—perched on the railing, flapping their wings against the glass, shrieking as they fought one another for something at the bottom of the pile of birds. They would rise a few feet off the balcony, circle, and then come in for a landing again. One of them started to fly away with a scrap of purple polka-dotted cloth in its beak, but then another bird snatched it away before he could escape with his prize.

Even with a quick glimpse, I recognized that scrap of cloth.

It was my—formerly—favorite bra, purple with a pattern of blue, pink, and white polka dots. It was the same bra I'd been forced to throw away yesterday because I didn't think I'd ever get the stench of garbage out of it. Except, I hadn't thrown it away, had I? I had tied it up in a garbage bag, along with the rest of the kitchen trash in the bin, and left it on the balcony to clean up later. And then I'd forgotten all about it.

But the seagulls hadn't.

I'm sure in a world without landfills, in a world where people composted and recycled and used resources wisely, seagulls would only be found on ocean beaches, fishing in clean, shallow waters. That world might exist someday, but not here and certainly not now. Instead, we've trained generations of seagulls and other creatures that were never designed to be scavengers that trash equals food. Seagulls were attracted to dumps like third-graders were attracted to pixie sticks.

And now they were coming for my garbage.

I grabbed the broom from the cubby next to the fridge and slid the door open just wide enough to squeeze the head of the broom outside without letting any of the huge, squawking birds inside. I waved the broom around, shouting, "Shoo!" as loud as I could manage. The birds were unimpressed.

I had no idea what to do. If I'd been back home, I would have turned the hose on them, but I was on the fifth floor, and I doubted my aunt owned a garden hose. Most people who lived in Brooklyn apartments never needed one. I could maybe get one from maintenance, but then I'd have to admit that I'd caused the problem in the first place. Besides, unless it was a *really* long hose and I had an equally long ladder, I had no way of reaching them.

If the broom and the cat and my screaming didn't scare them away, what would? They were New Yorkers. They weren't afraid of anything.

The idea of calling animal control crossed my mind, but I dismissed it. What would I say? There's a couple dozen seagulls fighting over my underwear? I'd be the laughingstock of Williamsburg.

I had to think of *something*.

"What's all the racket?" Izzy asked. I hadn't heard the bedroom door open over the melee on the balcony. "And do you have any idea what time it is?"

"It's early," I admitted. "And it seems that every seagull in Long Island has taken up residence on our balcony." Careful not to drop the broom or let the door open any farther, I yanked back the curtain and let her see the extent of the seagull circus.

"What do you think drew them in?" she asked, pressing her hands against the glass, as if feeling their wings slap against the door made them more real. "You didn't feed them, did you?"

"Of course not," I said. "Well, not exactly. At least, not on purpose."

"Odessa, what did you do?"

"I might have left a garbage bag filled with scraps and the clothes I was wearing yesterday when I was pawing through the park's trash-holding facility out on the porch to take care of later, but then there was the whole Huckleberry bath fiasco and the . . ."

"I get the picture," she said. And she meant it. Izzy took out her phone and started recording. After a few seconds, she hit the button to end recording. "This is gonna make a great TikTok."

"Gee, I'm glad something good came of this," I muttered. "What am I supposed to do?"

Izzy was already Googling. "It says here that seagulls are afraid of owls," she said.

"Which would be helpful if we were also being invaded by owls," I replied. "Wait a second." I read her screen over her shoulder. "Seagulls don't like anything bigger than them looking at them. They're not afraid of Rufus because he's smaller than they are, and they're not afraid of us because they're so used to humans."

I looked around the apartment with new eyes. All of my aunt's odd statues might not just be taking up precious space. "Here, help me." I opened the door a crack wider so I could pull the broom back inside.

"What do you have in mind?" Izzy asked.

"Give me a hand moving this closer to the door," I said, pointing at the seven-foot-tall metal giraffe statue in the corner. It took both of us, but we finally managed to position it so it was looking out onto the balcony. A few of the seagulls squawked and flew away, but the majority redoubled their efforts.

"What about that weird monkey statue in the bedroom?" Izzy suggested.

"Perfect."

We dragged the realistic chimpanzee statue out into the living room and pressed it against the glass. It took the seagulls a minute to notice it, but when they did, they all took flight at once. They hovered a few feet off the ground before coming back to land on the rails.

"It's working."

"Yeah, but not well enough," I said. "It won't be long before they realize they're not in any danger."

"What about that hippo trash can from the bathroom?" Izzy ran and got it, waving it at the glass door. The birds took off again, and this time instead of resettling, they circled warily. "This is our window. Our problem," she said.

"Agreed. Keep 'em busy." I dashed into the kitchen and pulled one of the heavy-duty black trash bags off the roll. The idea did not escape me that if I had used one of these bags in the first place instead of a flimsy white trash can liner, we might never have had this problem.

"I'm gonna go out first and keep them off you while you collect the trash," Izzy offered.

"You really *are* the perfect roomie," I told her as I steeled myself to follow her.

"Are you kidding? This isn't the first time I've lived someplace that was overrun by pests. Although, last time it was pigeons. Stay behind me, and whatever you do, don't let any of them inside." She slipped outside and waved the hippo trash can over her head, yelling obscenities at any bird that dared get too close.

While she did that, I was on my hands and knees, scooping up the remnants of my clothes, the garbage bag, and as much of the gloopy mess that remained of last week's kitchen trash as I could into the big black bag. When I got to my boots, I hesitated.

"What's wrong?" Izzy asked, shaking the hippo at a bird that looked like it was considering taking a run at her.

"It's my boots. They're the only pair of shoes I have here. I love these boots."

"And so do the birds," she pointed out. "If there's that much bird poop on the outside, just imagine what's inside. Be reasonable, Odessa. Even if you do manage to clean them up, every time you wear them, you'll be the Pied Piper to every rat and seagull in the New York metropolitan region. Raccoons are gonna take the train from Connecticut just to get a whiff of those boots. Now toss 'em!"

"Fine," I grumbled. She had a point. I could never wear those boots again. They might as well be haunted. I tossed them into the bag, trying to pretend I didn't hear the sloshing sound as whatever was in the heel splashed back and forth. I twisted the bag shut. "All done."

"Good. I think that big one over there is giving me the stink eye."

I retreated backward into the living room, and then slid the door shut as soon as Izzy was inside. Izzy passed me the hippo trash can and took the big black garbage bag from me and took it into the kitchen. She tied off the top, then nested it into another bag and tied that one, too, before handing it back to me. "Now go put this down the incinerator."

"Uh, we don't exactly have an incinerator in the building. We have a service. But they only come on Monday, Wednesday, and Saturday."

"I'm not fighting off seagulls for the next two days," she announced. "Go find a dumpster somewhere and get rid of it." She pulled the mop bucket out from under the sink and started running water into it, adding some dish soap that started bubbling immediately.

"What's that for?" I asked.

"I'm gonna try to get the slop off the balcony. Should keep them from coming back."

"All right. And before I forget to say it, thanks."

"For what?" Izzy seemed genuinely perplexed, which made me like her even more.

"Oh, I don't know. For doing the dishes. For washing and folding the towels. For helping me shoo off a gazillion angry seagulls."

"Least I can do, with you letting me stay here and all. Besides, it's what I do."

"What you do? You moonlight as a bird wrangler and I'm just now hearing about it?" I teased.

"No, I mean you can sew. That's your talent. Bethany could make soap. I take care of people. It's what I'm good at. It's what I enjoy."

"You're also a talented cook," I pointed out.

She shrugged and looked embarrassed. "I'm not as good as someone like Parker who makes up amazing meals from scratch, but I can follow a recipe." Izzy cocked her head. "I don't want to ruin a moment or anything, but can you do something about that trash? Even double bagged, it's pretty . . ." She waved her hand in front of her nose.

"Consider it done." I dressed and put on the pair of flip-flops I'd borrowed from my aunt's closet. I pocketed my keys and then dragged the bag downstairs.

"Good morning, Miss Odessa," Earl said, with his most professional smile.

I nodded politely in return. "Morning."

"Taking that bag out for a walk?" he asked, completely unfazed. Then again, this *was* Brooklyn. He'd probably seen much weirder. "We have people who can take care of that, Miss Odessa. Would you like me to print off the schedule for you? Again?"

"Appreciate it, but I'm fine."

"Miss Odessa," he said again, which set my teeth on edge. Which is probably why he did it. Down South, children often called elders that were family friends Miss Susan or Mister Jim, and near strangers by their last name like Ms. Smith or Mr. Jones. Earl, a man at least twenty years my senior, calling me Miss Odessa sounded . . . wrong. "You wouldn't happen to know anything about a flock of seagulls harassing the residents and causing a commotion, would you?"

"Should I?" I asked. Without waiting for his response, I bolted for the door.

17

Untapped Books & Café @untappedwilliamsburg · June 27
It's dangerously HOT outside—don't risk sunstroke! Instead,
beat the heat at UB&C & let us intro you to your new fav book &
brew! #hydrate #craftbeer #thatnewbooksmell

BY THE TIME I got back, Izzy was in the shower. The coffee in my mug was cold now, and the pot was empty. "You gonna want any coffee?" I yelled through the bathroom door.

"Already have some," she replied. Shower coffee drinkers, that's my tribe.

Rather than making another pot for just one cup, I microwaved my mug. I added a little non-sugar sweetener and nondairy almond milk, and it was good to go. It wasn't quite the same as it would have been fresh out of the pot, but I wasn't about to waste perfectly good coffee.

On the counter, Bethany's phone rattled and I turned it over to look at the screen. I'd found a compatible charger and left it plugged in overnight. The sheer volume of missed calls, texts, and other message notifications that scrolled across the screen boggled my mind. Even dead, Bethany was more popular than I ever hoped to be. Unfortunately, I couldn't access any of her messages.

The phone was locked, and was asking for a four-digit code. I stared at it, hoping for divine inspiration, but nothing happened. If I entered the wrong code too many times or too frequently, it would brick the phone and then what good would it be?

"Hey, I gotta run or I'll be late for work," Izzy said, emerging from the bathroom with one of the clean, fluffy towels wrapped around her. Her hair was plastered to her forehead. "And I might be a little late coming home tonight."

"Another date with the hot detective?" I asked.

She gave me a shy smile. "I really like Vince."

"He seems like a nice guy. I'm happy for you." And to my complete surprise, I meant it. Maybe I was a teensy weensy bit jealous, but I did want Izzy to be happy, and if Detective Castillo—Vince—made her happy, well, then, good for both of them.

Showered and dressed at last, I headed out to run errands. Cat food would be my last stop. Otherwise, I'd end up dragging a heavy bag of cans all around town. Besides, I had a more important stop to make first.

Cell phone stores in New York City were about as prolific as the Gap and Starbucks, only at least 90 percent of them were for carriers I'd never heard of before, or only sold cheap, disposable phones that came with reloadable minutes. Bethany's phone was connected to one of the big-name carriers and it was early enough that I was only the fourth person in line.

After explaining that I needed help unlocking a phone, the clerk—a guy a year or two my senior who had a bushy blond beard that could rival Santa's—shook his head. He wore his blond hair in a neat man-bun on top of his head, and had on a polo similar to the one I wore to work, but not in neon green. "Sorry, no can do. Unless you have a"—he counted out my options on his fingers as he talked—"death certificate and a court order granting you power of attorney, or you're a duly appointed member of the court with a search warrant, I can't open this phone."

"But you don't understand—" I said, but he cut me off.

"Don't bother. I've heard it all. There's nothing you can do or say that someone else hasn't already tried, and it didn't work for them, either. You're wasting your time." He pushed the phone back toward me without trying a single thing.

"You remember that viral flash mob video that was going around on Monday? The girl who fell off the elevated walkway at Domino Park in the middle of a marriage proposal?" I asked.

"Do I ever! Stuff like that never happens in this neighborhood. I must have watched that a dozen times."

"This"—I picked the phone up off the counter and waggled it in front of his face—"is her phone. The girl who fell." Now I had his attention. "The police think it was an accident, but I know it was a murder and the proof I need is on this phone. By refusing to help me, you're practically helping a killer walk free."

He sighed. "Tell you the truth, lady, I can't unlock it. Like it's not possible, especially if the last update's installed."

"But you can see her cloud account, right?"

"I can see that she has one," he admitted, "but it's encrypted. Wait a sec." He started typing on the keyboard under the desk, frowning at the screen in front of him.

"You do have a back door. I knew it!"

"Sit tight. I just wanna see . . . Let me check this one thing . . ." He typed frantically, but when he stopped and looked up at me, his expression was grim. "Good news and bad news."

"Hit me."

"I can't crack it." I sighed. "But," he added, one finger in the air, "she has Smart Lock turned on."

"What's that?"

"There are lots of options. Could be she set it up to unlock whenever she's walking, but that's buggy as anything. Chances are her phone automatically unlocks in certain locations or near another Bluetooth-enabled device."

"Can you tell where?" I asked, leaning over to see if I could catch a glimpse of the screen.

"Nope."

"All right, thanks." Painfully aware that the line behind me was losing patience, I pocketed Bethany's cell phone and stepped aside. I had a feeling he could give me more information if he had wanted to, but short of violating the Geneva Convention, I didn't have a lot of options.

Technically, I could turn the phone over to the cops. They had resources I didn't. But Castillo had made it perfectly clear that there was no case to investigate. At first, I'd gotten the impression he wasn't completely sold and was clinging to the hope that I could convince him. When he'd been in the lobby of my building last night, that hope surged front and center—and then came crashing down when I realized he'd come to take Izzy out on a date.

Cops didn't date possible suspects, witnesses, or coworker-slash-friends of the deceased. At least, good cops didn't. That he was free to date Izzy meant he wasn't investigating Bethany's death as a homicide. A phone in itself wasn't going to change that. I needed to find real, hard, actionable evidence. But to do that, I needed to crack the phone. Which I couldn't do without a warrant.

I was caught in a vicious circle.

Moaning about all the things I didn't have—a warrant, a cool hacker friend, any experience or training in the investigative arts—wasn't gonna get me anywhere. Maybe someone on YouTube knew how to unlock the phone, but chances were any links I clicked on would be loaded with viruses, not solutions. I tried to focus on what I did know. Bethany spent most of her time at her boyfriend Marco's place in Queens, the apartment she shared with Cherise and her other roommates in Bed-Stuy, and Untapped Books & Café.

Now would be as good a time as any to pop by the shop and see if her phone automagically unlocked for me. But if I did that, Todd would definitely rope me into working, especially since I'd skipped out on half of my shift yesterday. As much as I loved my job—and really, I did!—I needed a day off now and then to recharge, especially with Todd always getting me to do the odd jobs that he should be doing, the ones that had nothing at all to do with waiting tables and serving craft beer and artisan sandwiches.

Speaking of which, I should probably post something to the social media accounts. I never should have let Todd railroad me into taking responsibility for all of the advertising and outreach on the internet. But who else was going to do it? Todd? He probably still had a Myspace account. Andre? Unlike Todd, he had his hands full actually working.

I dashed off a quick tweet about escaping the heat with a cold beer and a hot new book and clicked post. Almost as soon as I did, a DM popped up. I hadn't been keeping up with notifications as well as I should have, but since the store got dozens of mentions a day, it would practically be a full-time job to reply to all of them. Other than scanning them to make sure none of them were spam or bots, I ignored them. If Todd wanted me to answer every reply, he was going to have to cover my tables and pay me minimum wage.

But a direct message was different. Maybe someone had a complaint and they were willing to report it privately instead of putting us on blast. To be honest, it was probably some rando with "genuine, honest, and caring" in their bio wanting to "make a special friend." Those accounts got an autoblock from me, even when I was logged in as the store.

I clicked on the message. It didn't appear to be a deposed foreign prince or a spam bot, at least not at first glance. In fact, the message appeared to have gone back and forth with the shop quite a few times. I assumed it was Bethany who replied to earlier DMs. The message came from someone named Stefanie99NYC—why did that name sound so familiar?—and the latest read, "Have u forgotten Bethany so soon? Did she mean nothing to u? Would it kill u 2 to say something? Or does that not match ur greedy corporate 'brand'?"

Yikes. That was a lot to unpack. I should have let Todd handle this, but if I knew him, he'd ignore the DM or block the user, even though previous messages indicated they were a loyal customer. I dashed off a quick reply, "Thanks for your concern. Bethany will always be a member of the Untapped family." I hit send before I could overthink it.

Stefanie99NYC did have a point. In addition to the wake that Izzy was planning, it would be nice to put some kind of tribute to her up on our social media accounts. Too bad Todd would never allow such a thing.

Since Untapped was out, I decided to try my luck at Bethany's apartment instead. The whole train ride to Bed-Stuy, I racked my brain, trying to figure out who this mysterious Stefanie99NYC was. I couldn't remember meeting anyone named Stefanie in Brooklyn. I tried to learn the names of the regulars, but if she was a bookstore patron only or liked to frequent the café in the evenings, our paths might never have crossed.

I got off the subway and headed toward Bethany's old apartment with the help of the map app on my phone, which had not failed me yet. Sure, I'd been to her apartment once before, but I always got turned around leaving a subway station and my GPS had a better sense of direction than I did.

I reached the building with no problem. When I pressed the buzzer, a male voice answered. "Sup?"

"Hi, my name's Odessa. I'm a friend of Bethany's."

"She's . . ." He hesitated, unsure how to proceed. "She doesn't live here anymore."

Well, that was one way of putting it. "I know," I told him. "I was wondering if I could have a minute?"

"I've gotta leave for work in a few," he replied.

"It will only take a sec," I assured him.

He buzzed the door open, and I hurried up the steps. A man stood in the doorway to their apartment. He was taller than me, which applied to at least 80 percent of the population over the age of fifteen, and was wearing a poufy white blousy shirt, black boxers, and nothing else. "I'm Tran Nguyen," he said, eyeing me warily. "What'd you say your name was again?"

"Odessa. Odessa Dean," I said, enunciating carefully. "I worked with Bethany at Untapped Books & Café."

"And?" he asked. Unlike Cherise, he didn't seem inclined to invite me inside.

"And I've got Bethany's phone. Before I give it to her next of kin, I wanted to double-check that there's nothing, you know, embarrassing on it." I'd lied more the last three days than I'd lied in my entire life up until then. I didn't know what was worse, the fact that I was doing it so much, or that it was getting to be so easy.

"So?"

"So, I think there might be something in the apartment that will help me unlock it. Mind if I have a look around?"

He opened the door wider. "Knock yourself out." Once I entered the tiny apartment that the four roommates shared, he pointed to five boxes of varying sizes stacked against the wall. "That's her stuff. You gonna take those, too? It's bad enough that Bethany took up half the apartment when she was alive and not paying rent. Now that she's dead and not paying rent, we're still stuck storing her junk."

Sounded like Tran wasn't Bethany's biggest fan. Then again, if she was as big of a slob as Cherise had said, *and* didn't carry her weight with the rent, I didn't blame her roomies for resenting her. The worst part was Tran had caught me in a lie even if he didn't realize it. If I admitted that I didn't know Bethany's next of kin, he would question why I was trying to unlock her phone. If I agreed to take the boxes, not only did I have to haul them back to Williamsburg, but then I had to figure out what to do with them.

I couldn't throw them out. This was everything Bethany owned in this world. Besides, something in those boxes might tell me why she died, or who killed her. "Sure. Can you help me carry them downstairs?"

"Whatever." He grabbed the two smaller boxes on top and headed for the door.

As soon as he was out of sight, I pulled out Bethany's phone and clicked the button to wake it up. It was still solidly, stubbornly on the lock screen. Drat.

I walked around the apartment, waving the phone around like I was in one of those high-tech spy movies and I was scanning for bugs. Nothing happened. The apartment wasn't large, and it only took a minute to cover the whole place. Nothing, with a side of nothing, and a glass of nothing on the side.

What was it that the guy at the cell phone store with the Santa beard had said about Smart Lock? It could be set to unlock to a specific location, or to a Bluetooth object. I'd hoped that she'd set it for her home, but with three roomies, she couldn't have had much privacy here. Maybe something in those boxes had Bluetooth enabled, and when it was powered on, would pair up with her phone. I crossed my fingers, grabbed a box, and lugged it downstairs.

I had to squeeze past Tran on the stairs. After depositing the box, I headed upstairs for the rest. Luckily Tran was on his way down with another box, leaving only one for me to lug downstairs. "Thanks," I told him.

"Sure. Is that all?"

"You wouldn't happen to know someone named Stefanie, would you?" I asked.

"Stefanie-with-an-f or Stephanie-with-a-ph?" he asked.

"Either," I said.

"Nope," he replied.

"Then why did you . . ." I stopped myself. Why would he care how Stefanie spelled her name if he didn't know any Stefanies? "Never mind. It's not important. Let me grab the last box, and I'll be out of your hair."

I retrieved the last box and carried it down to the foyer with the rest of them. Fans were blowing in the apartment, but the hall, without any windows, was stifling hot. I ordered an Uber—no way I was gonna be able to lug all of those boxes on the subway in one trip—and while I waited for it to arrive, I ducked into the kitchen to see if I could snag a drink of water.

As soon as I stepped across the threshold, Bethany's phone vibrated. I pulled it out of my pocket to see what new message had arrived, but instead of seeing the lock screen with a notification banner at the top, I was presented with her home screen, complete with a jumble of app icons.

204

18

THE KITCHEN WAS the key, of course.

Bethany was most at home in the kitchen, mixing the scents
and colors and various ingredients that would become her soap
creations. It made total sense that this would be the place where
her phone unlocked automatically. When she was making soap,
her hands would be too full to constantly be unlocking her screen.
Besides, when she was setting up videos and photo shoots, the last
thing she needed was her phone timing out and going to sleep.

Forgetting for a minute all about the glass of water I so desper-
ately needed, I opened the phone's security settings and tried to
pair the Smart Lock with my own phone to make it easier to access later. As soon as I went to save the changes, I was prompted

to enter a code. Great. If I knew that, I wouldn't need the Smart Lock in the first place.

I glanced at my own screen. The Uber was five minutes out, and I still needed to drag all of the boxes down the steps and out to the curb. I didn't have much time.

I scrolled through her text messages first. Many of the unreads were automated alerts from YouTube, Twitter, Venmo, and other apps, but others were friends reaching out. Either they'd heard the news and didn't want to believe it, or they were wondering why they hadn't heard from her in a few days and were starting to get worried. I would have dug deeper, but I was running out of time.

Juggling the phone in one hand to keep it from locking due to inactivity, I tried to carry the boxes out in the other hand, but they were too big and unwieldy. I gave up and dragged all of the boxes to the door, propping the front door open so I could get back inside. Once all of the boxes were piled up on the curb, I went inside one last time to unlock the phone again, but Tran was coming down the stairs.

He was dressed like a pirate, from black-and-red-striped pants to a tricorn hat and an eye patch. The only thing his costume was missing was a stuffed parrot on his shoulder. "You're still here?" he asked.

"Just waiting on my Uber," I told him.

"You might have better luck if you wait outside," he said pointedly.

"I'm gonna grab some water real quick."

"What? You don't have water in your own apartment? Look, lady, I'm gonna be late for work. You gotta go."

I glanced down at Bethany's phone. I was too far from the kitchen and the screen was dark. "Just one . . ."

He cut me off. "Now." I stepped outside, and he followed to make sure that the door closed behind us. "Bye, Felicia," Tran said. He walked down the sidewalk, looking like he was on his way to plunder the high seas. My Uber pulled up to the curb and the window for getting any more information from Bethany's phone today vanished.

I wrangled the boxes into the Uber—much to the driver's completely unhelpful amusement—and dragged them up to my aunt's apartment, more grateful than ever for her elevator. Most apartment buildings in New York didn't have elevators unless they were high-rises. Even then, they only worked on occasion. On scorching summer days, elevator service was limited and riding one came with the risk of being stuck inside during one of the common rolling power brown-outs.

Hardly a day passed without a new horror story of people trapped in elevators or elevators stuck in flooded basements. The more I thought about it, the more nervous I got. Then I remembered this building had backup generators and had been gutted and rebuilt from the studs up in the late 2000s, when safety codes were considerably stricter than during the construction of most of the older Manhattan apartment buildings.

As I spread the boxes around the living room, Rufus came over to investigate. Like most cats, he was obsessed with squeezing into any available space, especially spaces where he wasn't welcome. I did a cursory examination of the boxes and was disappointed—but not surprised—that Bethany's missing bracelet was nowhere in sight. Likewise, I found no laptop, video camera, or anything of value.

It wouldn't surprise me if her roommates had neglected to pack anything worth more than a few dollars, especially if Bethany was behind in rent like normal.

She had fewer clothes and toiletries than I expected. Either her roommates had tossed out her half-used shampoo bottles rather than packing them up for collection, or most of her belongings were at her boyfriend's. Or was that ex-boyfriend?

I wondered if Marco would want some of this stuff. Most of it looked like junk to me, but it might have sentimental value for him. I texted him and hoped he'd text me back.

The rest of the contents—a half-empty box of disposable gloves, several glass beakers, a variety of silicone molds, a pack of masks like the one I'd worn at the garbage facility, a scarred cutting board, and heavy-duty pink goggles—had a faint scent of sandalwood clinging to them. If I hadn't known better, I would wonder if Bethany was cooking up designer recreational drugs behind closed doors. But I knew from spending several unproductive hours on Bethany's YouTube channel looking for some kind of clue that these were common soap-making supplies.

Unless, of course, the soap-making was just a cover story? If Bethany had been making drugs, that could be a motive for murder. I shook my head. I was letting my imagination run away with me. If Bethany was selling drugs, she wouldn't need a waitress job at Untapped, now would she? I needed to concentrate on the few clues I *did* have without inventing wild theories.

Maybe Jenny Green could get some use out of Bethany's soap-making supplies? If they really were friends, Bethany would rather her molds go to her fellow soap maker than get tossed in a landfill. I packed it all up as best I could and set it aside for her. I knew that Izzy had her phone number, but rather than bugging her at work, I pulled Jenny's YouTube feed up on my phone, then followed her links to her Twitter account. I switched from the Untapped account to my own, and composed a DM saying that I wanted to talk to her if she had a minute.

My phone rang almost immediately, and I snatched it up and swiped to answer, not looking at the display name until it was too late. The caller ID was from Untapped, and the voice on the other end was Todd's. "Odessa, good."

I *never* answered the phone before checking the display screen, and I rarely ever picked up an unknown number. My only excuse was I was hoping to hear from Marco or Jenny, which had overridden my common sense. "Hey, what's up, boss?"

"I need you to take the evening shift."

"Tonight?" I asked.

"No, New Year's Eve," he said, his irritation thinly veiled as sarcasm. "How soon can you get here?"

"I don't know, Todd . . ."

"Cry me a river. You think you're the first person I called? You can hardly handle a morning shift." Ouch. That hurt. I was a good waitress. Well, a competent one, at least. It wasn't *my* fault that I'd been a little distracted lately. "You're the only one who picked up the phone. So tag, you're it." Before I could argue, he disconnected.

I guessed I was working that night.

All I needed to do was change, feed Rufus, and . . . Oh yeah. He was out of food. I had no idea when I was going to be able to get back tonight. It wasn't fair to Rufus to make him miss dinner. The café would have to wait.

Like almost every street in New York, there was a bodega on the corner. The tiny cramped convenience stores stocked the basics—milk, bread, cereal—at astronomical prices. But it still beat schlepping groceries from one of the few big supermarkets. The bodega half a block away sold cat food, carob covered peanuts, fresh flowers, and a selection of groceries with brand names I'd never heard of before.

I grabbed a variety of cans of cat food and paid cash at the register. They had a card reader, but it had been "down for maintenance" for as long as I'd been in the neighborhood. Instead, the owner directed customers to the ATM in the back, the one that charged an eight-dollar service fee. I wouldn't be surprised if the ATM owner was the same as the bodega owner. Good thing I remembered to bring cash.

Back in the apartment, I opened the cabinet where the cat food is supposed to go, and found a Post-It note on the empty shelf written in Izzy's handwriting. "Check the fridge." I removed the note and lined the cans up on the shelf. It would be so much cheaper if Aunt Melanie bought cat food in bulk or at least had it delivered as a subscription service. But even an apartment as nice as this one only had room for a few days' worth of food, and I wasn't sure if subscription services sold anything less than a month's worth at a time.

Cans put away, I opened up the refrigerator and found a medium-sized plastic bowl with "Rufus" written in black marker on the side. I pulled it out and examined the notecard taped to the top. "Serve 1/3c 3x/day." Underneath that was a list of ingredients, which was surprisingly simple—chicken, liver, rice, green beans, and broth. I opened it up and took a sniff. It wasn't what I would call appetizing, but it smelled better than what I normally fed him from the can, and it didn't have a suspicious oily sheen on top.

"What do you think, Rufus?" I asked, offering him the bowl for him to smell. He approached it tentatively, sniffed, and then finally licked it. Then he buried his face in the bowl, grabbed a huge mouthful, and ran into the living room. "I guess it's Rufus-approved."

I had no idea where Izzy came up with the idea for homemade cat food, but it sounded like a good idea to me. It had to be healthier than the fillers they shoved into the commercially produced stuff. She'd gone to all the trouble to make it, and he seemed to like it, so the least I could do was try it for a couple of days and see how it went.

After Rufus was fed, I got ready for work. I sure missed my cowboy boots. It was bad enough walking around Brooklyn in flip-flops, but to work in them? I couldn't begin to imagine how my feet would feel after a shift in the flimsy shoes, assuming that the glass-laced-sandpaper thong strap between my toes didn't kill me first.

I glanced over at the boxes. Among the miscellany that represented Bethany's entire existence had been several pairs of shoes. Two of them had been gorgeous and completely impractical, the kind that were designed to break a neck. But there had also been a pair of black orthopedic loafers. And they were in my size.

Wearing a dead person's shoes wasn't my first choice, but I was desperate. Besides, I'd worn clothes from thrift stores before, hadn't I? Lots of times! The chances that their original owner—or maybe owners, plural—had fled this earthly plane were pretty high. I grabbed a pair of my socks from my drawer—I drew the line at wearing a dead person's socks—and stepped into the loafers. They were ugly as dirt, but man, were they comfortable.

More comfortable than cowboy boots, if I had to be honest. Not that I would tell my beloved boots that, may they rest in peace. I was never going to make fun of orthopedic shoes ever again.

Even though I hurried all the way to work, the first thing I heard when I stepped inside Untapped Books & Café was Todd's whiny voice. "Took you long enough," he complained. "I thought you lived in that swanky building near McCarren Park, not in Jersey."

I was raised to respect my elders, but I'd had enough from Todd. "First off, I got here as quick as I could, as a *favor* to you."

He cut me off. "A favor? I'm doing you a favor. After that stunt you pulled yesterday? You're lucky you still have a job. Cutting out in the middle of the shift, and bringing Huckleberry back looking like a poodle with mange. I'm surprised you didn't paint his toenails and put a bow on his tail."

I caught a glimpse of Izzy coming around the counter to defend me. Technically, she had been the one to shave him, but I didn't want her getting into trouble, too. "You're welcome, by the way. He could hardly see before, and couldn't have been comfortable in this heat wearing all that matted fur."

"Well, he looks stupid," Todd argued. "You probably want a trophy or something now."

I ignored his barb. Todd never missed a chance to "own the millennials," as he liked to say. "And second, how do you know where I stay?" I knew that when I'd filled out my job application, I'd put down my permanent address in Piney Island.

"You don't think I'd miss Bethany's wake, do you? She was my friend, too. Are you gonna get to work, or what?"

"Yes, sir," I replied, too surprised to be annoyed with him any-more. Todd considered Bethany his friend? Bethany *hated* him, and had been very vocal about that fact, to his face. For that mat-ter, most of the employees despised him, and not just because he was a manager. Andre was a manager, too, but everyone adored him. Unlike Todd, Andre was upbeat and helpful. He directed us without being a bully. He didn't talk down to us or make us listen to his boring—and often offensive—jokes.

Izzy caught my attention as I headed back toward the café. "Hope you don't mind, but I spoke to Earl on my way out this morning, and reserved the pool for tomorrow night. Everyone has to clear out by ten and we're responsible for cleaning up after."

"Thanks for arranging that," I told her. She nodded and turned away, but not before I saw tears glistening in her eyes.

Everybody dealt with loss in different ways. Izzy and Bethany had been friends, but instead of letting her grief overwhelm her, Izzy was throwing a party in her honor. Todd and Bethany hadn't gotten along one whit, but now that she was gone, he could pre-tend that they were besties. Was that what I was doing, too? Maybe I was consumed with finding Bethany's killer so I wouldn't feel guilty that I wasn't more upset over the sudden passing of someone I barely knew, and by all accounts, might not have even liked that much if I had known her better.

After stashing my bag and putting on my apron, it was time to face the afternoon crowd. I almost bumped into Kim as she brought in a stack of dirty dishes from the courtyard. "Hey, I thought you were working days to train the new girl," I said.

"I was. She quit, and I ended up picking up a double." The bell rang from the kitchen window. "Now, if you'll excuse me." I stepped out of her way so she could go drop off the dirty plates and grab full ones to distribute to new customers.

I guess that was why no one bothered learning a new server's name for a few days. I wished Hana had stuck around a little longer, though. I'd never met anyone from Slovakia before, and I'd been looking forward to learning more about her native country.

Another waitress came up to me. "Odds or evens?" She was average height, but was built like a pin-up girl and even the baggy neon green polo shirt did nothing to disguise her curves. She had curly red hair that was caught up in a high ponytail that bounced when she walked.

I hadn't met her before, and had to glance at her apron to learn her name, Emilie. "Hi, I'm Odessa."

She rolled her eyes. "Not what I asked. Look, not trying to be rude or nothing, but we're slammed and . . ."

"Odds," I told her.

She winked. "Good luck." Then she turned and, ponytail bobbing behind her, headed off toward her tables.

There are lots of ways to divvy tables into sections. The easiest is when one server takes the right half of the room, and the other server takes the left. Then there's the first-come method which gets pretty confusing after a long shift and can result in one table getting overlooked. Apparently, Emilie's favorite was splitting it up according to table numbers, which was fine with me.

I scanned the odd-numbered tables. Three needed menus, so I dropped those off first. Seven had empty plates, so I cleared those away, got their check from Emilie, and dropped that off. She'd get the tip—she'd earned it. Then I saw who was sitting at

Table Nine, and realized why she'd been thrilled I hadn't chosen evens.

"Hey. Seth, right?" I said as I reached his table. As usual, Seth was drinking coffee, black. From the looks of the rings on the plastic tabletop, he'd been sitting here for a while, taking advantage of the free refills and monopolizing a whole table.

"Yup. Top me off, will ya?" he asked, not looking up from his laptop. He pushed his coffee cup toward me.

I didn't pay much attention to him when he always sat in Bethany's section before, but now he was my problem. "Look, Seth, if it were up to me, I wouldn't mind you sitting here all night nursing free refills, but people are waiting for a table. Why don't you move over to the bar?" There were several stools free, which was a minor miracle in itself. "Or, maybe, I can put this in a to-go cup?" I didn't like to be rude, especially not to a customer, but it wasn't fair to the other diners.

"Nah, I'm good here," he replied, leaning back in his chair. "Are you going to Bethany's wake tomorrow?"

Not answering him, I swept up his coffee cup. "I'll be right back with that refill." Then, instead of going back to the kitchen, I detoured toward the front desk to find Izzy turning the cash register over to Andre.

"Hey, Odessa, how's my favorite little Southern-fried Belle doing today?" Andre asked. If I didn't know better, I'd think he was flirting with me. The way he always made eye contact when he was speaking with someone made them feel special. "Didn't see you on the schedule for tonight."

"Todd called me in," I explained. I didn't think I'd ever worked a full shift with Andre before, and I was looking forward to it. Most of all, I was determined to prove to him—and everyone else—that I wasn't just a mediocre waitress. "Hey, has anyone named Stefanie ever worked here?"

"We've probably had a dozen Stefanies with an *f*, Stephanies with a *ph*, Stephs, Stevens . . ." His voice trailed off. "None in the last year that I can think of, but with turnover being what it is, well, you know."

I nodded. New Girl syndrome. "That's what I thought. Thanks." I turned to Izzy. "I'd rather you not invite customers to Bethany's wake," I told her. "You said you'd keep it small."

"I didn't invite any customers," she protested as she gathered up her belongings. "Just a few folks here, and a couple of her friends outside of work."

I frowned. "Then how did Seth hear about it?" I asked.

"You mean that creepy guy who only ever came in here to drink coffee and ogle Bethany all day? I would never invite him. Maybe he overheard a few of us talking?"

"How many is a few?"

"I don't know, a couple," Izzy said. "My shift's over, but we can talk about this at home, later, okay?"

"Sure. Don't forget, we also need to invite Bethany's roommates, her ex, and Jenny Green," I reminded her. Combined with whoever showed up from work, we already had a guest list in the double digits. And now random near-strangers were planning to attend as well. I had a bad feeling about this.

19

THE DIFFERENCES BETWEEN the morning and evening shifts were—
and I really don't want to say this—night and day. With people
ordering more beers than food, I finally had a chance to use some
of that craft beer trivia I'd memorized. Werewolf Pup had quite a
bite, as the name suggested. Yes, As Sour As Pickles got its signa-
ture tartness from the yeast, not from adding artificial flavors.
Pour Williamsburg Pale Ale was as local as it got—it's brewed and
bottled right here. Frankenbrew was a little like the Kitchen Sink
Dark Ale we had last week, only smoother.

I glanced over our remaining stock, noticing a trend. It must
have been a full moon or something, because half the names in
the refrigerator case had spooky names like Zomb-IPA. I took a
few pictures with my cell phone, but it looked more like a package

store than the Untapped "brand," so I grabbed a few bottles with appealing labels and carried them out to the bookstore section.

Few customers browsed the stacks this time of night. Mostly, they were café customers waiting for a table. But who knew? Maybe they'd find something even better than tonight's special— grilled apple, fennel, and tri-blend cheese on locally baked sourdough. I'd gotten to try a bite of it when a customer sent hers back because she hadn't realized that our sourdough bread wasn't gluten-free, and it was *delicious*. No offense to mom's grilled cheese sandwiches, but these were a whole different level.

"Whatcha doin?" Andre asked, watching me wander around the shelves with several bottles of beer tucked into my apron and under my arms.

"Oh, you know me, just goofing off." I set the beers down on a display table, artfully arranged around a stack of colorful books. Huckleberry wandered over to investigate what I was doing, and with a little bit of encouragement, he jumped up onto one of the big overstuffed seats we keep for customers, curled up, and laid his nose down on the arm of the chair. Framed by the big front windows, I got a few good pictures. "That ought to do it." I uploaded the pictures and caption to all of our social media accounts.

I know Todd only assigned me the task of social media manager because he didn't want to deal with it, but I had to admit that it was fun. I liked being creative, and I loved watching the funny comments pour in. Then I frowned down at my screen as a new comment from Stefanie99NYC popped up, worried that she was going to berate me again for still not posting a Bethany tribute, but instead she posted a heart followed by a beer mug emoji. Crisis averted.

"When you get a chance, mind taking out the trash?" Andre asked. "Kitchen's got their hands full, I'm sure."

"No problem," I replied, gathering up the beer bottles to return to the fridge. I made certain to always hold them by their label, not the pry-off lids. If I was a customer, the last thing I'd want was to be served a beer that tasted like armpit. Then again, to my unsophisticated palate, that described some of the most popular of the IPAs we carried, although our customers would fight me if I said that out loud.

Andre wasn't kidding. The trash barrel in the kitchen was overflowing, and even as I gathered the edges of the bag to tie them together, Silvia, the night cook, tossed a handful of apple peels into it. We needed a composting plan. It made no sense to throw away so much organic material that could be used to fertilize local gardens instead of taking up space in a landfill. I reminded myself to bring it up to Andre or Todd later.

I lugged the heavy bag through the narrow hallway and out the back door, musing over what a difference it made when Andre asked me nicely to do something versus Todd shouting orders. Either way, taking out the trash was a smelly chore, but at least this way I didn't resent doing it half as much.

Two customers I recognized as regulars were blocking the back door, and when I kicked it open—my hands were full—the heavy door almost hit them. "Watch it!" one of them snapped at me.

"What are you even doing out here?" I asked, then noticed that both of them were puffing away at vapes. Ever since New York made it illegal to vape or use e-cigarettes anyplace that smoking was already prohibited, the vapers were forced to huddle outside along with the few remaining cigarette smokers.

"Duh," the taller customer—I think his name was Jose or maybe George—said, gesturing with his colorful vape pen as he released a cloud of grape-scented vapor into the air. He was one of the few customers tonight who looked familiar to me. For the most part, the night shift regulars would remain strangers unless I graduated to one of the more desirable shifts.

I flung the garbage bag into the dumpster and heard it hit metal. I guess the trucks had been by recently. "Customers aren't supposed to be back here."

"We're just gonna be a second," the other customer replied. "It's all good." He held the door open for me. "Ladies first."

A sign on the inside of the back door announced "Alarm will sound if door is opened," but that was a lie. Short of installing an actual alarm on the back door, there wasn't much I could do about customers using it all willy-nilly. Even if the cheap-as-dirt owner could be convinced to open his dusty checkbook, the employees would disable it the first time they were inconvenienced by it, just like everyone—myself included—left the door propped open with a brick even when we weren't outside. It was easier, especially when we had our hands full with trash or deliveries.

As the door caught on the brick, a flash of red light in the hallway caught my eye. Mounted high up on the wall was a round black disk set into a white box. The red light I'd seen was a small power indicator on the bottom. I hurried back toward the front of the store, where Andre was finishing up a transaction with a customer. Once she left, I got his attention. "Since when do we have security cameras?" I asked.

"I dunno. A year, maybe?"

"So before I started?" I asked.

"Yeah. We had a break-in one night after hours. Todd thought it was an inside job, which is patently ridiculous. He had the cameras installed the next day."

I didn't like knowing that someone had been taping me every day while I was at work. It felt like an invasion of privacy. Had I been on camera the other day when I changed shirts in the stockroom? I shuddered. "How many cameras are there?"

Andre shrugged. "I don't know, why?"

"Because it's creepy, that's why."

"So, take it up with Todd," Andre said. Not exactly the response I'd expected from him, but he had a point.

"Yeah, alrighty then." As I returned to the café, I scanned the walls for more cameras. I didn't see any, but that didn't mean they weren't there.

The rest of my shift was uneventful. Tables took longer to turn over as people sat around chatting long into the night, sipping a selection of craft beers and ordering sharable plates from the kitchen. New customers joined existing tables, until six or eight people crowded around a four-top, making it challenging to keep checks straight.

Waiting tables, even at a café with a limited menu and so few seats, could be physically and mentally demanding. I had to concentrate to bring the correct order to the correct person, which was difficult when people started hopping from table to table. But even then, my mind started to wander.

I made decent money at the café. Not enough to afford an apartment in this neighborhood, but on the worst day, I still made about double what I'd make at the Crawdad Shack back home. On top of her job at the café, Bethany made extra cash from advertisers on her popular YouTube videos and had a side hustle selling the finished soaps on Etsy. So why was she always behind on her rent?

It didn't make sense.

I tried to recall the text messages I'd seen on Bethany's phone before I'd been forced out of the kitchen, but I couldn't remember if I'd seen any from a bank. She was a lot more popular than I'd imagined, judging by the sheer volume of texts she received even after she was dead. I'd only glanced at the previews—I hadn't had time to read them all—but they'd ranged from the "Hey, wanna catch a bite later?" variety to people who hadn't had a chance to say their goodbyes leaving one last message.

Mixed in with those were the annoying notifications I always turned off—so-and-so commented on/shared/liked your post. And there were lots of comments. There were also reminders that she had an upcoming hair appointment, that an Amazon order had been delivered, and that a payment had been sent.

Except that couldn't be right.

If she was dead, what was she doing sending money? For what? And to whom?

I needed to go back to her apartment, unlock her phone, and find out.

"Yo! Miss!"

I shook myself out of my stupor when I realized that one of my tables was trying to get my attention. "Sorry, must have zoned out for a sec."

I gave him an overly large grin, one that suggested I might be a little spacey, but gee I was nice and didn't you want to be friends? I may have never fulfilled my mother's dream for me of participating in the Miss Louisiana pageant when I was younger, but the few pageant prep classes I'd taken before six-year-old me decided this was *not* for me still remembered the basics. Lesson number one had been how to smile and influence the judges.

"No worries," the customer said, the slightly hostile tone he'd had earlier dissipating. "Can I get another?" He waggled his beer at me.

"Coming right up," I said brightly. I delivered his beer and made my rounds. The night was winding down, and several tables asked for their checks. The kitchen had closed ten minutes ago, and I could hear Silvia over the din, banging pots and pans around. Andre was squeezed into the tiny kitchen as well, washing dishes and checking inventory. He stuck his head out of the window and waved me over.

"How many tables do you have?"

"Just three now."

"Do you mind handing them over to Emilie, and then taking Huckleberry out for a walk before we close? I'd do it, but I still have to place orders for next week."

"No problem," I agreed. Truth be told, I *liked* walking Huckleberry. I would have happily volunteered to do so in a heartbeat. I just didn't like it when Todd ordered me to do it.

"Could you walk me to my car?" Silvia asked. "I hate walking around this late at night alone."

"Sure." By the time I'd gotten Huckleberry leashed up, Silvia was ready to go, too. "You have a car?" I asked her. "I didn't think anyone here drove."

She shrugged. "It's my dad's car." We walked briskly down the sidewalk. With his new haircut, Huckleberry seemed to have shed a few decades, which still put him in the hundred-and-fifty-years-old range, but he had more pep in his step than I'd seen since I'd met him. "I live out in Elmhurst, and working nights, it's easier driving, you know?"

"Elmhurst?" I asked. I was still learning all the neighborhoods, and I didn't think I'd heard of that one before.

"Queens," Silvia replied.

"That's quite a commute," I caught myself saying and had to laugh at myself. Back home, it was nothing to drive four hours to Dallas to see a play or something, because there was never anything going on in Shreveport. Now, after only a few weeks, I was starting to think that the adjoining borough of Queens, a mere five miles away, was on the other side of the universe. "Why not get a job closer to home?"

We crossed the street and Huckleberry made us stop so he could sniff the base of a streetlight. I wondered how far away she'd parked. Sure, street parking was a full-contact sport and spots were hard to come by, but we'd already gone four blocks. "I was living with my significant other and a few of their cousins here in Williamsburg when I took this job. Then we broke up a few weeks ago, and I moved back home. Temporarily. I'm still trying to figure out what I want to be when I grow up, comprende?"

"Do I ever," I agreed. I liked waitressing, don't get me wrong, but it wasn't exactly the career I'd pictured when I was little. "What did you want to be when you were younger?"

"A nurse," Silvia said. "Maybe an astronaut. Or an astronaut nurse. You?"

"A unicorn," I admitted.

"That's way cooler than an astronaut nurse. Well, this is my car. See you tomorrow?"

"Yup," I agreed. I was working the morning shift, which started a little more than nine hours from now, and she'd be coming in about the time I was cashing out for the day.

The walk back gave me time to think. Bethany had spent most of her time over at Marco's in Astoria according to everyone I talked to, and the fact that she hadn't kept much in the way of clothes or toiletries at her own apartment supported that. So why did she bother to pay rent on a place in Bed-Stuy? She'd said she liked the day shift at Untapped because it kept her nights free, but if Marco had been able to meet me on short notice for lunch, he had to work in the neighborhood, too. Maybe they commuted together in the morning?

And why had they broken up?

Four days had passed since Bethany's death, and I had more questions than I'd had in the beginning, and no answers at all. A tiny voice in the back of my head suggested that maybe I wasn't cut out to be a detective, but I squashed that as surely as if it were a cockroach in my kitchen. I didn't have time for that kind of negativity.

Sure, I hadn't had any luck finding Bethany's bracelet. Everyone I met had a reason to be mad at Bethany, but no one had enough motive to kill her. What was it the investigators always said in those true crime podcasts I loved to listen to? Follow the money. That was it. She used Venmo, that much I knew. She probably did all of her banking online, too. All I needed to do was take another look through her phone.

When we got back to Untapped Books & Café, the last of the customers were loitering around the front door, smoking a final cigarette or taking a pull on their vape pens before heading home. I had to knock on the door for Andre to come and unlock it. I settled Huckleberry in for the night and hung up his leash on the hook. After taking out the last load of trash, I nudged the brick out of the way and let the back door close. I pushed on it to make sure it was locked. It was.

Andre handed me a fold of bills. "Tips from your last tables," he explained.

I stifled a yawn. "Thanks."

"You want me to walk you home?" he asked, looking concerned.

"I thought you had to finish up orders."

"All taken care of. Come on, let's lock up."

As he finished his final checks, I felt around my messenger bag to make sure I had Bethany's phone with me. I'd thought about leaving it at home, but if it had rung and Izzy had found it, I would have to explain what I was doing with the phone. This seemed easier at the time. Maybe I should have left it in the apartment, because then I wouldn't have been tempted to take the subway down to Bed-Stuy in the middle of the night on the off chance that one of Bethany's roomies was awake.

"You live up near McCarren Park, right?" he asked.

I wished I hadn't agreed to let Izzy host Bethany's wake at my aunt's apartment building's rooftop pool. It felt weird that suddenly everyone knew where I was staying. It wasn't that I cared that my friends and coworkers had my address, it was that I didn't want them thinking I was some kind of bougie snob just because my aunt had a ritzy apartment in a swanky building. "Yup."

Andre looked concerned. "Isn't your building that way?" he asked, pointing his left arm.

"Yup," I agreed. "But I'm headed to the subway. I need to run a quick errand."

"This time of night? Maybe you should wait until morning."

I smiled and looped my arm around his. Most of the bars and restaurants were closing. Nearly as many people wandered the sidewalks as there would have been at high noon. More, maybe, since the only time it was bearable to be out on the street was after the sun went down. "I'll be fine," I assured him. "I know what I'm doing."

20

I THINK IT'S SAFE to say that I did not, in fact, know what I was
doing.

That went for life in general. I meant it when I told Silvia I had
no idea what I wanted to be when I grew up. This adulting business wasn't as simple as I'd thought it would be. My parents made
it look so easy. They met in high school, got married, got grown-up
jobs, bought a house, had a kid, and settled down for the important business of growing old together. They didn't take a less-than-
minimum-wage-paying temporary job that six years later was still
their only source of income. They didn't go to senior prom with a
bunch of other couples because they didn't have a date.

And they certainly didn't wander around Bed-Stuy at almost
three in the morning.

Don't get me wrong. Compared to twenty years ago, Brooklyn

is freaking Disney. Then again, a smart person wouldn't wander around Disney at three a.m., either.

Being in the service industry, I was used to working odd hours. Anyone who could work nine to five, Monday through Friday, was a mystery to me. Sometimes my shift would last four hours, sometimes it would be twelve. I could close one night and open the next morning. I could work ten days in a row, or get five days off straight, depending on the luck of the draw. The end result was that sometimes I forget that the rest of the world had a schedule.

Everyone else woke up at the same time every day, walked the dog, showered, and went to work. They ordered the same coffee at the same coffee shop every morning. They ate lunch at noon and then caught the rush-hour train home. They were in bed by eleven and asleep by eleven thirty. By the time it got this late—or was it this early?—there was no one out except for the weirdos, the insomniacs, and me.

New York may be called the city that never sleeps, but to be honest, after midnight on a Thursday, this part of Bed-Stuy was practically comatose.

As I made my way to Bethany's old apartment, I congratulated myself on finding it without any assistance from the map app on my phone. Maybe there was hope for me yet. I scanned the windows of her building for any signs of life, but it was dark.

I couldn't see any movement—no one getting up for a glass of water in the middle of the night. No one staying up late, glued to their screen as they binged Netflix. No one peeking out behind a curtain to see what the petite brunette wearing a dead woman's orthopedic shoes was doing lurking around their neighborhood at this unearthly hour.

I mounted the steps and checked the front door, hoping that it had miraculously malfunctioned and would spring open with the lightest touch. No joy. I should have known that was too much to hope for.

If it had been the middle of the day, I would have used the old tried-and-true trick of pushing each buzzer in succession until a rando decided to let me in. I didn't think anyone would fall for that in the middle of the night, though, and I imagined that their response if I tried would be less than polite.

I think it was safe to say that I had hit a dead end. I should have called it quits, gone home, and caught at least a little sleep before my morning shift tomorrow. That would have been the smart thing to do. The reasonable, adult thing to do. So of course, I chose Option B.

There were several possibilities for the Smart Lock on Bethany's phone. Without the password, I couldn't be certain if she was using Bluetooth, GPS location, or something else entirely, but when her phone was in her apartment, it was locked. Then when I went into the kitchen, it unlocked. Something about the kitchen unlocked her phone.

Maybe I didn't have to be *inside* her kitchen for the Smart Lock to work. I had no idea what the range was for Smart Lock. Maybe I just had to be near enough.

The apartment building was a four-story brownstone, a narrow house surrounded on either side by other narrow row houses. In lieu of a front yard, a smooth concrete surface was taken up by two large garbage bins and a broken planter that may have once held a decorative bush but was now home to dandelions. The front door had a narrow, barred window on either side of it. Each subsequent floor had two sets of windows—one a wide double pane and one narrow like the one downstairs. Each double window had a decorative architectural arch above it, and each single window had a narrow ledge below it that was too small to be a balcony, but had enough room to hold a potted plant or, in the case of the third floor, a bald mannequin dressed in a sequined evening gown.

I assumed that there were also corresponding windows in the back of the house, maybe overlooking a shared garden, but in all likelihood they would open into a few inches of space between themselves and the nearly identical brownstone that backed into it. There were no windows on the sides of the house because they shared a wall with their neighbors. It didn't bode well for privacy or an abundance of natural light, but it was practical in a city where every square inch was precious.

If I remembered correctly, the kitchen was on the left side of the house and the apartment that Bethany rented with Cherise, Tran, and her other roommate was on the right. I moved the large trash can out of the way and stuck my hand, clutching Bethany's phone, between the bars of the window I was 99 percent certain was the kitchen.

The phone sprang to life. I wanted to jump for joy.

I sat down on the cracked steps that led up to the front door and pulled up a list of apps on the phone. A jumble of icons, in no discernable order, for every ride share, delivery, and food service ever created crowded the screen. Either Bethany moonlighted as a delivery driver, or she ordered a whole lot of takeout. She had apps for events and individual rewards programs, along with icons for every social media site I'd ever heard of and some I hadn't.

It would have taken me weeks to go through all of her private message apps, but I saw the logo for a large chain of banks and knew I'd hit pay dirt. "Bingo," I said to myself, clicking the app.

In a world of technology and convenience, there's a balance between security and ease of use. I didn't want to have to enter my password every time I opened email up on my own device, but for more sensitive apps like banking and bill pay I used two-factor authentication. Bethany didn't. Her bank account app opened without so much as prompting me for a password.

I stared at the screen.

This couldn't be right.

The balance was a hair over sixty thousand dollars. I'd never seen so much money, even on a screen. Math had never been my strongest subject, but with my rough calculations, Bethany would have had to be working at least forty shifts a week at Untapped Books & Café for the past decade or three, and sold roughly a bazillion bars of soap a month to live in Brooklyn and still manage to accumulate a balance like this. The screen flashed, and the balance now displayed as twelve dollars and thirty-two cents.

I had a friend in high school that could max out a credit card in record time, but even she would have been hard-pressed to blow through sixty thousand in the blink of an eye. The fact that Bethany was already dead made the feat even more impressive. But where had the money gone?

I scrolled through her text messages until I found her money transfer alerts. The sixty-thousand-dollar transaction didn't show up, but the last successful alert caught my eye. Three thousand, five hundred dollars had been transferred from Bethany to one Cherise Deveaux. Unless Bethany knew more than one woman named Cherise, I assumed it was her roommate.

Thirty-five hundred dollars was steep—to say the very least—for a sliver of a five-hundred-square-foot apartment that didn't even have a kitchen, split between four roommates. It was astronomical. It wasn't realistic. If Bethany's portion of the rent was more than a thousand a month, she was being ripped off, and Bethany was more savvy than that. Besides, it wasn't only the amount of the transaction that was bothering me, it was the date stamp.

The transaction had been completed at midnight tonight, three and a half days after Bethany died.

Something was fishy in Bed-Stuy.

Bethany trusted Cherise enough to designate her as her emergency contact, but then Cherise turned around and pulled a healthy chunk of cash out of Bethany's bank account after her death. It was, at the very least, sus.

I stood and peered at the buzzer, trying to make out the numbers in the dark. I no longer cared what time it was. Cherise had some questions to answer. Right before I pushed the buzzer for Unit C, Bethany's phone went dark again.

Drat. I'd let the phone go to sleep and now it was locked. Again. I stepped off the narrow front stoop, maneuvered around the garbage can, and threaded the phone through the bars of the kitchen window. Just as the screen sprang to life, I heard a loud blip of a siren, followed by a bright strobe of blue and red lights.

"Put your hands up and step away from the window," came the instructions from a megaphone, and my hand clenched around Bethany's phone. I'd never in my whole life been as terrified as I was when I turned around, my hands held high, and faced the police cruiser.

"Drop the weapon," the megaphone barked.

"It's not a weapon! It's a cell phone!" I was staring directly into bright headlights, and couldn't see anything beyond them.

"I said drop it!"

I didn't want to get shot for not following orders, but I didn't want to drop Bethany's phone onto the concrete and watch my evidence shatter into a hundred worthless pieces, either. Holding my hands out, I slowly crouched and laid the phone down. I shoved it away from me with my foot.

"Hands behind your head. Turn around, and walk backward toward me!"

Shaking, I complied. I felt cold metal close around my wrists, and my hands were forced down. The officer then turned me around and had me sit cross-legged on the pavement. He shined his flashlight into my eyes. "ID?"

"In my bag," I said, voice quivering uncontrollably.

He lifted the shoulder of my bag, but the way I wore it cross-body, my hands were cuffed around it. The officer tucked his flashlight into his armpit and squatted in front of me so he could rummage through my bag for my wallet. When he found it, he let the bag drop heavily to the ground. He rose and shined the flashlight onto my driver's license.

I blinked as a hot tear escaped from one eye.

"Odessa Dean. Twenty-three. Piney Island, Louisiana. You're a ways away from home, aren't you?"

I'd never felt so far away in my life. Unable to answer immediately, I nodded my head and swallowed hard. "I'm staying at my aunt's in Williamsburg for the summer."

He made a noncommittal noise in the back of his throat. "Uh-huh. And you're here in Bed-Stuy at nearly three in the morning because . . . ?"

"'Cause my friend Bethany was murdered and no one believes me and then I found her phone but I couldn't unlock it but when it gets near enough to the kitchen it unlocks and that's when I found out somebody, and my money's on Cherise, has been draining her accounts and I think maybe that's why she was killed." It all came out in a rush, like the past three and a half days were compressed into one breath.

"Uh-huh," the officer repeated. "I didn't catch a word of that."

I dropped my head to my chest. My accent wasn't my only problem tonight. The first tear turned out to be one of many, and once the floodgates were open, there was no stopping them. I was crying so hard now, I could barely catch my breath between hiccups. Between the frustration of a futile investigation, Bethany's death, and the terror of being detained by the cops, I couldn't control myself. I couldn't calm down enough to enunciate clearly. "Call Detective Vincent Castillo," I begged the officer. "Please. He'll explain everything."

21

I'VE ALWAYS HAD certain talents. I can sew, and I've come up with designs that would put half of the outfits at New York Fashion Week to shame. At least all my designs have functional pockets. Despite what Kim and Todd thought, I was a good waitress. I could remember faces and orders and preferences of regular customers better than most. I liked to think I was responsible.

And I could sleep anywhere, under any circumstance. I'd once fallen asleep standing up. Taking a cat nap in the precinct was child's play next to that.

My head was resting on my arms as I hunched over the cold metal desk of an interrogation room in the local precinct. It was a similar design to the one where Izzy and I had first met with Detective Castillo, but this one was smaller. There were other differences too. Last time, I hadn't had one hand chained to the metal ring set into the table.

A noise startled me awake and my head jerked up. The cold handcuff bit into my arm when I moved too fast, and I rubbed at my wrist as the door opened and Castillo stepped inside. "Ms. Dean, I assume you have a good reason for dragging me out to Bed-Stuy in the middle of the night?"

I rubbed at my eyes with my free hand. I tried to speak but my voice was hoarse from crying myself to sleep.

"Hold on. Be right back." Castillo returned a minute later with a bottle of water, which he set in front of me. Then he leaned across the table and unlocked the handcuff from my wrist before settling into his chair. "What happened?"

"Cherise was stealing from Bethany," I told him.

"One step at a time here. Cherise?"

"Bethany's roommate." I closed my eyes and tried to recall what it had said on the screen. "Cherise Deveaux. She pulled thirty-five hundred dollars out of Bethany's account at midnight tonight. Wait, no, that's not right. Midnight yesterday. And then sometime around three a.m., someone pulled sixty thousand and change out."

"And you know this, how?"

"It's on her phone." I felt my panic rise again. "They did collect her phone, right? I had it at the brownstone. The officer wanted me to drop it. I don't remember if he picked it up before he shoved me into the backseat."

"Officer Bradshoe collected two cell phones at the scene. I'm assuming one of them is yours. He also has your bag and wallet," he confirmed. "How did you end up with Miss Kostolus's cell phone?"

"I found it shoved into a cabinet at work. I was gonna bring it to you if I saw anything incriminating on it to prove that you had to reopen the case."

Detective Castillo reached across the table again, but this time, it was to place his hands over mine. "Ms. Dean," he started.

"Odessa's fine," I corrected him. If he was dating my roomie, he could at least call me by my first name. Besides, gendered labels were so 2018.

"Let me guess, you read a lot of mystery novels."

I shook my head. "No, but I do listen to true crime podcasts."

"Listening to podcasts doesn't make you a detective."

"Why not?" I argued. "I taught myself how to sew a Renaissance Faire costume, complete with corset, by watching YouTube videos. I could get a whole master's degree online if I wanted to."

Castillo pursed his lips. "I understand how you feel. I've lost my fair share of friends, and it never gets any easier, especially when it's a senseless death. But that's all this is. Your friend Bethany Kostolus had an unfortunate accident. You need to accept that and move on with your life. She wouldn't want you to get into any trouble because of her."

"But it wasn't an accident," I insisted. "Just take a look at her bank records . . ."

"If you dig deep enough into anyone, you'll find something suspicious. That doesn't mean that she was murdered. Promise me you'll drop this, and I'll get all trespassing charges waived and drive you home."

Talk about a rock and a hard place. I didn't want to go to jail, but I couldn't let Bethany's death go unresolved, either. So instead of answering, I nodded.

"I need a yes or no. Can you let this go?"

"Heaven willin' and the river don't rise." It was the best I could do. Sometimes circumstances are out of my control. I wouldn't make a promise that I couldn't keep. What if the killer spontaneously confessed his—or her—guilt to me? Would Castillo expect me to pretend it never happened?

"Is that a yes?" he asked, narrowing his eyes at me. I did not envy the people he interrogated. He did not leave them much wiggle room.

"That's a yes," I agreed. It wasn't my fault that he didn't notice my legs were crossed.

"I don't believe you," the detective said. "I'm keeping the phone. And if you go getting into any more trouble, don't drag me into it because I won't bail you out next time."

"Bail?" I asked, blinking rapidly at him.

"Figure of speech. This time. Next time, it might not be."

"Can I ask you something?" He blinked at me, and I took that as consent. "Have you come across anyone named Stefanie in connection with Bethany's death?"

"No," Castillo said. "See here, Odessa, there is no investigation. No case. Come on." He escorted me to the front desk, where I picked up my messenger bag.

I verified my phone, wallet, and keys were inside. Bethany's phone was not. Castillo drove me home, graciously letting me sit in the front seat, which was a vast improvement on my last ride in an official police vehicle. The sun was peeking out over the horizon when he double-parked in front of my building. "Thanks for the lift," I said.

He nodded. "You're welcome. And, Odessa, next time you decide to lurk around a house at three o'clock in the morning, try to wear something a little more inconspicuous."

"Noted," I said, glancing down at my neon green polo shirt. I dragged myself upstairs. It felt like the lower half of my body was encased in wet concrete. The uncomfortable nap I'd managed to grab at the station wasn't nearly enough, and I needed to be at work in a few hours.

Izzy was up and awake when I unlocked the door. She was sitting at the island in the kitchen sipping a cup of coffee. The balcony curtains were drawn back and the first rays of the sunrise flooded the apartment. The balcony itself was blissfully seagull-free.

"Where have you been all night? And where did all those boxes come from?" Izzy asked as I dropped my bag on the floor by the door. Rufus jumped down off of her lap and came over to greet me. I barely had the energy to bend down and run my hand over his back.

"Long story," I replied.

"Want one?" she asked, gesturing with her coffee cup.

"I'd love a whole pot," I admitted, "but I need to catch at least an hour of sleep before my shift starts."

"Why don't you take the bed?" she offered. "That way I won't bother you."

"Thanks. I'll take you up on that." I looked over at the papers spread out in front of her, covering half of the island. "What's this?"

"I want to say a few words at the wake tonight," she replied. "I just don't know how to say them."

"I'm sure they'll come to you," I assured her.

"I hope so. By the way, I called around, and I found someone willing to come to the wake and give anyone who wants one a copy of Bethany's tattoo. Isn't that great?"

"*At* the wake?" I asked.

"Sure. Why not? Apparently, she and Bethany go way back. She did her tatt in the first place, so it's kinda fitting, don't ya think?"

I nodded. "That's poetic, actually." I yawned. "Hey, before I forget, you know anyone named Stefanie?"

Izzy shrugged. "Doesn't ring any bells."

"Drats." Yeah, I know I promised Detective Castillo that I was done investigating, but old habits die hard. "Well, I'm beat." I dragged myself into the bedroom and the next thing I knew, my phone alarm was blaring in my ear. I looked at the display and realized I could snooze for another fifteen minutes and still make it to work on time. So I did. When I finally dragged myself out of bed, I didn't have time for a proper shower. Instead, I twisted my hair up into a messy bun and slapped a couple of bobby pins in it to keep it in place.

Izzy was nowhere to be found, but she'd left a Post-It note on the door. "Fed Rufus already. Wake starts at seven."

With everything else that was going on, the wake was the least of my concerns, but true to her word, Izzy was handling all the details. And she seemed to need this. For all I knew, I needed it, too. Detective Castillo was a professional. He thought Bethany's death was an accident. The ME thought her death was an accident, too. Maybe they were right. Maybe I needed to find another way to grieve her death.

Feeling like a ton of bricks had been taken off my shoulders, I got dressed and headed to work. I dodged between cars that had no respect for crosswalks, swerved around a bicyclist who was inexplicably riding on the sidewalk even though bikes had their own lane, and resisted temptation when I passed Lucky Stan's Stuffed Croissant food truck—the same one that had almost run me over just a few short days ago. That reminded me that life could be short and brutal, and one should *never* pass up a stuffed croissant. I backtracked and bought half a dozen to share with my coworkers.

For the first time all week, Todd didn't yell at me as soon as I walked in the door. He was behind the cash register, actually smiling as he set up the till for the day. "Mornin'," I said, waiting for the other shoe to drop. When it didn't, I offered, "Want a stuffed croissant?"

He picked one and asked, "Hey, Odessa, how much does a hipster weigh?"

I shook my head. For a man who ran a business that practically catered to hipsters, he was clueless. First and foremost, the only thing hipsters hated more than corporate conformity was being called "hipsters." "How would I know? Everyone's different."

"About an *Instagram*," Todd said, laughing at his own flat joke.

"Oof." I gave him a disappointed look and headed back to the café. I offered croissants to Parker and Kim, who I was happy to see working with me on the morning shift. Todd needed to find a permanent replacement for Bethany soon, though. We couldn't keep swapping shifts and pulling doubles to cover for the hole in the schedule. The three of us stood around in the crowded kitchen, blissfully munching on our stuffed croissants. I'd gotten lucky and selected a chocolate-filled one.

As much as I wanted to heed Detective Castillo's advice and let the whole mystery of Bethany's death drop, lots of things still nagged at me. What had happened to her medical alert bracelet? And where had all the money in her bank account gone? For that matter, where had it all come from in the first place?

"Can I ask y'all a question?" I still hadn't gotten the hang of "you guys." Besides, "y'all" was gender neutral.

"Yes, I'll marry you," Parker quipped. "As long as you keep me in the stuffed croissants lifestyle to which I have become accustomed."

"Good to know. What would you do if you had sixty grand?" I asked.

"I'd get my little sister into cosmetology school," Kim said without hesitation.

"I'd drop ten dollars into every Patreon and GoFundMe account in my Twitter feed," Parker said. "Then I'd check my neighbor into rehab and relocate the roaches in my apartment to someplace nicer."

"If I had any money left over, I'd adopt all the dogs in the shelter and rent a big van and drive them up to Vermont and find them new homes," Kim added.

"What are you guys talking about?" Todd asked, sticking his head in the pass-thru window.

"What would you do with sixty thousand dollars?" I asked, as he nabbed the second-to-last croissant.

He bit into it and red jelly squirted down his chin. "I'd go to some little Caribbean island and sit on the beach drinking beer all day. You?"

"I'd go to all the second-hand stores and buy up as many books as I could find, and I'd put one of those Little Free Library boxes on every corner in Williamsburg," I declared.

"That's dumb," Todd said, shaking his head. "You wouldn't do anything for yourself?"

I shrugged one shoulder. "Who says that's not for myself? Making the world a better place *is* selfish, because I live here, too."

Todd rolled his eyes. "Millennials. We open in five, so chop-chop."

He walked away and we all collapsed into laughter. "Millennials," Parker said, in a fair imitation of Todd's nasal whine. "With your avocado toast and your fancy beard oils, it's no wonder you haven't bought a house yet."

"Don't forget man-buns," Kim added. Her impersonation was worse, but still identifiable.

"Do I need to get all of you trophies to convince you to get to work?" I asked, trying to replicate Todd's voice. "Chop-chop."

Parker doubled over in laughter. "Please, Odessa, don't ever do that again. With your accent, it hurts."

Kim nodded in agreement. "Let's never speak of this again. In your case, literally."

I stuck my tongue out at them. "Don't accent shame me." I grabbed a knife off the block and cut the remaining croissant into three pieces. Ooey gooey lemon custard oozed out of the cuts. I swiped a corner piece and popped it into my mouth. Parker tugged his long sleeves down over his scarred arms and snagged the middle piece. Kim snatched the last piece and tucked the empty box into the giant trash bin in the corner.

The bell over the front door tinkled faintly. I straightened my apron and washed my hands in the kitchen sink. We were open for business.

The first customer through the door was Seth. He made a bee-line to his favorite table. "Flip you for it?" Kim offered.

I shrugged. "I got this." As easy as he was to take care of, I didn't want to wait on Seth because I knew he'd sit for hours and not tip a dime. Our earlier conversation about how we would spend sixty grand was a good reminder that I could do more for my friends, coworkers, and neighbors. Saving the world didn't always mean composting every bit of organic material. Sometimes, saving the world was as easy as paying for someone else's subway ride or letting someone cut the line when they only had one item in their basket.

"Morning, Seth!" I said brightly. "Let me guess, you would like Parker's world-famous avocado toast with a side of fresh strawberries grown in the lush rooftop garden next door and a glass of fresh-squeezed guava juice?"

He frowned at me. "Allergic to gluten. You should know that by now. Coffee. Black." He powered up his laptop and made himself comfortable. As usual.

I guess Seth left his sense of humor at home this morning. "Coming right up."

We had a slowdown about eleven, and after updating each of Untapped's social media accounts, I found myself scanning Bethany's feed, too. Unlike before, when I was looking for some kind of clue that would bring meaning to her senseless death, now I was getting a real sense of her life for the first time.

Bethany was snarky, but she leaned toward funny rather than mean. At least half of her posts were filled with sarcasm and biting insights into the human condition. I'd always known that Bethany was street-smart, but diving deeper into her posts, I realized that she was also *smart* smart. But what really got me were her replies to other people's posts. She was encouraging. Honest. Thoughtful. Totally not the Bethany I thought I knew.

I wished I'd gotten to see more of this side of her while she was still alive. Many of her friends had offered touching tributes to her. I don't know who was cutting onions in here, but they needed to stop. The ones that got me the most were the ones that tried to be funny, but I could tell that they were hurting.

Izzy was right. We all needed this wake tonight. It was one thing for people to pour their hearts out on the internet, but they needed something more. We needed to be surrounded by other people who cared for Bethany, and take an hour or two to celebrate her life.

22

Untapped Books & Café @untappedwilliamsburg · June 28
ALERT—closing @ 6 today! #familyemergency #lastcall

HEY, ODESSA, C'MERE," Todd said, summoning me from across the room.

"Yes, sir, just a sec," I replied, distributing plates around the table. "That's one kale salad with strawberries, walnuts, and blue cheese; one free-range turkey and organic Swiss on whole grain gluten-free pita bread; and one black bean and quinoa wrap with carrot tahini dressing. Am I missing anything?"

I got a few responses of "looks great," and turned toward Todd. As usual, he was on his favorite perch at the top of the stairs. I had never noticed before, but my cowboy boots had a bit of a heel on them, and now that I was wearing Bethany's orthopedic loafers, I felt even shorter than I had before. "How can I help?" I asked, hoping he wasn't going to ask me to do something nasty like pull a hair ball out of the drain.

Then again, that would still be better than the time he'd had me go all the way into Manhattan to stand in line in thousand-degree weather at Madison Square Garden for tickets to some rock band that had one hit song back in the early nineties that I'd never even heard before.

"I need you to update the Twitter."

I bit my tongue. I was *not* going to correct him. Someday, maybe, but not today. "Already took care of it this morning. I pushed those hardback books you were complaining about taking up too much shelf space."

"Good, good. But I need you to announce that we're closing at six today." After years of waiting tables, I had a world-class poker face. I once dropped a butcher knife on my foot, and I never stopped smiling, not until the nice doctor at the walk-in clinic started putting in seven stitches. But I guess my confusion was evident, even to a person like Todd who wasn't exactly known for kid gloves. "You seem surprised."

"More . . . confused. You know it's Friday night, right?"

He nodded. "Yup. And we'll lose a ton of business, but as Izzy couldn't see fit to arrange Bethany's memorial for a decent time, say Monday between two and four, I don't see that we have much of a choice, do we?"

"You're closing early so everyone can attend the wake?" I asked, still not believing my ears.

"Of course. What do you think I am, some kind of heartless lowlife?" He clapped his hands. "Now get to it. I've got to call everyone scheduled to work tonight and tell them to go to the memorial instead."

"Wait a sec, if you were planning on closing the shop anyway, wouldn't it have made more sense to have the service here?"

"What, and have to clean up after all those people? No thank you," he said, turning and walking away.

Six o'clock finally rolled around. We gently shooed the last customer out the door, did a manic clean-up, and headed out together as a group.

When I was seventeen, I went to New Orleans on a family trip. We did all the touristy things. Beignets at Café Du Monde. A riverboat ride. A tour of St. Louis Cemetery No. 1. A mule-drawn carriage through the French Quarter. We even did a late-night ghost tour, including a stop at one of the famous voodoo shops, and one full block of Bourbon Street (just to say we did it). My parents were teetotalers, and I was underage, so Bourbon Street fell flat, but the rest of the vacation was amazing.

The day we were packing up and heading out of town, we got stuck on a side street as an authentic New Orleans jazz funeral parade marched down the crossroad, trumpets blaring and drums thumping. People were singing and dancing in the street, some dressed in ornate costumes and others in tank tops and flip-flops. Behind the big brass band, a horse-drawn carriage pulled a hearse. No one was crying. They were celebrating.

In a lot of ways, that's how it felt to march the eleven blocks to Aunt Melanie's building with my friends and coworkers in tow.

Parker brought up the rear of our ragtag procession, the cart of his electric bike carrying bags we'd filled up with ice from the café. In addition to everyone on the day shift, Silvia, Andre, and Emilie met up with us at Untapped Books & Café. We didn't have any tambourines, but we were laughing and remembering good times instead of dwelling on the bad. In lieu of feathered head-dresses, we all—even the folks who hadn't worked today—wore our UB&C neon green polos in solidarity.

We stopped at the bodega so everyone could run in and buy six-packs of beer. Kim, always one to shirk tradition, grabbed a box of wine instead. "I don't get it," I mentioned to Andre while we were waiting in the checkout line. "Why didn't we grab the good stuff before we left? A whole case of Pour Williamsburg came in today."

Andre hefted the red-white-and-blue pack of cans he was car-rying. "Bethany was partial to PBR. Troglodyte. Amiright?" He paused and his face fell. "I'm really gonna miss her, you know? She was fierce, even if she had questionable taste in beer."

"I know," I said. We paid for our purchases and I led the pro-cession into the lobby of Aunt Melanie's building. "Hiya, Earl."

"Miss Odessa," he replied, sounding grumpier than usual.

"Thanks for helping steer people to the wake." Izzy had told me that he'd agreed to let people up onto the roof as long as too many people didn't show up, but warned us that the first time any of the residents complained, he was shutting us down. "Can I get you anything? Snacks? Beer?"

"Thank you, no. Miss Izzy already dropped off a lasagna."

I smiled so hard my dimples hurt. That was so like Izzy. Here I was, offering him potato chips and cheap beer, and she'd gone to the trouble to make him a whole lasagna. I could learn a thing or two from her. "We'll be on our best behavior," I promised him as we headed for the elevator.

At least two dozen people were already milling around the

rooftop deck when we arrived, even though it wasn't quite seven yet. We deposited the ice and beer into coolers scattered around the pool. I wondered where Izzy had found the coolers. She'd probably bargained with someone for them or convinced a total stranger to loan them to her for the day.

I spotted Jenny Green hanging out near the potted plants. Her wheelchair was decorated with a pink boa, and she wore a fluffy pink dress than made her look like a little girl's third birthday cake. "Nice outfit," I said as I approached. "It's very pink." It was not at all what I expected, especially since the first time I met her, she was dressed in black from head to toe.

Jenny laughed. "Bethany always said she wanted people to wear cheery colors to her funeral. She thought black was depressing." She noticed my polo. "I'm not sure that counts as cheery, but she would have gotten a kick out of it."

"Thanks."

She fingered the material of her skirt, yards and yards of it arranged in big, poufy layers. If she hadn't been in a wheelchair, she would have been tripping over it or knocking things over anytime she tried to move. "Pink's really not my color. You want it when we're done here? I'm sure you could make something more practical out of it."

"I'm good," I assured her. "That would make some nice soap packaging, though. Speaking of which, I sent you a DM the other day. I've got all of Bethany's soap-making equipment in a box down in my apartment, and I hoped you could get some use out of it. I think she'd want you to have the molds."

"Sorry, I never check my DMs. Bethany was always so good at keeping on top of all that stuff, but I'm lucky if I remember to reply to my emails. It's too many different sites to keep up with, you know?"

I nodded. "Do I ever? I've got my own accounts, which get hardly any traffic, but then I'm also managing three different accounts for Untapped Books & Café."

"Try adding a YouTube channel and Etsy store to all that," she said. "But yes, I'd be honored to take Bethany's supplies. I always envied her molds. Plus, I teach a soap-making class down at the community center once a month, and there's never enough equipment to go around. You should come sometime. The invite's up on Facebook."

"Yeah, I'd like that. I've been watching your and Bethany's videos online, and it looks fun. Come grab me before you go, and I'll help you with the box," I offered.

A long shadow fell over us, and I turned to see Marco approaching. "Odessa, sorry I didn't call you back."

"No worries. I just wanted to make sure you knew about the wake, and to talk about a few things. Marco, do you know Jenny?"

He scowled at her. "Sure do. That's the reprobate that was trying to muscle in on Beth's business. Did you know that she stole the recipe to her maple bacon soap?"

"Oh, please," Jenny said with a huff. "Bethany and I developed that recipe together. It was her idea to make it look like we had some big online feud to hype up each other's sites, and it totally worked. My traffic practically doubled overnight, and if it weren't for all of that attention, we never would have gotten that deal."

"Deal?" I asked. "What deal?"

Jenny looked mortified. "Oops. I'm not supposed to talk about it."

Marco loomed over her. "What kind of deal? Look here, I'm her boyfriend. I have a right to know."

"Ex-boyfriend," Jenny corrected him with a hard edge to her words. "Why are you even here? You didn't care about Bethany. If you did, you wouldn't have broken her heart."

"That's not fair." I stepped in, trying to keep the peace. The last thing we needed was people fighting at a wake. "Who are we to say what is really going on in a relationship? Besides, Izzy said they broke up every other week, and always got back together in the end."

"Not this time," Jenny said, glowering up at Marco. "He accused her of cheating on him. He said he never wanted to see her again. He even threw out her best soap recipe ideas."

"So what if I did? We were supposed to be moving in together. She'd already moved most of her stuff in and was gonna break her lease. But then she started getting real secretive and was never home, and she wouldn't admit it, but I knew she was seeing someone else," Marco said, and my heart went out to him.

At the same time, I wondered if Cherise and Tran knew that Bethany planned on moving out, leaving them in the lurch. Was that why Cherise took thirty-five hundred dollars out of Bethany's bank account? If she was vengeful enough to steal from a dead woman, could she also have been responsible for Bethany's fall? I hadn't noticed Cherise in any of the photos on Instagram from the time of Bethany's death, but then again, I hadn't been specifically looking for her.

Wait.

No.

Stop.

I'd promised Detective Castillo I would stop looking for murderers when there were no signs of foul play. Tonight was supposed to be about Bethany's life, not obsessing over her death.

"Bethany wasn't cheating on you," Jenny insisted. "She wouldn't do that."

I tried to get between them and de-escalate before a full-fledged argument erupted. "Come on, you two. This is supposed to be a wake."

"Have you never been to a wake before? If the cops aren't called to break up at least one brawl, it's not a successful wake."

What? Izzy hadn't told me that part. I hoped Marco was kidding, but from the way the veins in his temple stood out and he was clenching his jaw, maybe he wasn't. Although, he wouldn't start an actual fight, would he? Not with a woman.

"I think I'm the authority on what my girlfriend would and wouldn't do," he continued, ignoring me to focus on Jenny. "And I'm telling you, she was seeing someone else behind my back."

"You big dummy! Bethany wasn't cheating on you! She was working on a big secret project with me! We couldn't tell nobody because we signed an NDA, but if you'd waited a few days, she would have told you everything."

"What on earth are you talking about?" he asked.

She bit her bottom lip. "The cat's gonna be out of the bag soon anyway, so I might as well tell you. But you have to promise me that you won't breathe a word of this to anyone."

"What's the big deal?" Marco asked.

"We sold the formula to the maple bacon soap we developed together to one of the big-name cosmetic companies. Those nights she came home late? We were in negotiations with their lawyers.

Bethany said she was gonna use that money to start a new life with you. Then you dumped her."

"I didn't know," he said, looking pained.

"She tried to tell you," Jenny said, "but you didn't trust her."

"I didn't know," he repeated. "I need a drink." Marco headed for the closest cooler. I still needed to talk to him, to see if he wanted to keep any of Bethany's belongings or if I should donate them, but this wasn't the time for that conversation.

"I didn't mean to upset him." Jenny sounded embarrassed. "But he needed to know that Bethany wasn't a cheater. She loved him. Like full-on head-over-heels cheesy love."

"I know," I said, patting her awkwardly on the shoulder. "Hopefully this will help him find some closure." Speaking of closure, Jenny's revelation had left me with more questions than I'd had before. "With Bethany gone, what happens to your big cosmetics deal?"

"It's already gone through," she said. "They're gonna make an announcement next week about their new product line featuring our maple bacon soap formula. We don't get any credit for it because we sold them the rights, but still, it's a pretty big honor, and then there's the money, of course."

That explained why Bethany's bank account was flush with cash, but not where it had all disappeared to so quickly. "What about residuals and royalties?"

Jenny shook her head. "We don't get any. Bethany said she needed the money and I've got medical bills like you wouldn't believe, so we negotiated for a larger price up front instead."

"Good for you. I'm really happy for you," I told her. "Can I get you a celebratory beer or something?"

"I'm more of a wine drinker," she said.

"Well then, come on, let me introduce you to Kim." I found Kim in the growing crowd and left Jenny with her, after discovering that they'd gone to the same high school, only Kim graduated several years after Jenny. Small world. I wasn't sure what the maximum capacity of the roof deck was, but we had to be getting close. If any more people showed up, I hoped they'd brought their bathing suits because the only place that had any room left to stand was in the pool.

I didn't recognize most of the guests. I saw several regular customers from Untapped Books & Café, including Seth, the coffee-drinking, laptop-obsessed, no-tipping table hog. A few faces I knew from Bethany's Instagram account, but couldn't recall their names. I had no idea Bethany was this popular.

The tiki hut had been converted into a makeshift tattoo parlor. A short line formed of people waiting for their owl tribute tattoo, and others were crowded around to watch the process. I could hear the faint buzz of the tattoo machine, and occasional laughter or shouts of encouragement when the person in the chair flinched. Several people walking around the party sported a new tattoo covered in Saran Wrap held on by tape. I guess people reacted differently to the process, because some of the fresh tattoos I saw were puffy and red, and others were merely shiny with whatever goo the tattoo artist smeared on them before wrapping them.

Then the elevator doors opened and I swear the temperature dropped from mid-nineties to low twenties as three people stepped out onto the deck—Cherise Deveaux, Tran Nguyen, and a third person who I assumed was the roommate I hadn't met yet.

"You okay?" Izzy asked, sidling up beside me. "Because you look like you saw a ghost."

I nodded. "Ducky," I replied, but my whole attention was focused on the elevator.

I wasn't looking at a ghost, but I had a feeling I was looking at a murderer. Maybe three of them.

23

IZZY GRABBED MY arm, and then flinched. I noticed that she had a
wrapped tattoo on the underside of her wrist, and her movement
must have irritated her inflamed skin. "What are you about to do?"
she asked. "You've got that look in your eyes."

"I'm not gonna do anything outrageous," I insisted.

"Oh yeah? Like you'd tell me if you'd gotten arrested trying to
break into Bethany's old apartment building?"

"Huh?" My head swiveled toward her. "Who told you . . . ?
Castillo."

"Vince said . . ."

I cut her off. "I wasn't breaking in. I wasn't even attempting to
break in. And I wasn't arrested." Handcuffed, read the Miranda
rights, and tossed into the back of a police cruiser, yes. Photo-
graphed and electronically fingerprinted, yes. Chained to an interrogation room table, yes. But not arrested. Not technically.

"Vince asked me to keep an eye on you."

I forced myself to grin and let the tension drain out of my shoulders. I'd never get any answers out of Bethany's old roomies as long as Izzy was on Odessa watch. "That's sweet of him. But I'm fine. Pinkie swear." I'd never broken a pinkie swear before, but this was a summer full of firsts for me.

"All the same, it might be better if you went and checked on the ice situation. I'll go greet our latest arrivals," Izzy suggested.

"Suits me," I agreed, my grin plastered firmly in place. To prove I was going to cooperate, I turned and made a slow sweep of the rooftop deck, checking the coolers as I went. Parker was sitting on one of the coolers, nursing a beer and talking to a pretty redheaded woman I didn't know. She was laughing and leaning in to touch his elbow. "Hey, guys, hate to interrupt, but I need to get into the cooler real quick."

They both jumped up. Parker looked sheepish as I opened the lid. "Need a beer? Don't blame you. It's awful hot out here."

"I'm just making sure we have enough ice." Like the others, this cooler was half-melted, and the beer cans sloshed around in the icy water.

"Do I need to make a run?" Parker volunteered.

"Thanks, but I think we're good." Something was different about him, and it took a minute for me to figure it out. "Hey, I don't think I've ever seen you wearing the Untapped polo before."

"Well, no. Kitchen staff aren't required to wear them. They're impractical, with the short sleeves and everything." He held out his bare arms, which were covered in scratches and scars as usual. "That and back when we used to have to wear them like everybody else, they were always getting stains and cuts and burns until Todd caved."

"You look good in the polo," I told him, and I meant it. I hadn't thought that anyone could pull off that shade of green, but it kinda worked on Parker. "Are you gonna say something later?" I knew Izzy was working on a speech, but I wasn't sure if everyone was planning to speak or just a few people.

He shook his head and took a swig of beer. "Last time I tried public speaking, I puked and then passed out."

The girl he was with giggled as if he'd said something clever. "I'll let you two get back to your cooler," I said. Then I winked at Parker and mouthed, "Good luck." He blushed, and I returned to my rounds.

I found Marco near the back of the crowd, resting his palms on the lip of the wall that ran around the roof deck and staring off into the city. When I paused next to him, he said, "I bet that's one heck of a view at sunset."

"It sure is," I agreed.

"Sorry about earlier, me losing my temper and all."

"No worries. It's not easy, losing your bae."

He took a deep breath before saying, "Yup."

"Are you all right?" Yes, I know. It was a stupid question. Out of everyone here, he was probably the most affected by Bethany's sudden death.

He nodded. "I will be."

"Good." I leaned forward, admiring the view. Being more than a foot shorter than Marco, my elbows hit the wall about where his wrists did. "Can I ask you a question?" He didn't respond, so I proceeded. "On the day that Bethany . . ." I wanted to say "was murdered" but I didn't want to stir him up any further. ". . . died, she went to meet someone in Domino Park. You were working nearby, right?"

"A few blocks east of there, yeah. We're revitalizing an old department store. By this time next year, it will be mixed-use commercial space and high-end apartments."

"Did she go to the park to meet you?" I asked, even though I was fairly certain I knew the answer to that. None of the photos I'd seen from Domino Park that day featured a seven-foot-tall bearded man in an orange construction vest and hard hat. I might have missed something, but I wouldn't have missed that.

"Nope. I was pouring concrete all morning. Ask anyone." Talk about a rock-solid alibi. Literally. "Besides," he continued, "she went to meet some chick named Stefanie."

"What?" I turned to face him. The mysterious Stefanie I'd been looking for was the one in the park with Bethany? "Are you sure?"

He turned his face away and sighed. "I feel like such a chump, especially now, but it was all hella suspicious. She was staying out late and there were all these guys sliding into her DMs. I needed to know who Beth was cheating on me with, you know? Wanted to give him a piece of my mind. So I kinda hacked into all of her accounts and read her private messages, okay?"

"You did what?" I asked. I wished I'd been able to do that. It would have saved me the trouble of trying to get into her phone.

"The morning she died, a message came in from this Stefanie person asking to meet at the park. Something about a flash mob. Beth was always a sucker for those."

He had my full attention now. "And you didn't think to tell the cops this?" I asked.

Marco shook his head, "Why would I? Her death was an accident. Besides, I don't know any Stefanie. Do you?"

"No. I mean, I don't *know* know Stefanie, but I know who you're talking about." It had to be the same woman, the Stefanie-99NYC stan that liked or commented on practically all of Bethany's social media posts. Other than that, they didn't seem to have any interaction online. Bethany didn't reply to any of the comments or tag her in anything. So why would Bethany go to meet her in Domino Park in the middle of the morning?

Unless it was for the same reason *I'd* agreed to meet Marco in the park.

It was a public place. It seemed safe.

"I could use a refill," Marco said, shaking his empty can. "Get you something?"

"No, thanks." I didn't understand how anyone could drink beer in this heat. It would go right to my head. Give me a big reusable bottle of water instead.

Marco moved out of the way and I found myself face-to-face with Cherise. "Oh, there you are!" she exclaimed. She pushed her sunglasses up onto her head. Her short hair had to be more comfortable than my long hair, which had been pulled up into a ponytail or bun almost every day of this infernal heat wave. "I've been looking everywhere for you."

I glanced around to be sure Izzy wasn't lurking nearby, ready to tackle me if she saw me interrogating Bethany's ex-roommate. "Glad you could make it."

"Wouldn't miss it for the world. Tran told me you came by to pick up Bethany's things. Thanks for that. I didn't know what to do with them."

"Did you know that Bethany was moving out?" I asked her.

"Of course. She was moving in with her boyfriend. Even agreed to catch up on the rent she owed and pay a little extra to break the lease with no bad feelings."

"Thirty-five hundred dollars?" I asked.

"How'd you know?" Cherise asked.

"Just a hunch."

"It was kinda creepy. It hit my bank account yesterday. Guess she set up an autopay before she died."

Oh. That made sense. It explained the payment I'd seen. If Cherise wasn't stealing from Bethany, and Bethany was moving out on good terms, then I couldn't see any reason why any of the roommates would have to hurt her. Sure, they had to go out and find a new roomie to replace her, but judging by all the "room needed" notices I saw everywhere, that wouldn't be too hard. Then I remembered that the thirty-five-hundred-dollar payment wasn't the only one that had come out of her account. "Did she owe anyone else?"

"Not that I know of. In fact, she got a letter this morning from a bank. I didn't know what else to do, so I opened it. It was a statement showing that her student loans were paid off in full. Such a shame. She finally finished paying off all that money and she doesn't live long enough to enjoy it." Cherise shook her head. "Makes you think."

"Sure does," I agreed. At least now I knew why Bethany had wanted to take the money for the maple bacon soap formula up front instead of waiting for royalty checks. She wanted to pay off her student loans and settle up with Cherise so she could start fresh with Marco. "One more thing. Do you know anyone named Stefanie?"

"Nope. Should I?" Cherise waved at someone over my shoulder. "Hey, I see someone I need to talk to. Thanks again for everything. This is a nice wake. Bethany would have appreciated it."

"Izzy did all the work," I said, but Cherise was already walking away and didn't hear me.

This Stefanie nonsense was bugging me. How was it that no one knew who she was, when everyone seemed to already know everyone else? I pulled out my phone. Bethany was active on multiple social media platforms from Snapchat to Tumblr. She had Pinterest and a blog. But as far as I could tell, she spent most of her free time on Twitter.

It didn't take long to find where Stefanie99NYC had commented on a post. I clicked on Stefanie's name and opened up her profile. Her banner was a generic snapshot of Manhattan taken on a clear day. Her profile picture was a stuffed pink bunny. Cute. All of her likes and replies were to Bethany, but she had few original posts. She'd joined a week ago, and most of her feed was retweets.

If I didn't know any better, I would have assumed she was a bot or a fake account. Then I read a recent tweet and despite the stifling temperature, a shiver ran down my spine. Is it too much to ask for a million dollars in uncut diamonds, and a gluten-free donut that doesn't taste like ash? #mood #williamsburg

I'd heard that phrase before.

I hurried toward the elevator and jabbed my finger on the button. Only a few seconds had passed, but I was too impatient, and decided to take the stairs instead. It was only one flight down to my apartment. The air-conditioning was on full blast in the hallway, and I paused long enough to appreciate it before unlocking my door.

Rufus came to greet me, as usual. He meowed loudly, winding his way around my legs. "When's the last time anyone fed you?" I asked him. I knew Izzy had given him breakfast, but I had no idea if she'd been home since then. She'd been so busy setting up for the wake, she might have forgotten. I knew I'd gone upstairs straight from work without checking on him.

I got a double scoop of the fresh cat food in the refrigerator and put it on a dish on the floor. Even if he had eaten lunch, it wouldn't hurt him to get a little extra. "Sorry, Rufie, I haven't been home a lot lately, have I?" I asked. He meowed in response, then turned his full attention to devouring his meal.

Detective Vincent Castillo's business card was on the fridge. I pulled it down and dialed the number. It went to voicemail. Ugh. I hated leaving messages. "Detective, this is Odessa Dean," I said after the robotic greeting. "I know who killed Bethany Kostolus. Call me back."

24

·.·•°•○•··○·•·•··•·•·○•○•·•·○•··•·○•·•·○•·•·•·

Odessa Dean @OdessaWaiting · June 28
Always b yourself. Unless u can b Wonder Woman, then
always b Wonder Woman. #girlpower

·•·•·•○·°•··•·•··•·•○·•○·•··•·•·•·○○•·•·•·

I HEARD A RAP on my door, and I jumped. "Nine-one-one, open up!"
came a man's voice from the hall, and I relaxed.

Strange how much difference a few days made. Less than a
week ago, when Detective Castillo had first knocked on my door,
I'd panicked. This time, I opened the door eagerly. "That was
quick," I said.

Only it wasn't the detective on the other side of the door.

It was Seth, the most annoying regular at Untapped Books &
Café, Bethany's biggest fan, and—unless I was very much
mistaken—Stefanie99NYC.

"Hey! Sorry, didn't mean to scare you," he said, shuffling forward until he was blocking the open door. He spoke with the
rapid, clipped pace of a lifelong New Yorker. "But it's an emergency. Need to borrow the bathroom."

I moved so I could grab the door frame and block his way. "There's a bathroom on the roof."

"Yeah, and it's got a line longer than the folks queuing up for a tattoo." He tapped his chest, where I could see a bit of tape and Saran Wrap peeking out of his collar. His fresh tattoo didn't interest me. The half-healed scratches on his wrists did. "Good thing I got in early, while the artist was still fresh. Her hand has to be cramping up by now."

"You can't be in here," I said, closing the door.

He wedged his foot against the door. "I know, but I can't hold it any longer." He ducked under my arm and pushed past me, into Aunt Melanie's apartment. The door clicked shut behind him. "Man, this place is extra." He made a beeline for the giraffe statue. "This is a Waxby, isn't it?"

I shook my head. "I wouldn't know. Bathroom's that way." I pointed toward the open bathroom door with one hand. With the other, I swiped at my phone screen. I'd intended to close the app so Seth wouldn't see I'd been surfing Bethany's comment history on my phone, but when I'd fumbled around, I accidentally opened the livestream option instead. I clicked the broadcast button, and then as casually as possible, propped my phone up, camera facing out, between two cookie jars—one a nineteen-fifties-style robot and the other a Day of the Dead sugar skull—and moved away from the counter.

"This is totally a Waxby," he said, nodding to himself, still fascinated by the giraffe sculpture.

"Seth, I'd like you to leave. Please."

"Just a minute," he said, stepping around Bethany's boxes of possessions to pull open the curtains. He slid the balcony door open and peeked outside. "What a great garden view." Leaving the door open for the air-conditioning to escape, he turned and directed his attention to the bookshelf. "Wowzers, you really like to read, don't you?" He ran his finger along the spines of the books. "This is a bookworm's dream. What's your favorite genre?"

"I prefer true crime podcasts. You need to go now." On one hand, my Gammie would be appalled by my lack of manners, but on the other hand, Klaxons were going off in my head.

"Slow your roll," Seth said, still examining the bookshelf. "What's this one?"

Out of sheer habit, I took a step toward him before stopping myself. "I don't know, what does it say on the spine?"

"Geez, rude much?" he asked, and I wilted inside. I'd been raised to believe that a good Southern woman always had a clean house, never offered guests store-bought iced tea, and was never *ever* rude under any circumstances.

"Please, Seth, just leave," I begged. I moved to the other side of the kitchen island. The farther away from the phone I stayed, the less chance of him noticing it, I reasoned. "My aunt doesn't allow visitors, and she'll be home any minute now."

"Tsk, tsk. I thought you were such a sweet, nice girl. But here you are, lying to me?" He shook his head to indicate his disappointment. "Your aunt's in France. You should see the photos she posted on her Facebook account of her at the Eiffel Tower just now. Looks like she's having the time of her life."

Fire ants are a particularly nasty insect that live primarily in the southern part of the United States. They aren't big, but their bite feels a little bit like being injected with acid. Worst of all, like most ants, they're a co-op. That's why no one ever gets bitten by just one fire ant. I stepped in a patch of them once, and didn't notice as half the colony swarmed up my legs. I felt something tickle my thigh and swiped at it without thinking, triggering them to all attack en masse. It was probably the worst pain I'd been in ever, and then for days after, the bites itched so bad I thought I was gonna lose my mind.

I'd rather have my wisdom teeth pulled with no anesthetic while covered in chicken pox than ever go near a fire ant again.

Seth's casual mention of my aunt's travels felt for all the world like that half-second of warning before that swarm of fire ants stung the devil out of my legs. I froze in place, waiting for the other shoe to drop. "People should really pay more attention to their privacy settings," Seth said casually. "It's ridiculous what anyone can find online."

"You're right," I agreed with him. I'd tried being nice. I'd tried being firm. And I was done playing games while this jerk who couldn't be bothered to tip on a lousy three-dollar cup of coffee was standing here *in my own home* tossing around not-so-veiled threats. "Like when I found that message from Stefanie99NYC asking Bethany to meet her at Domino Park the morning she was killed. I already called the cops and told them everything, Seth. Or should I call you Stefanie?"

He growled at me and advanced. "You think you're so smart, don't you? How'd you figure it out?"

"You and Stefanie99NYC used the same odd phrase. I don't get it. Why pretend to be someone you're not? Did Bethany not like you for you, so you had to invent another persona?" I moved behind the table.

"It's just a username, don't read too much into it. It's kinda like those ship names," he explained. "It was supposed to be flattering—Seth plus Bethany equals Sethany. Only my phone autocorrected it to Stefanie and I didn't notice until later." It was kinda on the nose that Seth would use the word "ship"—a fantasy relationship that only happened in someone's imagination—to describe his pretend connection to Bethany, but I didn't think he would appreciate it if I pointed that out, so I kept my mouth shut.

Seth reached the other end of the table and ran a hand over my sewing machine. I was going to Lysol every single inch of this apartment after he left. "You know how you girls are. Sure, you say you want a nice guy, but then you block the nice guys and go for those meatheads like *Marco*." He said "Marco" in a mocking, sing-song voice.

"I get it." I nodded and tried to look sympathetic. "You went all full-on stalker mode online and Bethany blocked you, so you invented Stefanie so you could keep tabs on her, knowing she was more likely to let her guard down with a female username."

"She didn't just block me. Stupid girl *reported* me, and for what? Nothing. But *no*, according to the powers that be, I violated the"—he made little air quotes—"'Terms of Service' and my accounts were, *poof*, gone."

"Seriously?" I asked, unable to stop myself. "You got your feels hurt over that?"

He gave me an exasperated look. "Chuh. Do you even know what I can get for an account with over fifty thousand followers? It takes weeks to build up a Twitter handle so it's worth anything. Months, sometimes. It's a full-time job. My personal handle wasn't the only account they deleted. They deleted *all* my accounts. Even the ones I'd already sold, and boy did I have some angry customers demanding a full refund."

My head swam from trying to follow his train of thought. "Is it even legal to sell Twitter accounts?"

"Everyone does it. Besides, while I'm building accounts, I'm always online. When I saw Bethany's Facebook relationship status change to 'single' I knew that this was my chance to get back in her good graces." He grinned and a shiver went up my spine. "I'd heard a flash mob was about to go down, and I used that to lure her out to the park."

"But, I thought she blocked you?" I said.

"She blocked *Seth*. So I invented Stefanie. I knew once we were on that bridge, I could convince her to give me a chance. I could even forgive her for ruining all those accounts I was building. Then I was gonna make her see that I was the man she needed in her life. Not that Marco clown."

"And how did that go?" I asked, although I was pretty sure I knew the answer.

Seth's hands balled up into fists. "She laughed at me. Can you imagine? Stuck up little . . ." His voice trailed off. His cheeks reddened, whether with rage or embarrassment I couldn't be sure, remembering the moment she rejected him.

"I'm sorry she did that to you," I said. Every time he took a step, I did, too, keeping the table between us.

"So was she." The furrow in his brow relaxed and I realized he was actually smiling now. I shivered. "That look in her eyes when she realized . . ." He shook his head. "That's a moment neither of us will ever forget."

"Sounds like her death was sorta like an accident," I said, careful not to let my poker face slip.

"Sure. Yeah. Totes. I *accidentally* shoved her over the rail." Seth made air quotes around "accidentally." "Had to make sure she went over hard enough to kill her, didn't I? You should have seen her. Pathetic." He held up his scratched wrists. "Trying to grab me, like I was gonna save her or something. Well, I guess I did save a little part of her," he said. Seth reached into his pocket and withdrew a short length of stainless-steel links.

"Seth, is that Bethany's medical alert bracelet?" I asked. I had crawled under bushes and dug through a mountain of garbage looking for that fake medical ID bracelet—the one declaring Timothy O'Shay was allergic to bullets—when Seth had it all along.

"It certainly is. Although, maybe she should have gotten one that said she was allergic to major head trauma, instead." He laughed at his own sick joke. "Catch."

He tossed me the bracelet, and I caught it out of habit.

"When the police find you dead with Bethany's missing bracelet in your hand, it won't take long for them to put two and two together. Sweet little Odessa Dean, consumed by guilt after killing her dear friend Bethany, swan dives off her own balcony." He clucked his tongue. "Such a tragedy."

"Detective Castillo will never buy that," I said, shaking my head. We were halfway around the living room table and I was desperate to do or say anything to buy me enough time to round the table and sprint for the front door. "He knows how hard I've been trying to find Bethany's killer."

"Haven't you heard? The perp always tries to insert himself— or herself, as the case may be—into the investigation." Seth shoved the table, hard. It hit my stomach and I stumbled backward toward the open balcony door.

"I've already told the cops everything!" I shouted, grabbing the lip of the table and inching back the way I'd come. It was either get closer to a madman or to that open door, and I was willing to take my chances with Seth. I'd seen what a fall had done to Bethany, and that was just fifteen feet. We were five stories up. "Even if you kill me, and we both know you don't want to do that, Seth, the cops know you were with Bethany on the walkway before she died. Besides, I have an airtight alibi. I was in the café when she died."

"So was I," he said with a grin. "Or at least, that's what everyone will remember."

I stared at him. That couldn't possibly be true. He was in the café pretty much all day, every day, playing on his laptop—apparently using Untapped's free Wi-Fi to build up his scammy Twitter accounts—and drinking coffee. He was such a fixture in the place, I hardly noticed him unless he was in my section, and even then I didn't check on him half as often as I would a tipping table. Had he been in the café before Bethany died? I couldn't remember. But I do vaguely remember talking to him after the flash mob proposal video was posted online, and telling him Bethany wasn't coming back.

Would I have noticed if he'd slipped out before Bethany left, and returned after he'd killed her? Apparently, many of the regulars knew there was a back door, and that we kept it propped open with a brick during business hours because we were too lazy to do things the right way.

But what kind of absolute monster could commit cold-blooded murder and then go out for a coffee afterward?

The kind of monster in my living room, apparently.

"There're video cameras," I blurted out. Bless Todd and his paranoia. I sure hoped he hadn't cheaped out on the cameras like he did with everything else, and had paid for more than a day's worth of storage. "Front and back doors. The police will be able to tell exactly when you came in, and if you left at any time."

"You're lying," he hissed.

"Nope. Todd had 'em installed after a break-in a while ago, but now he uses them to watch everyone coming and going."

"I don't believe you."

"The cops also have security footage and cell phone pictures from Domino Park that morning. They've got everything they need to place you at the scene, Seth." At least, I hoped that was true. All it would take was a glimpse of Seth in the background of one of the hundreds, if not thousands, of Instagram pictures to prove he was at the park.

A movement behind Seth caught my eye, and my pulse spiked. Seth must have seen it, too, because he started to turn around, but Rufus jumped up on the table, purring as he slunk around my sewing machine. "Come here, Rufie," I said in a saccharine voice I typically reserved for babies and small animals.

Seth cocked his head to one side. "I didn't know you had a cat."

There it was again, that skin-crawling sensation. Despite the fact that our longest conversation before now had been me asking if he wanted a refill of his coffee or not, he thought he knew me because he'd checked out my online presence. I didn't even know his last name, but he probably knew my cowboy boot size.

"Rufie, baby, c'mere" I repeated. I didn't know what terrified me more, the idea that Seth might hurt Rufus, or that Rufus might escape through the open door and possibly fall off the balcony. Either way, I wasn't going to let anything bad happen to my aunt's cat. When he got close enough, I snatched him up and held him to my chest.

Rufus, not used to being manhandled, hissed and scratched at my arm, crisscrossing the marks he'd left the day I'd brought Huckleberry home with me. I yelped, and almost dropped him.

"I don't think the cat likes you very much," Seth said, a wide grin blossoming across his face.

"And I don't think I like you very much," came a man's voice right next to Seth's ear. Seth jumped, but Detective Vincent Castillo clamped a hand on his shoulder and shoved him face-first into the table. Seth writhed in discomfort as his freshly tattooed chest smacked into the hard wood. The detective pinned him down with one hand as he reached for his handcuffs with the other. "Nice distraction, Ms. Dean," he said, winking at me.

"I think Rufus deserves all the credit," I said through chattering teeth.

Before the detective had opened the front door and Seth had started to turn around, I was sure that I was about to do my best impression of Humpty Dumpty. If it weren't for Rufus jumping up on the table at that exact moment, I don't know what would have happened. Just thinking about it, the world got fuzzy around the edges, and it sounded like a bunch of Parker's bees were buzzing around my head.

I wobbled, but Castillo was there with his arm around my waist, easing me down into one of the dining table chairs before I could lose my balance. "You okay?" he asked.

"Uh-huh," I nodded. "Just ducky."

He closed the balcony door before rejoining Seth, who was now standing with his hands cuffed behind his back. "You can put the cat down now, Ms. Dean."

"Odessa," I corrected him faintly. I tried to swallow, but my throat was as dry as a creek bed in August.

The detective nodded as he looked me up and down. "You're bleeding."

I glanced at my arm. It was barely a scratch. "It's just blood," I assured him. "I'll make more. You got my message."

"Sure did," the detective said. He pulled a laminated card out of his wallet. "Sorry I missed your call, I was up on your roof with a couple hundred of Bethany's closest friends. It's so loud up there, I didn't hear my phone ring. Then Izzy saw your livestream, gave me her keys, and I got down here as soon as I could. Quick thinking, repeating his name every time you could and getting him to confess on tape."

"I didn't think anyone would believe me otherwise," I told him.

"Sorry I didn't take you seriously earlier," Castillo said.

I shrugged. "I wouldn't take me seriously, either," I admitted. "Kinda fitting, though? A case that started with an accidental video of Bethany falling to her death ends with a livestream of Seth confessing to everything. I'm just lucky that Izzy saw it."

"Are you kidding?" Castillo chuckled. "You were logged in to the Untapped Books & Café account. Thousands of people are watching live right now. I think you have a new viral video on your hands." He winked again, and read Seth his rights.

25

Odessa Dean @OdessaWaiting · July 5
I did another thing, y'all. Whadya think of my new ink? #tattoo
#owie #sorrynotsorry #YOLO

A WEEK AFTER SETH was arrested and charged with murdering Bethany, I was sitting on a vinyl-covered chair in a tattoo parlor, staring at the stencil on the underside of my wrist. It was the same outline as Bethany's cute little owl tattoo, with a few minor tweaks. Bethany's tattoo had been turquoise. Most everyone who got the memorial tattoo got theirs in black and gray, but remembering what Jenny had told me about Bethany's dislike of somber colors, I went with bright purple. Also, in place of the comically large eyes, I wanted big green buttons to express my love of sewing.

"You don't have to do this," Izzy said. She stood on the other side of me, holding my sweaty hand.

The shop was clean, well lit, and smelled faintly of soap. The walls were painted complementary shades of bright, cheery colors, and instead of examples of common tattoo designs like butterflies and anchors—apparently called "flash"—taped to the walls, the owner had hung framed original artwork. Swing music was piped in over Bluetooth speakers mounted in the corners, and my foot tapped unconsciously to the beat.

"I know," I said. "I want to do this." And I did. Yes, I was nervous. And yes, I knew getting an almost exact copy of someone else's tattoo wasn't unique. But it would always be special to me, and that was the only thing that mattered.

"The wrist is a bold place to get a first tattoo," Parker warned me. He stood by my knees, opposite the tray table where the tattoo artist was squeezing colored inks into tiny caps. Parker looked a little green around the gills. He'd offered to come as a show of support, but now I was afraid he was going to throw up or something, and he wasn't even the one getting inked.

"True," I replied. "I want it to be visible. I want to see it every day." It was both a tribute to Bethany and a reminder that life was short. It wouldn't be much of a reminder if I couldn't see it, would it? "Besides, go big or go home, YOLO, and all that other stuff, right?"

"You about ready?" the tattoo artist asked, tapping a foot pedal so that the machine in her hand buzzed.

Before now, I'd always pictured a tattooist as a big burly forty-something man in a motorcycle jacket with "I heart Mom" tattooed on his enormous bicep. I don't know where that image had come from, but the artist who'd drawn Bethany's original tattoo and had inked dozens of copies onto her friends during the wake last week looked *nothing* like that. She was in her early twenties with jet-black hair styled up in big vintage glam curls held in place with a bright pink headscarf. She wore a full-skirted dress, the kind that needed petticoats, topped off with a short white sweater with an enamel long-necked cat pin near the collar.

All in all, she looked like the perfect nineteen-fifties house-wife, if the perfect nineteen-fifties housewife had almost every inch of their visible skin covered in brightly colored tattoos. Even her temples were tattooed—an ice cream cone on the right temple and a simple blue heart on the left.

She pushed up the sleeves of her sweater to reveal a long pink flamingo that ran the length of her arm and snapped on a new pair of gloves. "Say the word," she told me.

"Ready," I confirmed.

I braced myself for the agonizing pain to come as she dipped the tip of the tattoo machine into the little pot of ink and brought it to my arm. Then the buzzing needle touched my skin and to my surprise, it wasn't bad. I'd had worse papercuts.

Just like grief, everyone processed pain differently. What was a mild annoyance to me could have felt like a root canal without anesthesia to someone else, or vice versa. Then again, my grandma taught me how to sew when I couldn't have been six or seven. Since then, I'd probably pricked my fingers a hundred thousand times with a sewing needle. Maybe that had desensitized me over time, or my artist had a gentle hand, or I'd inadvertently selected a location that had few pain receptors. In any event, it wasn't any-thing near as bad as I'd expected.

"You okay?" the artist asked, bent over and concentrating on the design.

"Ducky," I replied.

"I'll wait for you outside," Parker announced, and left abruptly.

I didn't blame him. I'd felt a little squeamish before she started, too. The fact that Parker had come along to provide moral support was enough.

"Men, am I right?" the artist asked. Beside me, Izzy giggled. I didn't move a muscle. The very last thing I wanted was to twitch and end up with some random line across my wrist. "I do need you to hold still, but you can breathe," she told me. "It's okay."

I took a couple of shallow breaths, and once I realized it didn't seem to affect what she was doing, allowed myself to breathe normally. "This isn't nearly as bad as I thought it would be," I told her, and then flinched as she ran the needle along a tender spot. It wasn't quite like getting tickled with a feather, but it wasn't being swarmed by fire ants, either.

As she worked, my mind wandered. When Detective Vincent Castillo dragged Seth out of my apartment in handcuffs last Friday, a huge crowd had been waiting at the door. They burst into applause as soon as the door opened, as if my brush with death had been a reality TV show. Then again, I guess by broadcasting the whole thing to the world, I had sort of set myself up for that.

As Castillo had predicted, Seth's video confession went viral, but later that evening, someone released a TikTok of ferrets swarming over an obstacle course and my five minutes in the spotlight was forgotten.

I had to go down to the station and give my testimony, but between Seth's video confession, the bracelet that had been in his possession, and the police tracing Stefanie99NYC back to his laptop and the café's IP address, it was an open-and-shut case. Just as I'd hoped, one of the security cameras in Domino Park *had* caught him leaving the elevated walkway while everyone else was rushing to Bethany's side. The footage from Untapped Books & Café was useless—Todd's cheap surveillance system was too grainy to make a positive identification—but one of the regulars that day had noticed Seth coming in the back door when he'd come out of the restroom.

Castillo never outright said so, but I knew he was glad I helped put Bethany's killer behind bars. I'd been tempted to rub it in, to remind him that he'd been convinced that Bethany's death was an accident, but I thought that might be in bad taste.

Besides, I was seeing a lot more of him now that he and Izzy were officially an item. I liked having him as a friend, and would prefer to stay on his good side as much as possible. "Is Vince coming over for dinner again tonight?" I asked Izzy.

"Depends on what time he gets off work. I was thinking of making caprese pizza with vegan mozzarella on cauliflower crust. How does that sound?"

Horrible, I thought to myself.

"I'll try anything once," I told her reluctantly, glancing over at my arm. Before coming to Williamsburg, I would have never even considered eating *anything* with a cauliflower crust, much less vegan pizza. I wouldn't have tasted stuffed croissants, raspberry Nutella crepes, or avocado toast, either. I wouldn't have developed an appreciation for craft beer. I certainly wouldn't have gotten a purple owl with button eyes tattoo.

"Speaking of dinner at the apartment . . ." Izzy sucked on her bottom lip for a second. "I got a text from my roomie at the schoolhouse. It's safe to move back in now, and if I don't act soon, I'm gonna lose my spot."

"About that," I said. "I talked to Aunt Melanie last night. Took some cajoling, but she's good with you staying. At least for the next two months, until she gets back." I didn't love the idea of Izzy going back to a situation that sounded neither safe nor sanitary. And to be completely honest, I didn't want to go back to living on my own just yet.

"That's sweet, but you can't keep sleeping on the couch," she told me.

"Don't worry about me. The couch is plenty comfy. Besides, I've already started making black-out curtains for the sliding glass doors." After delivering Bethany's soap-making supplies to Jenny and donating the rest to charity—turned out that most of her stuff was already at Marco's and he didn't want anything from the remaining boxes—the apartment had breathing room again. "I like having you around."

"Are you sure?" Izzy asked.

"One hundred percent," I assured her, and then fought the reflex to flinch when the tattoo needle, now putting in color, hit the already sore outline. The artist wiped the area and the soapy liquid stung for a second before providing cool relief. "It's only for two more months, until my aunt gets back, but that gives you plenty of time to figure out what you want to do."

"What about you?" she asked. I was grateful for the distracting conversation. The longer the tattoo went on, the more uncomfortable the constant stinging on my inflamed arm got. "Where are you going to go when Melanie gets back?"

"I'm not sure. I assumed I'd go back to Piney Island, but the longer I'm in Williamsburg, the more I don't want to leave." The thought had been growing in the back of my head for the past week, and I still didn't know what to do. "I'd love to stay in Brooklyn, but I don't think I can afford it."

"You worry too much," Izzy said, flapping her free hand in a dismissive gesture. Her other hand was still holding mine, providing comfort and support even though the tattoo turned out to be a lot easier to handle than I'd feared. The artist hadn't exactly been overwhelmed with joy when I'd shown up with two friends in tow, but since she'd already met—and tattooed—Izzy, and Parker hadn't lasted more than a few seconds, she didn't seem to mind the extra spectator now. "Like you said, we've got two whole months. We'll figure something out."

By the time the tattoo was finished, my arm was slightly swollen and sore, like someone had been vigorously rubbing fine-grit sandpaper over it for the past hour. Which wasn't far from the truth, I guess. The artist cleaned my arm, and before she could rub another layer of goo over it, I snapped a quick picture and posted to my Instagram account.

It was a good thing that my mom didn't use social media, because she was gonna kill me when she saw this. Then again, I wasn't a kid anymore. If I was old enough to solve a murder, I was old enough to get a tattoo, move to New York City, or do anything I put my mind to. I guess this adulting business wasn't all bad.

Once the fresh tattoo was wrapped and the artist had given me detailed care instructions, I tipped her and we headed outside. As someone who survived off tips, I always tipped in cash. Besides the obvious drawback of business owners that skimmed a little off the top of tips left for their employees on a credit card for "service fees" or some such nonsense, cash tips were immediate money. That could sometimes mean the difference between eating ramen noodles and purloined ketchup packets for dinner and nothing at all.

Speaking of eating, "I'm starving," I declared. Parker, who had been waiting outside on the steps, joined us. He must have been really wigged out to prefer to stay out here in the blazing heat instead of the cool air-conditioned shop.

"I don't blame you. I'm always famished after a tattoo. Don't know why," Izzy said. "We've already got all the fixings for pizza if you want to make it for lunch instead of dinner."

"Or, I know this little café nearby," Parker suggested. "Best sandwiches in Williamsburg, and an impressive selection of cold local craft beer."

"This café wouldn't happen to feature a waitstaff in atrocious neon green polo shirts, would it?" I asked.

Parker nodded, "Oh, you know the place?"

"It is close," Izzy agreed. "And you can't beat the family discount. What do you say, Odessa?"

I grinned. Before coming to Williamsburg, I'd had a narrow definition of "family," and I'd always wished I had a brother or sister, or at the very least, some nearby cousins. But recently, I'd discovered that the amazing people I met here weren't just friends or coworkers. They were family. "UB&C it is. But in the event that Todd is shorthanded, we might want to sneak in the back door so we don't get pressed into working."

Todd and Andre had hired not one but two new waitresses to fill some of the gaps in the schedule. If one of them worked out, I would be ecstatic. If both worked out? I'd be downright delirious. But just in case they had both quit already, I didn't want to end up serving on my day off.

"Agreed," Izzy said, looping one arm around my right arm—the one that wasn't still stinging from a fresh tattoo—and the other around Parker's left. Her owl memorial tattoo was already well on the way to healing, the metaphor of which was not lost on me.

Together, the three of us headed toward Untapped Books & Café, my mouth watering at the promise of a savory sandwich on locally made artisanal bread, washed down with a cold bottle of Pour Williamsburg Pale Ale. Here, in the heart of Brooklyn, surrounded by friends, I was living my best life.

#TheEnd.

Acknowledgments

This book exists because the lovely and talented Karen MacInerney encouraged me to find my voice writing quirky, unconventional, character-driven cozies.

Special thanks goes to my cheerleaders-slash-advisers-slash-therapists-slash–critique partners, Dare, La, Ris, and Liz, and of course to my weird and wonderful Potassium, who makes me laugh every day. I'd also thank my little writing buddy, Bailey-cakes, but puggles can't read. At least I'm pretty sure she can't.

I'm beyond grateful for my incredibly supportive agent, James McGowan; the BookEnds Literary Agency; the amazing Kristine Swartz; and the entire Berkley team.

But most of all, thank YOU for giving Odessa a chance.

Recycle. Hydrate. And always follow your dreams.

Photo courtesy of the author

Brooklyn Murder Mysteries author OLIVIA BLACKE writes quirky, unconventional, character-driven cozy mysteries. After shuffling around the USA from Hawaii to Maine, she currently resides with her husband and their roly-poly rescue puggle, but is forever homesick for NYC. In addition to writing, disappearing into a good book, and spending *way* too much time on social media, she enjoys scuba diving, crocheting, collecting tattoos, and baking dog cookies.

CONNECT ONLINE
OliviaBlacke.com
🐦 OliviaBlacke
📷 OliviaBlackeAuthor
f AuthorOliviaBlacke

Ready to find
your next great read?

Let us help.

Visit prh.com/nextread

Penguin
Random
House